DEAD GIRL FIGHTING

ANN M. NOSER

IMMORTAL WORKS
SALT LAKE CITY

Immortal Works LLC
1505 Glenrose Drive
Salt Lake City, Utah 84104
Tel: (385) 202-0116

© 2023 Ann Noser

Cover Art by Ashley Literski
http://strangedevotion.wixsite.com/strangedesigns

ISBN 978-1-953491-67-1 (Paperback)
ASIN B0CKPFXWYH (Kindle)

Dear Dad,
How can you be gone when we've got so much left to say?

ABOUT DEAD GIRL RUNNING

Eight years ago, SILVIA WOOD's father died in an industrial accident. After suffering through years of Psychotherapy Services and Mandated Medications dealing with her loss, she longs to work in Botanical Sciences. When the Occupation Exam determines she must work in Mortuary Sciences instead, she wonders if the New Order assigned her to the morgue to push her over the edge.

To appease her disappointed mother, Silvia enters the Race for Citizen Glory, in hopes to stand out in the crowd of Equals. Once she begins training with "golden boy" LIAM HARMAN, she discovers he also lost his father in the same accident that ruined her childhood. Then Silvia meets and falls for Liam's older cousin, whose paranoid intensity makes her question what really happened to her dad. As the race nears, Silvia realizes that she's not only running for glory, she's also running for her life.

THE NEW ORDER BRINGS PEACE AND PROSPERITY TO ALL

Prejudice, greed, and an overemphasis on self-worth led early, unenlightened American Administrations to engage in Aggressive Warfare Tactics with other similarly misguided nations.

Without the ingenuity of the Great City Founders, World War III would have resulted in the complete Destruction of Life here in the Northern Americas.

The New Order rescued us from certain death and saved us from ourselves.

In their great wisdom, the Founders voted to provide All Citizens, by decree, the rights of Equality, Public Safety, and Provision of Basic Needs.

To fill these needs, a League of Representatives was appointed to oversee the Fair and Equal distribution of goods.

What The New Order has banded together let no one put asunder.

1

HAPPY BIRTHDAY

I didn't always hate my birthday. In fact, I used to love it. The day I turned nine, I hurried home after school to search our front hallway for clues. Smack dab in the middle of the front rug rested one of Mom's shiny black flats. Yes! That meant chocolate for dessert. Further down the hallway I spotted Dad's worn brown shoes, one toe set on top of the other. Double yes! We were also having spaghetti for dinner—my favorite. This was going to be the best birthday ever.

And it was. Seconds after I dumped my school bag on the floor, bouncy notes from *The Music Man* floated in from the living room, followed by my dad sashaying toward me, his right fingers snapping overhead and left hand outstretched. I grasped his hand, and we twirled in circles, turning our front hallway into an impromptu dance floor. Mom joined us, clapping to the beat and chanting "Happy birthday to you" so many times it became a part of the song. We were a party of three, but that was enough. We ate all my favorite foods, talking and laughing together before curling up on the couch to watch *The Music Man* from start to finish. Dad and I loved watching recordings of old musicals, while Mom—the only real musician in the family—snoozed. She *insisted* that it wasn't on purpose, that she *wanted* to see the movie with us, but she just couldn't keep her eyes open. It happened every time. No matter what day of the week or time of the year, Mom was *always* tired.

But it didn't matter. I could always count on my dad.

Until I couldn't.

Until exactly one year later—on my tenth birthday and the worst day of my life—when he left for work and never came home again. Supposedly, he had to work late because his replacement—Jack Harman—didn't show up on time.

But I found out later from his nephew Franco, that wasn't true.

In the worst factory accident of modern times, fifty-three people burned to death in the Wardrobe Production District. The New Order investigation found faulty wiring to be the cause. Due to this horrific incident, new regulations on the use of electric heat and lighting have been implemented. This will never happen again.

Dad disappeared, taking everything that was good with him. Mom and I were left all alone, both so lost and confused, while the rest of the world moved on as if nothing had happened. For the two of us, life became a void—something to tolerate, rather than enjoy. Like a huge vacuum had removed our happiness and joy and it was impossible to feel either emotion ever again. We had to move to a smaller, darker apartment. All of Dad's green plants died from lack of sunlight—or maybe they missed him too, even more than they missed the sun's warmth on their leaves. Mom lost her job because she couldn't play violin anymore. Her heart withered and shrank. There was nothing left for her to care about anymore—not the violin and not me, either. She was a fractured, broken shell, as if she had died too.

Dad was gone—killed by stupid faulty wiring. My amazing, crazy father who made everything an exciting game was no more.

After Dad's death, Mom seemed to forget she was still alive. I kept hoping that someday, somehow my father would return, even when I knew he never would.

Until eight long years later, when Gus told me what really happened.

Your father's alive. And you're going to see him again.

Both my father and Liam's father, Jack Harman, had been injured in the "accident" staged by the New Order to get rid of the rebels working in that sector of the clothing industry. Both our fathers had gone to secret meetings—meetings I never told my mother or the Suits about. After the accident both men—presumed dead—were delivered to the morgue, where Gus protected them. He drugged them and used stage makeup, courtesy of his past in the theater, to make them look deceased.

Gus was the Underground Railroad for those persecuted by the New Order. My genius, kind, brilliant Gus helped people—including my dad, Jack, and now me—escape Panopticus.

But he never, ever saved himself.

Well, that was going to change—I was going to save him.

I swear it, Gus. I'm coming back for you and my mom at the very least.

And I meant it.

But first I had to find the others, a life and death game of hide and seek in the wilderness.

2

RUNAWAY

All you have to do is find the others.

I don't know if I can do this.

Sure you can. You're smart. Plus, you have no other option.

Gus believes I can find them out here in the woods. He's risked far too much by saving my life for me to let him down. And he's right, I don't have any other option—except for death and starvation out here alone in the woods.

Smoke clogs the sky, streaking across the moon and scratching my throat. Hidden within a cloak of tall black trees, I pause to watch fumes rise from the Incinerator. I wish Gus had escaped along with me, to tell me what to do each step of the way in this strange new world. And even though she hates exercise and would complain the whole way, I wish Mom was out here with me so we could go find my father together. And why couldn't Franco escape the city he cursed, to stand here by my side and give me the courage I need to survive?

My unsteady feet stumble away from the flames and hurry me further into the darkness deep between the trees. The screaming sirens and alarms fade into the distance. Gus has done all he could, working miracles to find me in the hospital, where they had bound and drugged me and held me hostage. Then he'd concealed me between dead bodies on the way to the Incinerator. His final move (always the drama king) of setting the Incinerator on fire disguised my escape.

My strong leg muscles obey my fight or flight response to crash through the scratchy underbrush. I push myself onward, despite my shaking hands and woozy head. No doubt the sedatives haven't fully left my system. This terrain is rough on my ankles. I miss my flat treadmill. This is much worse than the pothole filled training road out to the greenhouses. Here I am in the Dark Woods—a mysterious place filled with life-giving trees and life-taking monsters that I wondered and dreamed about as a child. My fuzzy head fills with pictures of wolves feasting on human flesh, their teeth ripping muscle from bone. Could they be out here right now, watching and plotting their next murderous move?

I shiver, wishing again for Gus to be by my side. After a lifetime spent surrounded by thousands of faceless strangers every day as I walked to work or the gym, I have never once been this alone. No Gus, no Mom, no Franco... and now, never again Liam. Tears sting my eyes at the memory of his body lying pale and cold on the gurney.

The New Order killed Liam just because he tried to get ahead in life. What would they do to Gus if they found out what he had done to save me? Gus, the master keeper of *way* more secrets than I ever imagined, saved my life by helping me escape just like he'd done for my father eight years before. How has he managed to cover his tracks for all these years?

The moon glows brighter and whiter, my eyes adjusting to the darkness. An owl hoots nearby, startling me. Thanks to all the nature programs Gus forced me to watch, I recognize the sound. He had me watch so much programming—not just about the Underground Railroad and difficult surgeries. Most of my wildlife knowledge came from Gus, as if he was coaching me for this very day. But everything he showed me was supposed to help me take over for him, not travel this path on my own. Maybe he wanted me to know how to prepare those I sent out into the wild. Maybe that's what it was all for. How I hate leaving behind the best friend I ever had, even if I barely knew half his real story.

Gus's words resonate in my mind: *I expect I will get in a whole heck of a lot of trouble, but I don't care about that anymore. I'd rather be killed for doing the right thing than die inside by turning the other cheek.*

But I don't want him to die. Ever. He may not believe what I said, but I *will* come back for him. And I *will* bring an army to burn it all down. The entire New Order.

I'll see Gus again. I won't leave everyone I care about behind. Not like my dad did.

I stumble, falling to my knees. I can't keep running through this forest full of stumps and twigs and branches ready to catch and trip me at every turn. Hurting myself alone in the darkness would be a very bad idea. As the lights and sirens fade behind me, I downgrade to as brisk a hike as I can manage, hoping I'm heading in the right direction. Should I stop now to take out Gus's compasses and maps and figure out which way to go? But then I'd have to use the flashlight, and what if they're already searching for me out here in the woods and spot my light?

Maybe I don't know what direction I'm heading, but that's okay. For tonight, all I have to do is get as far away from the Incinerator as possible. Tomorrow, when daylight arrives, I'll stop to organize and plan. Once I've found the others, I'll figure out how to destroy the New Order.

One thing at a time.

My pulse races, my heart rate elevated from both fear and excitement. Finding the others means finding my dad. How is that even possible? All this time, when I'd felt he just couldn't be dead, I was actually right. That secret part of me that kept hoping someday Dad would come back is now alive and kicking again. This is amazing. I can't believe this is happening to me—and my mom, too.

I'll bring him back to Mom, and we will all be together again, just like I always wanted.

Whack. A tree branch whips me smack in the face. My steps falter and my hands fly up to inspect my stinging cheek. The sirens, once deafening and terrifying, have faded to a harsh whisper. There's just my breath, my heartbeat, and my hesitant crunching footfalls once I start again.

My mom's scared face floods my mind. Gus said Franco told her Dad's still alive. How did she react? What will she do? Will she be okay? She fell apart before. Who's going to help her now that I'm gone? Franco? What will she do if the Suits come after her?

If Gus visits her like I begged him to, will that cause more problems for him? I hope not.

What if they hurt her? Or him? What if they kill her? Or him? What if I've made things worse by connecting them to each other?

Tears sting my eyes, and my hands tremble. Swallowing becomes painful, and I don't think it's just from the smoke Gus poured into the skies. I stumble and catch myself just in time. I can't get hurt. There's no one here to save me if I do. This is all on me, just me, so I need to calm down right now and get myself together. I can't think this way. I can't fret about my mother and everyone else I've left behind. All I can do is move forward and find my father. After that, we'll make a plan together to come back and fix everything.

Remembering my yoga classes, I calm my breathing and heart rate as I hold my arms out in front of me protectively, seeking the thinner areas between the trees to pass through. Hiking as fast as I dare, I move on. If I could survive my past and win that stupid race, I can manage a cross-country trek without starving or getting lost. Gus believes in me, and he's the smartest person I know.

He's never been wrong before.

Let's hope this won't be the first time.

3

ALONE

"*North, south, east, west...*" *Gus points at the crazy collection of maps crowding the floor-to-ceiling bulletin boards on his main office wall. The Museum of Fine Arts hung between Narnia and some national forest.*

"Sorry, Gus, but why should I bother learning how to read a map? I know you loved hiking as a kid, but I'm stuck here in Panopticus, running in place and going nowhere on a stupid treadmill every day of my life."

Gus frowns. "What's wrong today? Did you have yet another fight with that long-suffering mother of yours?"

I sigh. Gus knows me so well. "So I happened to mention that cool video you showed me about kayaking, and Mom told me—once again —that I needed to stop wasting my time dreaming about what I couldn't have in life and work on what I could have instead. Like how I need to make more friends, get a boyfriend, and, you know, try to get a different job, preferably one that doesn't involve dead bodies."

Gus nods, knowing how much my mom wishes I worked somewhere other than in Mortuary Sciences with him.

"And the worst part about the fight was that I got so mad I said something horrible."

"Oh, boy. What was it this time?"

I mumble a confession, eyes downcast. "I said that I wished Dad was here instead of her."

"That's pretty low, Silvia, even for you."

"I know, it was a terrible thing to say." I release a long breath. "And I'm sorry now, but I'm so sick of fighting with her all the time over every little thing. If Dad were around, he would just join in and watch whatever video I liked. Not everything would turn into an argument like it does with my mom. She doesn't like anything I say or do, period."

"Silvia, you never give your poor mom any credit."

"Well, she doesn't give me any credit, either. She's never interested in what I want to do, just in what she wants me to do."

"And the two things never seem to agree."

"That's right." I step away from the maps. "But I know it doesn't give me the right to say such mean things to her."

"No, it doesn't. She's doing the best she can. Sometimes you have to accept that love doesn't always look like you want or expect it to."

I slump in my chair, mad at both myself and my mom, and pretty much at life in general. "But she's never happy with who I am. She's always pushing me where I don't want to go. It doesn't feel like love. It just feels like she's disappointed in me. And I hate feeling like I'm never good enough. I can't help getting mad sometimes."

Gus shrugs. "You can't help what you feel, but you can certainly help what you say."

"Yeah, I know. I'm a bad person."

"No, you're not. You're in a bad situation, you've got a bad temper, but you're not a bad person. Trust me. I know you."

"But I could still use a little improvement." I offer him a weak smile.

"Maybe just a little." Gus claps his hands together. "Now, enough fooling around pretending I'm a psychiatrist. Let's get back to work.

You should learn how to use a compass, if only to stretch your brain capacity."

"Okay, fine. Go ahead and teach me this pointless skill since you've got your heart set on it. But I don't need a compass to find my way from here to home and back again. I'll bet I could manage it in my sleep."

"Oh, quit your whining. Knowing how to read a map legend and measure scale might prove useful someday."

As usual, Gus had been right.

THE SKY LIGHTENS as pastel waves dance across the eastern horizon. As the sun rises on my right side, I sure hope north is the direction I'm supposed to be heading. The dawn casts pink rays of sunshine between dappled leaves. It's like being reborn after spending the night in a blur of fire, fear, and flight. Birds sing, their red and yellow feathers flickering among the tree tops overhead. I have never seen so much green before in my life. The world around me wakes up with the sunlight. Even the wind rustling through the leaves resembles music.

It's almost like a dream—if it wasn't such a nightmare.

Since I'm not sure I'm heading in the right direction, I take a break to unpack, reassess, and eat. My dry mouth waters in anticipation of Gus's promised sandwich. After checking the ground for dampness, I settle down on a fallen log covered with a carpet of moss, surrounded by fern. Dropping the backpack before me, I unzip slowly. Bags of dried fruit, snack bars, hard crackers, and bottles of water tumble out. Once I find Gus's magic sandwich, I devour it immediately. It's perfect.

I shouldn't be surprised that Gus put a lot of thought into the contents of this backpack: three small flashlights with plenty of extra batteries, a compass, a map, small notebooks filled with directions and notes in his handwriting. Several water bottles, matches, bandages, extra socks, water purification tablets, salt capsules, binoculars, pens, and a knife. I shrug my way out of Franco's jean jacket. The interior pockets contain small books full of detailed illustrated pictures detailing which berries and plants are safe to eat. Only obsessive Franco would include footnotes crediting a 1956 Bradford Angier book on surviving in the wild.

On the very last page of the third little book, again, I read his plea: *Please wear this jacket at all times. I need to know you made it out alive.*

Touching his jacket almost feels like he's here with me. But he's not. I'm all alone. And out here I've no idea if he's still alive. After all, they killed Liam. And Franco's such a hothead, he won't stay quiet for long.

I clench my hands to stop their shaking. It's all too much. Franco's words swim before my tired eyes. Setting down his books, I reach for Gus's maps. I can't take another step until I figure out which direction to go, but a quick glance at them overwhelms me even more. My head aches, and I can't stop yawning.

I need to rest, but I'm afraid to stop moving. What should I do?

Trembling, I load everything back in the pack then search the sky above me, making sure I'm hidden from view by the trees before I slump into position to sleep.

Last time I woke up, Gus was at my side. Next time, I'll be alone.

4

WALKING ON SUNSHINE

With a rush of terror I wake up, grasping at my wrist, searching for the GPS training watch the New Order gave me for the Race for Citizen Glory. But that wrist is now bare—except for the self-inflicted scars that will persist forever. Breathing hard, I scan the surrounding trees to make sure no one's found me. That watch is long gone, so they can't trace me now. I feel my upper right arm for the familiar blip of the embedded microchip. At least I hope they can't trace me now. I think this was just for identification purposes, but I guess I don't really know.

At least if I had a watch, I'd know what time it was. Not that it should matter, but I'd feel a little more anchored if I could figure out the date and time and everything. But not if it meant the New Order could find me out here. They sure seemed to know my every move while I wore that training watch, which led them to believe I was Liam's girlfriend and an easy candidate for producing a child for one of their high-up political elites

Poor Liam. He thought he was bettering himself and lost everything because of his great ambition. And poor Franco. He gave up everything to help his family and ended up losing his cousin anyway.

I didn't protect him. I promised Jack I would.

Of course, Franco blamed himself. No wonder he pushed me away. But I don't want to think about that. I gotta get moving.

Groaning a little, I stretch and rub my eyes before diving back into Gus's backpack. Still hungry, I grab a bag of dried fruit and nuts to snack on as I examine two Rand McNally laminated maps.

"Wisconsin state map and Minnesota Easy Finder," I read aloud. Although we don't use state names anymore, I remember these were both in the Midwest where Panopticus is located.

A red circular sticker denotes a city named Kenosha, with the words "You are HERE" in Gus's handwriting alongside. I smile, remembering where he kept his thick, black permanent marker in that "trust me, I'm a doctor" cup perched on his desk. I scan the rest of the Wisconsin map, turning it over, folding and unfolding it, but can't find any other stickers. Setting that map aside, I open the Minnesota Easy Finder, and there it is—another big, red dot—this time to the left of a city once named Rochester. "THIS is where you WANT to be" written again in Gus's black scrawl.

This is where my dad went. This is where he stayed instead of coming back to get me and Mom. This is where I'm going. Quickly, I measure out the miles from eastern Wisconsin to southeast Minnesota, but there are multiple routes to consider. Since I can't fly like a bird straight over there, I'll need to walk, relying on landmarks I'm not even sure will still be around. It's been at least twenty-five years since the major highways on this map have seen traffic. Maybe longer. Some of them could have been blown up during the war, but there's gotta be a few road signs left. At least I hope so.

If I'm right, it looks like I should travel north on 94, then follow 94 west and then northwest into Minnesota. That's about three hundred miles based on the map scale. The food Gus packed will only last so long, so I'll have to find more to eat along the way. Next, I page through Franco's books to figure out what berries and fruit might be ripe this time of year. Looks like late summer I might find raspberries or blackberries or early apples. I'll also need water. Gus tucked quite a few bottles away in this backpack, but I'll need more. Gus even included a bottle of iodine tablets with a sticker that's says they can be used to purify water.

Okay, first things first. I need to use the bathroom, except there aren't any bathrooms out here. Everything's just out in the open, and I better make sure I don't end up squatting on some poison ivy or anything. That would be a disaster.

Once that awkward morning business is over and done with, I focus on finding that highway. Finishing my snack plus some water, I replace all the contents of the pack and hoist it onto my back. Then it's one step in front of the other through all this beautiful nature. No buildings, no skyscrapers, no streetlights, no roads, no people—just me, and plants, and sky.

Warm sunshine filters through the treetops. Thank goodness it's the end of summer and I don't have to worry about getting cold. There's so much green I just want to stand still and drink it all in, but I must keep moving. My old self would have been ecstatic to have been surrounded by so much green: the ferns, the trees, the moss growing on the north side of the trees (another fun fact Gus once told me). My dad would love this too. He loved plants and filled our old apartment with as many as he could find.

I should be beyond thrilled to see my father again, but the thought that he never came back to get us still eats at me. Why didn't he come back? What stopped him? Unless he *did* try and something bad happened to him. Gus wouldn't know about that, I don't think. Or would he? How much did Gus know about what happened when people got outside the walls of the city? How much communication did he have? He said our goodbye was forever, like I shouldn't even give him another thought. But that's impossible. Who does he think I am? I would never give up on him.

But first I have to find the highway. Despite all my wandering last night, I'm pretty sure that if I keep moving north I'll eventually hit 94 as it veers west. If I happen to be just east of 94 as it moves north, I'll run into Lake Michigan. Then I'll just redirect my path. No problem, right? Once I get to the highway, walking on a road will be so much easier than trekking through the woods. But I'm much more hidden here in the woods. I could be spotted pretty easily on the open road from the air if anyone from Panopticus is searching for me.

Birds fly overhead, calling out to each other. Squirrels climb high in the trees, jumping branches with ease. I come upon a narrow strip of dirt that leads me further into the woods. I believe Gus would call this a deer path. Good thing I obsessed over everything that man said. His endless knowledge on every single topic comes in useful. Although I have enough drinking water for now, I remember he taught me that game trails often lead to water, and I wouldn't mind bathing away some of this smoke and grime.

The sky is so blue and the air so pure. Nothing's fake here. The sheer beauty puts the Northwest Citizen Park to shame—except, of course, for the disappointing lack of lilacs. I remember now that in the real world they just bloom in spring, but the genetically modified ones bloomed in the Panopticus parks all summer long. I guess they got one thing right.

I always spent as much time in the park as I could with whoever would take me there—whether it be my mom or dad, or even Franco.

Let's walk around and pretend this is what the whole world looks like. Forget there's row after row of identical gray apartment buildings outside the gate.

There's no rows of buildings here. This is what I always wanted—or thought I wanted, anyway. But maybe I didn't know what I was wishing for. All this green isn't enough. Being left alone isn't what I wanted after all. My vision blurs with images of everyone I've left behind, then clears as the trees thin to tall grass.

The deer path has led me right to the highway.

5

LIFE IS A HIGHWAY

This highway stretches on forever, two lanes on either side, separated by a wide strip of tall grass in between. I can't see any signs from where I stand, but I hope this is highway 94. The road's not in great shape with the edges eroding and the asphalt faded and worn. Nobody's maintained it for years, but it's not bad for walking.

I set off at a faster pace than I could manage through the woods, hoping to cover good ground before nightfall. It's warm, but there's a nice breeze, even better now that I'm out in the open. My head is clear now, so I think all the drugs the Suits injected into me have finally worn off. Gus is right. I can do this. I'm in good shape from training for that race, so I can handle traveling cross country on my own to find my dad. It shouldn't be too difficult to convince him to help me take Panopticus down, destroy the New Order, and establish something better for everyone. It's not impossible. Gus might be brilliant, but he's wrong about me not coming back for him. Maybe I couldn't take over for him like he planned, but I can set him free.

Man, there's a lot of pot holes here in this road. I guess maybe one thing the New Order is good at is road maintenance, but I still hate them. Occasionally I spot deer, their white tails flashing as they scamper away, spooked by my presence. Seeing all these animals and plants out in the real world feels like I've fallen into one of Gus's nature shows. I wonder why the New Order kept those shows available for us to watch. Didn't they worry we would yearn to escape, or did they just assume we were so dependent on them it didn't matter what we saw? That we'd all remain stuck under their thumb because we weren't brave enough to break free? I know I never dreamt of leaving until it was forced upon me.

Forlorn buildings line both sides of the highway, so I must be nearing a city. Tall weeds creep up the walls of homes with broken windows, peeling paint, and gaping doors. All worn-out shells of what they once must have been. Individual houses seem so strange to me. I'm too used to the tall apartment buildings of Panopticus. Here, even buildings that look like multi-family dwellings are only three or four stories tall, not ten or twenty. This type of living seems surreal and foreign, like it never really happened and this is all just fake. But, deep down, I know it's real, or at least it used to be. Now it's just sad and lonely. Where have all these people gone? What were their lives like? What was the war like?

Sometimes all that's left behind on the side of the road is just rubble. I wonder how widespread the bombing was here in the Midwest. They taught us about it in school—naturally, from the viewpoint of the New Order, so you never knew what to trust. So many war pictures of flattened homes and massive destruction. Long hospital hallways crammed with rows of stretchers filled with dying patients. Photos of burned bodies, the patients' skin and faces almost unrecognizable as human. It must have been so awful. Even Gus— the bravest man I'll ever know—could barely talk about it. He lost everyone he loved either during the war or because of its lasting health effects afterwards.

Be thankful we have peace now. You have no idea what it was like, always being at war—and with so many countries at once. Everyone throwing bombs at everyone else. After the nuclear fallout, everyone rushed to the nearest radiation treatment center. My family came here, but everyone died except for me.

So many died. No wonder those left behind were lost and scared and ready to follow the organization they believed had saved them.

Before World War III America had a population of about four-hundred million. And now, it's a tenth of that. Millions died instantly in the direct nuclear attack. Millions more died soon thereafter with horrible, incurable ailments. So many people dying with no way to treat them. No way to stop their pain.

That's why Gus switched from studying theater to medicine. He wanted to help. But his education in theater ended up helping people escape the New Order instead. He had so many tricks up his sleeves. He was always there for me, no matter what I needed. He was my best teacher, a shoulder to lean on, and someone to talk to who really listened and let me think for myself. Maybe I took him for granted. I miss him so much already.

So much endless walking. And thinking. I've never spent this much time alone in my own head before. I can't believe nothing has been rebuilt out here. No windmills, solar panels, or greenhouses. The worn roads, the buildings falling apart—everything's been neglected. It all seems so wrong. There's so much space here, but no one (or almost no one) dares to live outside the Great City of Panopticus. I wonder if any of the other supposed Great Cities even exist. Is Argos, the Great City to the south, real, or is that just another big lie?

Up ahead I spy a faded road sign announcing the exit for the town of Racine, so according to Gus's old map I'm headed in the right direction—north on highway 94. I'm officially on my way. It's not so bad. I'm not bored. There's plenty to see. Weeds fill in the cracks and flourish amidst the debris surrounding the abandoned buildings, cracked roads, and fallen electric poles. Everything is so quiet you can hear the wind rustling the grasses and leaves. No human or electronic voices, no bells or alarms—just birdsong. I listen to my own breathing, my clothes rustling as I move my arms and legs, and my solitary footsteps taking me away from my mother and closer to my dad.

Everything is so still, so peaceful, so calm.

Until the screaming begins.

6

HUNGRY EYES

I sprint toward the howls of fear and pain, expecting to find wolves circling a terrorized child. The backpack feels twice as heavy as I gasp for air racing up a steep hill. I can't see anything except black crows swirling overhead as I reach the top.

Catching my breath, I approach the bloody scene. A glassy-eyed deer lay flat on its side, front legs akimbo and chest covered with dark red blood. It has to be dead. Please let it already be dead. Don't let it linger in pain. But then, who is screaming?

A half dozen rough-looking dogs, at least sixty to seventy pounds each, circle the poor creature. In the middle, crouching in a defensive position and yowling its head off, is a scrawny little dog. The larger dogs snarl and snap at the smaller one, clearly wanting the deer meat for themselves. The skinny runt holds its ground as the bigger canines advance with teeth bared. Pretty soon that deer won't be the only dead body on the road. What a stubborn little dog! I'm not sure if it's brave, or just plain stupid, for standing its ground when surrounded by so many much bigger than itself.

All of a sudden, I'm that little girl again, back in the library with the dark Suits circling, all of them so much bigger and stronger than me. I was all alone, and no one came to help. Well, that isn't going to happen here.

I hurry to the side of the road to grab a couple medium length, thick fallen branches.

"Get away!" My voice cracks from smoke and disuse as I shove my way into the fray, arms swinging. "Leave him alone! Back off!"

Everything pauses for a moment as the wild dogs turn my way in surprise. Then that little twerp dog growls at me, not at all appreciating my interference. Oh, why did I bother? Now I'm positioned with the dead deer behind me and the six snarling big dogs in front, blocking any hope of escape. I'm so stupid for getting involved. I could get bit or injured by any of these dogs. Even the little one barks and snaps at my ankles, dancing back and forth between me and the dead deer and the big dogs.

"Shut up, you idiot!" I yell, which makes him stop for a second and whine.

I slam the sticks down on the ground in front of me, trying to drive the larger dogs away from their meal, which isn't working. I need to get out of here, but how am I going to pick up this mongrel without it biting me? It's already covered in blood—I'm not sure whose—and probably injured, so maybe this whole thing is pointless, and I won't be saving anyone today anyway. But it's worth a try.

"Let's go!" With one stick I nudge the snarling little dog away from the deer and keep the larger dogs at bay with the other stick, trying to remove us from this dangerous equation.

The small one keeps trying to dash back in to get a bite of the deer, but finally we make it to the side of the road.

"You're an idiot. You know that?" I inform the dumb dog.

It whimpers, glancing back at the others already gnawing on the fallen deer, still snapping at each other.

"But you're brave. I'll give you that." I set down the branches and my backpack. "If you're so hungry, I'll give you something. Just give me a minute."

I dig out another sandwich, take one bite myself then pull off a good sized chuck to hand to the little dog.

The mongrel backs away from my hand at first, then sniffs the air and dashes in to snatch the food.

"Hey, there, watch it! You almost took my finger off."

The next piece I toss on the ground near the dog to avoid getting bit. The poor thing's ribs undulate with every breath. It's that skinny. There's blood smeared across both flanks, but so far I don't see any open wounds. He's not lame or anything, so maybe it's just deer blood after all.

"Are you hurt, buddy? Let me see you."

The determined little thing keeps inching closer to the dead deer in the road.

"Don't be stupid! Hold on. Wait a minute." I listen intently. "What's that noise?" A mechanical engine grumbles in the distance, but the noise keeps increasing, so it's definitely coming closer. Hands shaking, I grab my backpack and dash for tree cover, sneaking glances overhead for a plane or helicopter or whatever the New Order might send after me.

"Come on, dog!" I urge, but am ignored.

The rumbling increases, roaring so loud now it's pounding in my head. I can't think straight. It's all over now. Over before I even got started, before I even found my dad. They figured it out. They know I've escaped. They know Gus helped me. I knew they'd come. I knew I'd never see Dad again. Or Gus. Or Franco. Or my mom.

Ducking into the woods, I crouch behind some bushes hoping against hope to not be seen. Maybe I should hide further in, but I must at least know what's going on. Who's coming for me? Is it a plane or a car or what? What's the best way to hide?

The noise takes over. There's no more peace and quiet, just the thunderous roar of an unseen engine. The sky remains clear, but there's something heading this way fast on the road from the west. The strange looking vehicle sports four big black wheels, no doors or top, just a camouflage patterned open frame. The odd contraption screeches up to the dead deer, the engine kills, and two passengers jump off. One shoots a rifle once into the sky, scattering the larger dogs.

But that smaller, idiot dog remains on the side of the road, barking its fool head off. I hope they don't hurt it. I wish it would've followed me, but it's too late now to do anything about that.

"I'm telling you, Nate, this deer just came out of nowhere and ran smack into the four-wheeler. There was nothing I could do."

"Nothing, huh?" The dark-haired, dark-skinned young man with the rifle crouches down to examine the deer. "Looks like you took your sweet time telling me about it. We should've been here earlier. It's a shame to waste fresh meat."

"I knew you'd be mad..."

Nate levels a gaze at the light-haired kid who is maybe in his mid-teens. "You need to be more careful. We can't afford to damage what little working equipment we have."

"I know..."

"Let's load it up and take it home."

The two men struggle to lift the deer onto the back end of the large four-wheeler, the stupid little dog yapping at their ankles the whole time.

"Just shut up, you stupid dog!" grumbles the younger guy, sweating and grunting in effort.

I cringe, hoping they don't harm it. I can't break my cover. Or should I go talk to them? Maybe they'd help me find my dad. What should I do? Hide because they're strangers, or ask for help? For starters, they have a vehicle, which is a lot faster than walking.

"It's just hungry." Nate digs into a pocket and tosses the dog a morsel which gets devoured in the one quiet second before the barking starts all over again.

"Now *you're* the one wasting food!" teases the younger guy, shaking his head as he gets back on the vehicle.

Gulping down my fear, I decide to approach. There's no Suits here, just two guys who probably don't like the New Order any better than I do. Plus, the one named Nate just fed the scrappy dog instead of hurting it. He could be safe. I take one step forward, then hesitate. Taking deep breaths, I clench my hands.

I burst out from my hiding place and wave my arms just as Nate jumps on the vehicle and starts the engine. The ensuing roar of the motor drowns out my greeting.

They take off down the road without a backwards glance.

7

THE TRICK IS TO KEEP BREATHING

After the War, some people resisted the move to the cities. Ben's brother was one of them. His name's Harry. He's the one who sets off the fireworks show every Fourth of July, just to let me know he's still out there.

Although Gus had informed me that not everyone moved to the Great Cities, he didn't have enough time to explain what to do if I happened to find strangers out here in the wilderness. The great wide world out here is intimidating, and I'm alone and vulnerable in it. So instead of tearing off down the worn out road, screaming after the deer laden four wheeler, I retreat back into the woods, slipping in between the green leaves. Watching the one vehicle I've seen so far shrink into the distance, my spirits sink knowing that I've just ruined my best chance at finding my father before I run out of the food Gus packed for me.

That fence was built to restrain you, not protect you.

Gus meant to reassure me and give me much-needed confidence. So why does some small, scared part of me yearn for the false security of the familiar world I knew so well?

Happiness comes from security, not freedom.

I shake my head, annoyed at my moment of doubt. How can any part of me want any part of Panopticus, especially after what the leaders have done to me, my dad, and Liam? And, quite possibly, what they are doing right now to my mom.

At the moment, your mom will have to fend for herself. But she could be in trouble. Franco told her everything.

Remembering Gus's warning is like a punch to the gut. I collapse to the ground, focusing on breathing, as my thoughts spiral. My poor mom shut down when we thought Dad died. It's still so hard to wrap my mind around the idea he's still alive. At least I hope he is. All I know for sure is that last time Mom broke apart, and I'm the one who took care of her, even though I was just a kid. But who's going to step in now? Gus? Franco? And will that make the New Order suspicious? It's not like Franco is super stable or great at dealing with grief.

If I lost someone I loved, I'd hide or destroy every picture. I don't think I could bear seeing them at all if that was all that was left for me. Denial's not such a bad place to live. Sometimes it's the only way to survive.

I'm not sure I can count on Franco to save my mom. He's got his own family to worry about, especially after they lost Liam. Plus, he's kind of crazy—brilliant, but erratic. I never knew what he was hiding, what he was thinking, or what he'd do next.

I'm not holding back anymore. I'm taking it all down. Everything. The whole city of Panopticus—where there is Liberty and Justice for none.

There hadn't been any Liberty or Justice for Liam. Tearing Panopticus down sounds very reasonable to me right now, although I don't want to end up half crazy like Franco. And I don't want to lose any more people I care about. Losing Liam was bad enough.

Poor Franco. He lost both his cousin, Liam, and his Uncle Jack due to Panopticus. Come to think of it, what happened to his own parents? He never talked about them. His grief and guilt over Liam turned him into a rambling drunk, but hopefully that was just temporary. Too bad he had to be drunk in order to kiss me. My cheeks warm at the thought. Afterwards, he pushed me away and told me to leave him alone—which broke my heart at the time, but maybe that doesn't matter in light of everything else that happened.

The next day, after I'd already been kidnapped by the Suits, Franco went searching for me. He found my mom instead and told her everything he never told me. How did she react to the news that my father is still alive? I can't even imagine. I just hope she's holding herself together this time. I shudder thinking about what I'm leaving behind as I search for help.

I adjust the backpack straps, intent on finding another deer trail. I'd like to find a clean-looking water source before tonight. I'll use the compass to make sure I don't veer too far south of the highway as it heads west. I've got to find my dad as fast as I can. And if I find anyone else again before then, maybe I'll try harder to ask for help.

Branches crunch behind me. I whirl around with my fists in the air. I can't see anyone, but I can hear them moving closer. Somebody's coming.

8

SOMEBODY'S WATCHING ME

Heart hammering in my chest, I sneak between trees and shrubs, wincing every time I step on a stick, the resounding crack ringing through the air. There's nowhere to hide, nowhere to run. Why don't I have any weapons?

The rustling continues behind me, but no voices, no footsteps, no sirens or alarms, nothing mechanical or robotic. Who's out there? Did those two guys come back? Did the New Order find me with a drone? Pausing to peek between the leaves of a very big shrub, I shiver in terror until I notice that the movement comes from near the ground. Low branches shake, but nothing higher than two feet. Must be a rabbit or a squirrel or a skunk—not that I relish the idea of encountering a mad skunk.

The ferns rustle one last time, and that rotten little dog emerges from between the lush greenery, stopping to shake its head before trotting toward me as if I'd called it to my side.

"What do you want?" I ask, hands on my hips and relief in my heart.

It licks its lips, looking up at me expectantly.

I'd been afraid of this little runt? How brave is that? I sigh.

Apparently, I have a new companion. "When's the last time you ate a real meal, buddy?" I dig in my pocket and toss some flattened leftover sandwich bits to the gaunt dog.

Maybe I'll regret this later, but for the moment I'm not as hungry as this starved creature in front of me.

"You're pretty good at begging, so maybe there's more people out here than I realized, enough to bum scraps from, anyway."

The little scrounger gulps down my bread and imitation sliced meat (yet another Panopticus-designed alternative protein source) sandwich in seconds. Then it stares at me again with big, pleading brown eyes.

"That's all you're getting for now. And if you'll excuse me, I'd better find some water to sanitize." I push away a branch and continue along a deer path, hoping it leads to a small stream.

I glance back to see if I'm being followed. Yes, I am. Onward we hike, with me in the lead and the little dog trotting behind me. If I stop, it stops. If I hurry ahead, it catches up but hangs back at a slight distance. The sun overhead beats down on us through the trees. The backpack chafes my back, but I don't want to stop for that. I need to find water first, then I'll rest. I don't know how hard it is to find water out here in the wild, and I can't remember the last time it rained, assuming it would be the same here as in Panopticus.

On we travel through the forest, me sweating under the heavy pack and swatting at an occasional mosquito. I watch my footing, not wanting to trip on a stick or root with so many of them cluttering my chosen path. To help pass time, I sort the sticks in my head. Long ones, short ones, fat ones, and skinny ones. Black ones and brown ones. Some freshly fallen with green leaves and some crispy old dried gray ones. And, oh, look, here's a different one, this one starts out light gray, but it has such cool reddish-brown spots bordered with black on it. Is that mold or something?

I bend down to pick it up for closer examination, my fingers hovering.

The stick moves.

9

THE BIRDS AND THE BEES

My mouth goes dry as I back away, bumping into the little dog.

"Stop! Snake!" I point, as if that will help the dog understand. "Stay back!"

The dog's ears perk up as it steps closer and leans in.

The coils of the snake slither hypnotically.

This stupid dog is so keen for this snake. Why can't it sense the danger?

"Don't—" There's no time. I crouch down. "Okay, then. Just don't bite me!" Cringing, I slip a hand under the dog's belly and lift it up and away from the twisting reptile. "It's okay, pooch. It's okay. I'll protect you."

Backing a few steps away from the snake, I veer off the trail, watching my footing in case fellow serpents are hiding nearby. When I think we are far enough away from those slippery coils, I set the dog back down.

"Thanks for not biting me, and don't even think of running back there," I warn as it glances back in that direction.

What a macho dog. It's so brave, wanting to go investigate, and here I am shuddering just thinking about the undulating muscular coils of the snake. I don't know if it was poisonous. I suppose Franco might have something in one of his books about it, but I didn't have time to look it up before running away. Better to be safe than dead. I've read books making fun of city girls, and growing up in Panopticus, that's who I am—very much out of my comfort zone here.

"Let's go," I command. "And let's hope all we find now is water. No more snakes, please."

Onward we hike along yet another deer path. My sweat-drenched ponytail drips down my back. The muggy air has no breeze. I'm sure I reek something awful—the one benefit to not having Franco here, I suppose. Every time I glance back, that little pooch trails after me. We often stop for water breaks, further depleting my supply. I chug from the bottles, knowing that if I don't keep myself well-hydrated I'll be toast out here in the hot August sun. But with every bottle I empty, the fear grows that I won't find more water in time. Crossing my fingers that I won't regret this later, I rest a little plastic red cup I discovered in my backpack down on the ground and fill it with water for my four legged friend. Watching the little pink tongue lapping the cup dry, I know I've done the right thing.

Hours tick by. If I still had a watch I'd be able to keep better track. I never realized how much I focused on what time of day it was until now. Maybe total freedom isn't all it's cracked up to be. I need some sort of structure. Maybe most people do. My back aches. The foliage grows thicker between the trees, further blocking any welcome breeze. Birds sing from on high. The buzzing of insects hangs in the air, although the heat of the day seems to have stopped them from pestering me for a while. There's more mosquitoes out here than there were in the city. One of the very few benefits of living under Panopticus rule.

The little dog continues to follow me even though it didn't seem to like me too much at first. Perhaps the few bits of food I've given it were enough to convince it to stick close by. Thank goodness I haven't come across any more snakes. And if more snakes are hiding out there in between all the rocks and leaves, but I can't see them, and they don't bug me and I don't bug them, I'm okay with that. I just don't want to find any more of them.

On the other hand, I *would* like to find some water. By my calculations, I have a day or so left before I run out. I'm not sure how many miles I've covered today. I could head back to the highway and look for more road signs to figure out how far west I've gotten. But I need the water first, and I doubt I'll find it while walking the highway.

Gus said that deer trails often led to water, and the best sources of water should have lots of healthy plant life surrounding them. If everything looks half dead around it, then it's not safe to drink. That's all I know about how to find water. Back in Panopticus, I never had to worry about it. It was just there. Yes, you had to take short showers for conservation purposes. Right now I'd give just about anything to take a shower—get rid of this backpack, clean away all this sweat, and put on fresh clothes. Sounds like a dream.

What am I doing dreaming about Panopticus? How can I care about the few good things there?

The deer path I'm on narrows and foliage encroaches even more, making it hard to pass. Protecting my face with my arms, I push through.

"You coming?" I peek back to check on the dog.

Not even breaking stride, it ducks underneath the leafage and forges ahead of me. I guess there are some benefits to being short.

"Ow!" A sharp whip-like branch slices my right arm, leaving a long, bright-red bleeding scrape. "Idiot plant!"

I pause to reassess, not wanting to get injured further, and hear chewing. Glancing down, I spy bright red berries being swallowed whole by the dog, one after the other in rapid succession.

"Raspberries!" I am saved. There should be plenty of moisture in these berries.

As I pick the berries, I realize the sharp, cutting vines are from the raspberry plant itself. Of course, I should've remembered they had thorns, but I've never seen it growing in the wild before. The vines are everywhere, stretching out of control. Stuffing my face, I pick clean the top half of the bush while the dog clears the lower half. There's a bounty here. We can both eat our fill without any worry about depleting our precious supplies.

With each delicious bite, my fears and worries fade. I can find water tomorrow. I'm okay for today, especially when I can gorge on such luscious fruit in unlimited quantities. I want to find a good place to rest before night falls. It's okay if today isn't the day to find water. There's always tomorrow. I have time. We will both have our fill today, thanks to Mother Nature.

Once the dog has eaten everything it can reach, it starts begging again. I empty a handful of berries on the ground next to my foot. The dog dives in greedily. I smile, because there's plenty more where that came from.

I reach out for a luscious berry when a stabbing pain plunges into my right hand.

I've been shot.

10

ZOMBIE

Ducking down, I cradle my injured hand, expecting blood to spurt through my fingers. But there's no blood at all, just a raised pink lesion that hurts like someone's stabbed a sharp knife into my hand. What the heck? Searching warily through the raspberry patch, I spy a yellow hornet. Then I spot another one. Holy hell, do bee stings hurt. I had no idea. I've never been stung before.

I guess it's better than being shot, but it sure makes eating berries less fun. I'm so done with all this wilderness crap right now. My back hurts, my feet ache, and now my freaking hand burns. I'm sweaty and crabby, and I've got a headache. I'm so tired. I've never been this tired before in my whole life.

"Let's find somewhere to rest, buddy. I can't take any more today. Today sucks." I stalk off, hunting for flat open ground with no bees, no snakes, and nothing else waiting to bite, sting, or chew me up into little bits. I'm so sick of nature and would be ever so grateful for an actual bed.

After maybe another half hour of confused hiking where I can hardly remember my name or my reason for being here, I drop down.

Shrugging off the backpack, I can barely stay awake long enough to dig out the mosquito netting and what very well might be my last water bottle. Swallowing eagerly, I almost down the whole thing when a small whine stops me.

Those begging brown eyes. I stop drinking to dig in the pack for the little red cup. I'm so weary and muddled that a bunch of other crap falls out instead. But I do find it and pour the last of the water into the cup, my hand shaking and throbbing in pain. The little dog laps up the water as I shove everything else back in the backpack. My unsteady hand pauses on a full bottle of capsules with Gus's perfect handwriting in bright red pen across a large white sticker on the side:

SILVIA: Be careful in the heat! Hyponatremia causes nausea, muscle cramps, confusion, headaches, etc. Best ward it off by taking two electrolyte capsules per hour during exercise. Don't forget!

I unscrew the lid and swallow two capsules dry, letting them scratch down my throat. Stupid me. I haven't taken any of these yet. I don't even remember seeing this bottle before, but every time I sat down to open my pack I was in such a hurry that maybe I just didn't pay enough attention. I'll do better tomorrow, but right now I'm going to get some sleep. I'll deal with everything else in the morning. Nudging the pack to one side, I lie down and drape the bug netting over my body as I curl into a ball.

"Good night, pup," I mumble, already half asleep.

MY EYES FLY OPEN, waking with a start, something fuzzy and warm curled at my side. First I tense, then relax. That's right. I'm lost here in the woods, and I've made a friend. Sensing my movement, the hairy light-brown creature stretches out all four paws and yawns, its little pink tongue uncurling. Man, this little thing is cute. No wonder people used to have pets. Of course, I've never had one. I don't think anyone in Panopticus did—at least no one I knew. Gus's family had dogs long before I knew him.

We had a dog named Albert. He wasn't beautiful to look at, but he was the best dog ever. Scruffy hair every color you can think of—brown, black, white, gray, tan. He had dark brown eyes, a long black tail with a white tip, and tall gangly legs. He wasn't what you'd call proportionate. Not very graceful, either. But he was my little sister's best friend, especially once she got sick. He could be there when I couldn't because of work or school. Beth was so weak and in such pain. She slept all the time with Albert at her side. Near the end, she couldn't get out of bed and wouldn't eat. Her hand rested on Albert, never moving.

That last day, I watched as her breathing grew weaker and jagged. Her pale skin changed from pink to rose to purple. It was awful to watch her cough and choke and not be able to do anything to stop it.

Albert never moved. I couldn't convince him to eat, or potty, or anything. He simply refused. Not until the end. Seconds after she took her last, gasping breath he got up and walked away. I knew without checking her pulse that she was gone.

Albert was already so old by then. He died soon after Beth left us. I figured he couldn't see the point of life here without her.

Gus talked of Beth every winter, because that's when she died. He had lost everything: his family, his partner, and maybe his belief that his life could get any better. Was that why he never tried to escape himself, and why he didn't believe I'd come back for him? Maybe he was so used to losing those he cared about, he just expected it.

Well, I want a happy ending for Gus, so I will make it happen. But first I should carefully go through the backpack and assess what's left of the supplies and what I need to do to avoid turning into such a zombie like I did last night. For starters, I will remember to take electrolyte tabs on a regular basis.

I stretch, smiling at the little dog watching me expectantly. "You need a name. You're a boy, right? Yes, I can see you are. And don't worry, I'll find you some breakfast while I decide."

As I dig into Gus's backpack, the choice becomes obvious. "Let's call you Albert."

11

HIT THE ROAD, JACK

First thing out of the backpack is a medical kit. Time to peel off these smelly socks and shoes and cover up the blisters on my heels and toes. It's harder to address the wounds on my lower back from the pack rubbing because I can't see what I'm doing, but hopefully I'll slap the bandage tape on the right spots. Gus packed me a fresh set of clothes, and it feels a little bit like heaven to put on a pair of clean socks.

After folding up the mosquito netting, I tuck it deep inside the pack and tie the socks to the outside so they can air out. I've got two full water bottles left, plenty of water purification tablets, lots of salt capsules, three small bags of dried fruit, and four granola bars. Sadly, I've run out of sandwiches. I've got just a day of water and two days of food left, and so far I haven't had any luck finding water. Maybe I've just been an idiot wandering down the deer paths, thinking I'd happen upon a stream that way. Would the map help me find the water faster? Unfolding the Wisconsin map over my backpack, I scan the lower half of the state. Lake Michigan is way over by Milwaukee on the right, but I'm so far away from that now it's no help. After that, there's nothing obvious until I get to the Madison area, where there's a couple lakes called Mendota and Monona.

My best bet is to go back to the highway so I can head west faster than I can here in the woods, hoping I make it to Madison before I run out of water. After last night, I know too well that if I don't drink or eat enough and don't get enough salt, I'll get weak and disoriented. I can't risk that again. I can't let Gus down after all he did for me, including putting a lot of thought into packing this bag. In addition to everything else, there's a small box of safety pins, matches, a knife, binoculars, a fish hook and line, and a baseball hat. I slip the lightweight gray hat on right away to help keep the sun off my head and out of my eyes. I put everything else away except the compass after splitting a granola bar and half bottle of water with Albert and taking another pair of electrolyte capsules.

"Let's hit the road, buddy." Using the compass, I work my way north to northwest, hoping to hit the highway sooner rather than later. We need more water ASAP. Albert trots after me. It's not the easiest thing to plow through these woods, since I'm not always on a deer path and the undergrowth can get pretty thick.

"This is like the most disorganized park in the world," I chat to Albert to pass the time. "You can tell Franco didn't have anything to do with this. See those vines climbing up that tree like a snake? Franco would chop those down for sure. I hope we don't see any more snakes. I'd rather find more raspberries. Keep your eyes peeled. I know we're both hungry. Not that I want to get stung again. I'll be more careful next time."

Compass in hand, we march onward. Once we find the highway, we can figure out where we are and how long it will take to get to water. We need to hurry. After what seems like a few more hours and a few hundred more mosquito bites and plant scratches, Albert and I emerge back where we first met—on the highway.

"Oh man, I could just kneel down and kiss this road. We're here, buddy! What a relief! Now, what does that sign say? Lake Mills? Okay, let's take a super short rest, eat something, and check the map." I struggle to sit down, every muscle stiff and sore. We split another granola bar, dried fruit, and water. I take another electrolyte capsule, then hesitate. "Albert, you might need these too, but I've no idea what the correct dose is, and I don't want to make you sick."

I lie all the way back on the bare ground to stretch out my sore back, wishing for someone real nice to come along with a car and drive us to the nearest water source, but I don't think that's going to happen. "Okay, where's that map? Let's see here. Looks like Lake Mills measures out to be maybe just under thirty miles away from Madison. We're still so far away. Oh, well. Break's over. Let's move. The sun's still high in the sky, so I think we can reach it before it gets dark."

I head straight for the pavement and start at a brisk pace. Albert lingers in the ditch, glancing at me and sort of following, but not right by my side as usual.

"What's going on, buddy? Wait a minute." I crouch down to place my hand on the road to check the surface temperature. "Woah, that's hotter than I expected. Albert, I'm joining you in the ditch. There's a bit more shade, and that highway is way too hot for your feet. We can't have you burning your paws, big guy."

Albert seeks as much shade as he can. Time passes slowly when you know it's going to take you about eight hours to get where you need to go, even if you don't have a watch to see the seconds tick by. There's no dead deer on the road, no stray dogs (thank goodness, wouldn't want Albert to get into another fight), and no four-wheeled vehicles to break up the endless asphalt. Passing the exit signs for deserted towns is a bit gratifying, but I'm still tired of walking. I sort of expected I might need to carry him at some point, but so far Albert has been keeping up.

Finally, the Madison/Monona/Middleton signs come into view, just as the evening air catches a cooling breeze. August days are so ungodly hot, but the nights are a relief. We take another little break to finish our last bottle of water and take in more food and electrolytes.

While we sit, I flip over the Wisconsin map to find the city of Madison guide to help me find the lakes.

"All right, this is it. Let's both go jump in the lake, okay? I know *I* stink. How about you, buddy?"

As the sun loses its strength, we travel deserted streets passing empty buildings with broken windows, a faded carousel, and countless weeds climbing up and taking over everywhere. Everything's so dull and worn until a sliver of blue shimmers in the distance. A lake! We are saved! I break into a stiff legged run with Albert meeting my pace. At the shoreline, I ditch my backpack, hat, shoes, and socks to dance in the refreshing gentle waves. But it isn't enough. I push out further, dunking my whole body into the cool, shallow depths. It's liquid perfection. I've never appreciated a shower or bath more in my entire life. I don't even care that I don't have any soap.

Wait. Where's Albert? Does he know how to swim? I burst out of the water, yelling his name. "Albert! Buddy! Where are you?"

I scan the beach. Where on earth did he go? I didn't lead him into the lake to drown, did I? Crashing through the water, I search the shallow depths along the shoreline. I can't find him anywhere. Finally, I spot him frolicking further down the beach. My moment of panic evaporates. He's okay. He's okay.

He spots me and comes running back.

"Good boy! You're a good boy. Here's another piece of granola bar for you, buddy. Okay, my little overconfident stud muffin, let's stop fooling around and focus on sterilizing some drinking water."

I line up all the water bottles, dropping iodine tablets in each one. Then I fill them with lake water and shake them like crazy. Now all I have to do is wait. The label on the iodine tablet bottle claims it takes twenty to thirty minutes to disinfect the water, but maybe I'll wait longer than that, just to be safe. Albert laps at the water's edge, which looks tempting, but I'll be patient.

As nice as it is right here where we are, the shoreline further on gleams even more invitingly, so I hoist up the full backpack and move out. We reach a deserted college campus, according to the faded signs, starting with a big hill. I can picture how charming it must have been here in its heyday. The buildings still look interesting, even if they are run down. We find a lovely limestone trail along the southern edge of Lake Mendota. As the college buildings thin out, we reach a picturesque part of the lakeshore with worn docks reaching out into the water.

"We should stop here to rest. I'm exhausted. You must be too."

Albert circles once and sits, looking out at the lake. Every color in the rainbow floats on the water.

"It's pretty here with the sunset, isn't it? I sure wish I had more food. Should we split another granola bar now, or... Wait. Where are you running off to? Hey, come back! Don't go!"

I charge after Albert, but he's too darn fast. He disappears just as darkness falls. I can't see him anywhere. Where did he go? I found him last time, so maybe I shouldn't worry. But it's too quiet, like the world holds its breath. The eerie silence breaks with Albert barking wildly. He sounds scared. I bolt toward the awful noise even though part of me (maybe the smarter part) wants to sprint in the opposite direction. Racing along the lake's edge, the trees and their lengthening black shadows block my view as the path curves to the right. Albert's terrified barking grows louder. Screaming out his name, I round the curve and have to veer sharply to avoid running into him.

But he's not alone.

He's growling at an old man half hidden in the shadows, pointing a gun in our direction.

12

SOLITARY MAN

Albert stands his ground, teeth bared and paws firmly planted.

"Don't hurt Albert!" I beg.

The old man chuckles, sending shivers down my spine. "That's one badass little bodyguard you've got there, young lady."

"Please don't hurt him," I repeat, my hands shaking.

"Why would I hurt him? I *like* dogs."

"Okay, then." I take a deep breath. "Put away your gun."

He cocks his head to the side. "Call off Cujo."

"Albert—"

"Never mind. I'll take care of this." He lowers his gun, turns toward the water, and yells, "Rachel! Get over here!"

Who's Rachel? I tense as a smattering of footsteps approaches in the falling darkness. Out of the encroaching shadows emerges a tall black dog with wavy hair.

"Good girl." The man rests a hand on the dog's head. Tail wagging, the big dog takes a moment to lean into the petting before glancing first at me then at the small, growling dog before her. Albert stops barking immediately. After a half-hearted glance in my direction, he shyly approaches Rachel, mesmerized.

"Traitor," I grumble.

Once again, the stranger chuckles. "Never met a dog that doesn't immediately fall in love with my Rachel. You're a good girl, aren't you, sweetheart?" He scratches behind her ears.

My thoughts jump all over the place. This somewhat creepy old man hasn't shaved or cut his hair in years. And I'm not used to guns being pointed at me. But is he dangerous or not? He aimed a gun at my dog, but adores his own. What should I do? Should I stick around and see if he can help us? Or run away right now and hope Albert follows? No, I won't leave him. Not now. Not here.

"So, young lady, while our dogs are getting better acquainted, why don't you tell me what you're doing out here all alone? And my name's Clark, if you're interested."

"I'm Silvia Wood." I clench my hands. "And what makes you think I'm all alone?"

"Well, let's just say I don't come across too many pleasure hikers anymore." He sighs sadly, which makes me think he might be concerned for me and not such a bad guy. "Who are you looking for, my dear?"

"My dad." The truth bursts out of me before I can stop it.

"I see." He nods. "And where did you come from? I haven't seen you or your dog before in any of the nearby Groupings. I may not get out much, but I never forget a face, and I'm even better at remembering dogs."

"I'm from Panopticus."

"Ah. You're a city girl, then. How are you managing out here? I'll bet you're hungry. Do you have enough water in your pack?"

"I just collected some." I gesture at the lake. "I'm sterilizing it with iodine tablets."

"Well, then. The fishing was pretty good today, and I don't live too far away. Would you like a hot meal before you head out again?"

My stomach says yes, but I still hesitate, glancing at Albert and Rachel playing together on the lakeshore path. It took them half a second to become friends.

"Don't worry. I don't bite. It's just... sometimes I go months without talking to another person, so I get kinda jumpy. Sorry if I scared you. I'd never shoot your dog. You just can't be too careful out here. You can't trust everyone. You've gotta be careful and watch out for yourself."

"Yeah. It's been an education so far, that's for sure. I guess I'm used to being coddled by the system. You work, you eat, you have someplace dry and warm to sleep. You don't have to think about it much, you know? It's just provided... as long as you obey all their rules."

"Well, now. I was never too keen on joining any Great City, so I'll just have to take your word for it. I'm too stubborn and set on making my own way and having my own way."

I smile. "My mom always said I was too stubborn for my own good, so maybe we have something in common."

He pauses. "So she's dead, then? I'm sorry."

"I hope not." I stiffen at the thought that he might be right. "Actually, I don't know what happened to her after I escaped."

"So you left without her?" His soft voice sounds understanding, rather than accusing.

But I get defensive anyway. "I didn't have any choice. Everything happened so quickly. And they were trying to kill me."

"But your father's out here somewhere?" His brows furrow like he's worried this might not be true. "So at least you'll have him?"

"Yeah, he's in Minnesota. But I'm not just going to have him. I'm gonna convince him to go back and save my mom so we'll all be together again. She didn't do so well eight years ago when we both thought Dad died. Things were pretty... bad. I can't leave her there alone."

"Eight years ago?" He clears his throat. "I see. Well, the offer for dinner is still open, for both of you. And I'm not a bad cook, if I do say so myself. Of course, there's usually no one else around to complain, so who knows."

"Thank you. We're both quite hungry and almost out of food."

"Then it's settled." He turns toward the lake to call the dogs. "Rachel! And what's your little furry bodyguard's name again? Oh, right, it's Albert. Albert! Let's go! Want some supper?"

The dogs join us. We head away from the lake, back through the deserted campus, over a small bridge that reaches over an old road into some housing that looks like it used to be pretty fancy back when people lived here. For a while, we don't talk at all.

"You know, don't feel bad if you can't save your mom," he says quietly.

"What?" I shake my head. "I'm going back for her. I won't leave her there alone. I won't."

"You might not have much choice," he says gently.

"You sound just like Gus." Tears flood my eyes. "He told me it would never happen. He said my dad never came back for us, so why would I come back? But he's wrong!"

"Gus. Is he the one who helped you escape?"

"Yes. I worked for him in Mortuary Sciences. He was my best friend, and yet even *he* doesn't think I'll come back. I thought he knew me better than that."

"Do you mean Gus Andrews?"

"Wait a minute. You *know* him? How do you know him when you live way out here?"

Clark shakes his scruffy head. "Can't say that I've ever had the pleasure of meeting him in person, but out here, that man is kind of a legend. I've heard his name from several people he's helped escape that I've run into as they're passing through. It's not often. In fact, I can go months without seeing a soul. But once a year or so, I might find someone in need of food or water or something to help them get where they're going."

"Have you ever met anyone going the *other* way—back to Panopticus?"

"Sorry, kid. It's kind of a one way road out here. There's no going back."

13

TAKE ME TO THE RIVER

"I don't understand why no one goes back." I sigh in frustration. "It doesn't make any sense. Don't they miss their family or friends at all?"

Clark winces. "I'm sure your father misses you. That's not the issue."

"Then what *is* the issue? I've missed my dad every single day of my life. I just can't believe he's been out here alive for eight years and never even tried to come and get us."

"It's not that easy. Panopticus is so controlled, so regimented. From what I hear, there are eyes everywhere—every street and hallway under constant surveillance. Have you figured out some great plan to save your mother?"

"Not yet." I cross my arms. "But I'll think of something. And it sure as heck won't take me eight years to figure it out."

"You know, eight years is a long time." Clark pauses. "You might not even recognize your dad when you see him."

"I'll recognize him. His picture was the first thing I looked at every morning. I've got his face and red hair memorized."

Clark chuckles. "People change. Take me for example. I used to have real short brown hair, but I've gone gray and let things go. I hardly recognize my own self whenever I bother to look in a mirror."

"You're right. Dad might look different, but that won't matter to me."

"It's not just appearances I'm talking about." Clark shrugs. "I'm not the same man I used to be. Living out here changes a person. And don't be in such a rush to blame him for something you might end up doing yourself."

"You're wrong there." I clench my teeth, trying not to let my temper flare. "I *will* go back for my mom. And Gus. And Franco."

"You could die trying." Clark turns to me in the darkness. I can't see his face anymore.

"I'd rather die than leave them behind." I straighten my shoulders. "I'm not afraid."

"You should be." Clark starts off again at such a fast pace I struggle to keep up. "Going back to Panopticus would be a death sentence if you're caught. You know just as well as I that Gus risked everything to help you escape. Don't make his sacrifice mean nothing."

My mouth goes dry. I can't bear the thought of hurting Gus.

"Okay, here we are." He stops abruptly, and I bump into him. "Watch your step. The yard's a bit overgrown—on purpose, of course."

I shadow his path past a brick home and head for the backyard, continuing past a fenced-in garden and several small trees. Clark crosses the yard toward a smaller two story structure behind the house.

"I live above the garage," he explains, unlocking the side door and letting both dogs bolt ahead of him.

Just inside the door, he grabs a small lantern and lights it, leading us to a staircase in the back left corner. The lantern illuminates tall stacks of small wooden logs lining the back wall of the garage. Parked in front of the logs is a heavy-duty four-wheeled machine.

"You have a car?" I ask breathlessly.

Clark points a thumb at it. "Well, it's not really a car. That's an ATV—an all-terrain vehicle. You can drive it most anywhere, which comes in handy. I'm glad I know enough to keep it running."

I keep staring at it, afraid to ask.

"I suppose you want me to drive you all the way to Minnesota."

"Yes, please."

"Can't do it, I'm afraid."

My shoulders droop. I knew it.

"I make a strict rule of not crossing any bridges that haven't seen any maintenance in decades, which pretty much includes every bridge there is at this point."

"I hadn't even thought about that. Are the bridges dangerous?"

"And here I thought you were never afraid." Clark gives me a small smile. "Don't worry about that now. It's late, and I'm hungry. Let's eat. Tomorrow I'll take you to the river, but once we get to the bridge, you're on your own."

14

BREAD AND BUTTER

I wake to the soft clink of metal on metal. I'm so tired. I hope it's not time to get up yet. Something rubs against my arm. Something soft and hairy. Something that pants hot stinky breath in my face.

"Stop it, Albert," I mumble.

He whines. How on earth does this little dog have so much energy all the time? He should be tired like me. I could sleep forever. My eyes fly open when I notice a mouth-watering smell.

"What is that? Is that butter?" I jerk upright into an awkward sitting position in Clark's recliner, trapped by the sheets twisted around my legs. "How do you get butter out here? Do you make it or something?"

"Well now, don't get too excited." Clark focuses on the pan sizzling over a small wood-burning stove in the corner of the room. "This is plant-based butter. I don't have a cow hidden in the garage or anything, although I do have a few chickens in a coop in the backyard."

"Don't worry. I wouldn't know any different. All I've ever had are plant-based proteins and fats. Gus has informed me that my life is incomplete since I've never had *real* ice cream."

"I'd have to agree with him." Clark chuckles. "Brings back memories of maple nut and mint chocolate chip. Oh, boy. Haven't had any real ice cream myself for a very long time. But it's eggs and toast this morning, young lady. Hope that sounds good."

"Sounds good, smells good. It's all good." I struggle to get out of the recliner. "What's *wrong* with this thing? It doesn't make any sense. How do I get out of here?"

"Like I told you last night, you're making this harder than it should be. The handle's on the right side. Just flip it forward."

"Oh, right." I get up, fold the sheet together, and set it on the chair before crossing the small room to peer over Clark's shoulder. "How can I help?"

"Well, you can start by escorting those two furry whipper-snappers back outside to finish their jobs. They've already been out once, but got distracted. Sorry to say, there's no indoor potty in here."

"Got it. Come on, dogs."

We barrel down the garage stairs with Rachel in the lead and Albert close on her heels—both of them three steps ahead of me. Rachel sits right by the door, looking first at me then the door then back at me as if to inquire what's taking so long.

"Okay, here we go." I open the door, and the two of them bust outside like it's a race.

The chicken coop sits to my right, with the chickens milling around in their fenced area, pecking at the ground. The chickens don't pay any attention to either dog. Rachel dashes right past them without a glance. Albert pauses a moment to gawk before tearing after his new girlfriend. They both rustle through some tall grasses where they potty as I survey the rest of Clark's remarkable yard. Everything's well thought out, fenced in, groomed, organized. Everything has a purpose. There are fruit trees with apples just starting to redden—must be close to harvest time. Rows of corn next to clumps of raspberry canes separated from pea pods and flowers. So much food interspersed with the beauty of blooming purple coneflowers and black-eyed Susans. It reminds me of Franco's greenhouses with vines and sunflowers climbing to the ceiling. So many tables and workers there, dedicated to providing the masses with food. This is just as meticulous, but so much more alive and inspired out here in the real world under the warm summer morning sun.

My stomach rumbles. "Okay, dogs. Let's head back in now that you've gotten things taken care of."

They hurry back, and we head upstairs to the tantalizing smells of Clark's cooking. "You're spoiling me." I gaze at the eggs and toast on my plate.

"It's nice to have someone around to listen to an old man talk once in a while." He taps the table. "Sit down. There's the jam. Help yourself."

"Do you grow all your own food?"

"Most of it." Clark talks with his mouth full, but it's my fault since I asked him a question right after he'd taken a big bite. "That and fishing and a little trading with some other folks who grow things or have livestock I don't. Works out pretty well."

"So you know other people out here?" I ask. "This is wonderful, by the way. Thank you for feeding me."

"You're most welcome." He takes a drink of water. "And, yeah, I know people. Some are worth knowing, some not, but I know them just the same."

My fork pauses midair as a thought occurs to me.

"And before you bother asking, I can't remember seeing anyone the right age to be your father sporting red hair. So I can't help you out there. You'll just have to keep looking."

"Guess I'll just have to go all the way to Minnesota like Gus said, then."

"Guess so." He chews a bit before continuing. "You'll have to cross the Mississippi River to do that. We'll travel 94 to 90, then I'll leave you at the bridge with my best wishes."

"This is so nice of you."

"Well, I'm only part way nice. I'm not driving you the whole way. I reckon you'll have another seventy miles or so to go after that."

"I'll take what I can get." I glance around the room. "You've got a pretty nice set up here."

"Yeah, I do," Clark agrees, as we both survey his home.

Most of the wall space is taken up with packed bookshelves. Maps and wildlife prints crowd the wall-space above the bookshelves. There's a wood-burning stove with a small stack of slender logs nearby. We eat at a small wooden table with matching chairs. There's a couple buckets of water, one comfy chair, and his bed.

"I like your garden."

He nods. "It's a lot of work, but it feeds me. Hard to keep the pesky rabbits out. Some of the plants are perennials and come back each year. With the annuals, I have to gather the seeds, but it all works out. Getting water for the garden and for washing up can be a pain, but it's all manageable. Winters are long, but it's okay."

"Are you lonely?"

Clark pauses. "Not much I can do about that."

"You did say there were others out here. Why don't you join one of those Groupings you mentioned so you don't have to be alone all the time?"

"Yeah, well, I don't trust people. Most people, anyway. I've seen too much of folks turning on each other. Everyone's so close to the edge because some years it's hard to get enough to eat. I don't know, it just seems more peaceful to be by myself."

I shrug. "Fair enough."

"But you don't agree, do you? You're determined to find both your parents and leave me far behind, because I'm just a silly old man, stuck in my ways."

I raise my eyebrows. "You could come live with us."

"Why would you want me?"

"For starters, you're a good cook." I count off on my fingers. "And also, I'd like you to meet Gus. You remind me of him."

"I'll take that as a compliment, because after listening to you last night, it's clear he's your favorite person on the planet."

I smile. "Thirdly, I think Albert and Rachel would prefer hanging out together on a permanent basis."

"Ha! I guess I'd do most anything for my Rachel, but I'm pretty set in my ways." He leans back in his chair. "That said, maybe the real reason I'm alone is that I'm too old and stubborn to care anymore about anyone but myself."

"Are you sure about that? You took me in and fed me."

"Plus your dog. Don't forget about Albert. I fed him too."

I laugh. "Yes, I'm sure he appreciated getting more than just my scraps." Although I'm not a hundred percent sure he knows his name yet, it seems like Albert can still tell we are talking about him because he ambles over to get a pet from Clark.

"That's why he followed you, you know." Clark points at me with his other hand.

"Because you fed him out there on the road when you didn't have to and when you didn't have much food even for yourself."

"Yeah, I suppose. But I like having him around, I guess. It's nice to have company."

Clark nods. "That's why I have Rachel. Don't know what I'd do without her. And, you know, I've been thinking about what you said last night. I might know that Nate fella you saw on the highway. If he's the one I'm thinking of, he's a young guy—a real good hunter, smart, and the head of his Grouping. I don't know them well, mind you. Just go there to trade for some cooking spices with a nice lady named Sarah. Haven't been there for a while. It's been a few months at least. Last time I was there, they had a new member. Some angry looking fella I didn't care much for, so I've stayed away. Real creepy guy. Don't know what Nate was thinking by taking him on. He's sure to cause trouble."

I shiver a little, thinking of how I almost ran down the road after them. "Good thing I asked you for help instead of them. I don't need any creepy guys in my life."

"That's right. Wise decision. Okay, let's clean up here and head out. I've packed you a few more supplies—should be enough to get you to that red-headed father of yours at least."

I smile. "You're the nicest guy—you know that?"

"Ha! Shows how little you know. Now let's get going. Time for you to find your dad."

⚹

"THIS IS JUST A *FEW* MORE SUPPLIES?" I hoist the heavy backpack over my shoulders, groaning at the weight. "Just how much food did you give me? This thing weighs a ton now."

"A simple thank you will do just fine." Clark collects his keys. "It's not like I want you to starve to death or run out of water before you reach your father."

"Yes, of course, thank you—from the bottom of both my and Albert's hearts." I adjust the straps on the backpack so they don't pinch as much. "You're more than generous."

We head down the stairs.

"Why do you think I collect all this junk?" Clark waves at boxes of clean water bottles and plastic food containers. "Now, I'm not a hoarder or anything. I just collect useful things, clean them up, and then I've got them when I need them."

As he opens the garage door and preps the ATV for travel, I examine his garage. He's got stacks of crates filled to the brim with items.

"How many people have you helped?"

"Guess I don't rightly know." He shrugs. "They come and go. A handful return to say hello now and then, but not many."

"You're a good man, Clark. I feel bad for being scared of you at first last night."

"Ha! That makes two of us. It sure doesn't hurt to be careful when you're out here alone."

"That makes sense." I pause, looking around at this perfect little oasis Clark has created for himself. "I don't suppose, then, you'd want to come with me?"

"For protection, you mean?" He looks straight at me, a worried look on his face.

"Yeah, plus, you know how much the dogs like each other." I really want him to come with me. I don't want to lose him. Feels like I'm losing everyone.

Clark takes a few breaths, and at first I think he's going to agree. But then he shrugs. "I'm sorry. I've just got so much work to do here. The chickens need feeding, and there's weeding to be done in the garden..."

He frowns and looks down, and I feel bad I pushed him.

"Don't worry. I'll be fine. I mean, we'll be fine. Albert, you're still coming with me, right?"

He glances at me, then back at Rachel, and now I'm not sure he's coming with me either.

"Hop in." Clark clears his throat as he gets in the ATV. "Let's get going. Come on, dogs."

Rachel gets up on her own, but Albert needs a little boost, so first I help him up, then take Clark's hand for support. Once I climb aboard, I remove the backpack and tuck it at my feet for storage. The dogs have a little perch behind us.

Clark backs out, then hops down to close the garage door behind him and lock up. Then we are off, heading through the deserted town of Madison and onto the highway. Both of us glance overhead to check the skies as we race northward on Interstate 94. The wind blows around Clark's shoulder-length gray hair. He squints in the bright sunlight, then reaches over to grab some of the biggest sunglasses I've ever seen and puts them on.

"Those things are enormous."

"What? These? Hey, these are classics, retro '80s style. The bigger, the better." He grins. "Sorry I didn't think to find you a pair before we left."

"That's okay. You've given me enough already." This ATV is so loud I have to yell everything. This makes it harder to talk, so we spend most of the time checking the sky and the woods to each side as we drive on. I'm not sure what we're searching for but can't help but remain vigilant, just the same.

I keep glancing back at the dogs to make sure they're okay.

"Don't worry, I built up the back seat with dogs in mind. Plus, I'm not going that fast, and there's no other traffic out here, so we shouldn't crash or anything. They'll be fine."

"I just don't know if Albert's used to riding in cars. I'd hate for him to jump out and get hurt or something."

"He's probably not used to it, but he trusts Rachel. He'll be fine. Don't worry." Then Clark's tone changes as the ATV screeches to a halt. "Oh, crap. Hang on. Could you jump back there and keep a tight hand on them both? Whatever you do, don't let them follow me."

I leap in back to grab hold. "I've got them."

"Promise you won't let them go." He digs in a side compartment, then jumps down and disappears, gun in hand.

15

ANIMAL

Clark's gone, and I'm stuck here clinging to the dogs. I crane to hear anything, desperate to know where he went, what he's doing, and when he'll return, but the world holds its breath and is silent except for the occasional lone birdsong. The dogs become restless as time drags on, raising their heads to sniff the air. What is it? What do they smell? Clark should've told me what he was doing. I've no idea how long this will take or if he's in danger. He grabbed his gun, so it's not like he's just bird watching or something else easy and safe. I crouch in the backseat with Albert tucked into my lap and my sweaty hand clenched around Rachel's collar. She begins a low whine, and Albert joins in. Her muscles tense like she's about to spring, so I grip even tighter. I can't see much from where I sit, but I don't dare stand up to look around for fear that I might accidentally lose hold of her leather collar. My hand cramps, but I'll never catch her if she runs off, so I remain frozen in place.

A gunshot rings out, then another. I jump both times. The dogs grumble and fuss. Then nothing more. No noise, no sign of Clark. What happened? Is he okay? Should I go after him? What should I do?

Where *is* he? I feel exposed out here in this lone vehicle on the open freeway. This is such a vulnerable location to be stuck in, but I won't leave the dogs behind or set them loose. I promised to stay put, but I sure wish he wasn't taking so long or that I knew what he was doing.

After what feels like hours, I spot a lone male figure far ahead on the road. Clark approaches slowly, arms hung down at his sides, one hand holding the gun pointed to the ground and the other carrying what looks like a small shovel. A ways off he stops to bend over, resting his hands on his knees and breathing hard.

"Are you okay?" I yell, upsetting the dogs, who whimper and strain to get away from my hold.

He waves limply. "Yeah. Just tired."

"Can I set the dogs loose now?"

"Yeah. Sure. Let them go. They're safe now."

The moment I release my grip, both fly down the road to meet him, Rachel in the lead and Albert trying his best to keep up.

"What happened?" I follow the dogs to Clark's side.

"Rabid raccoon. Or maybe distemper. Either way, they're both terrible diseases." Clark runs a dirty hand through his gray hair. "Couldn't risk the dogs going after the poor sick creature and catching something fatal."

"Then why stop to shoot it? Why not just drive on?"

"It's not right to let an animal suffer." Clark shook his head. "Wasn't going to get any better. Not when they're in that state— drooling and hissing and stumbling around. Racoons are nocturnal creatures. It had no business wandering around in broad daylight. I was suspicious when I saw it had such a hard time crossing the road. Then when I got close, I knew for sure."

The dogs circle Clark, sniffing him over.

"In case you're wondering what took me so long," He holds up the undersized shovel. "Please observe the size of this shovel. It took forever to dig a deep enough hole so no other animals would get exposed. And don't worry, I was careful not to touch any blood or saliva."

"I did wonder if you were ever coming back."

"Well, I'm back, not smelling the best, but here I am." Clark slaps the side of the vehicle. "Come on, dogs. Stop your sniffing so we can get going. This young lady has places to go and people to see."

Rachel hops up gracefully, and again I assist Albert up into his seat.

Clark examines his dirty hands. "Maybe I can rinse off once we reach the Mississippi."

"How many hours until we get there?"

"Not long now." Clark climbs into the ATV. "Soon you'll be rid of both me and this smell."

I'm slow to smile because I don't want to leave him behind. What if I never find him again? And what if he's right, and I end up stuck out here with my mom and Franco and Gus left inside? What if I end up like my father and never go back? Why *didn't* he come back? I thought he loved us so much he couldn't live without us. But what if...

"What is it?" Clark studies me before starting the engine.

"Listen... Do you think my dad's dead?" My throat tightens around the words. "Do you think that's why he never came for us?"

"There's a good chance." Clark grimaces. "And I'm sorry, but I can't pretend that the thought hadn't already occurred to me."

"So you think he's dead?" I repeat, my voice trembling. "Then everything I'm doing now is pointless. My hiking all the way to Minnesota is stupid if there's nobody there for me. Maybe I shouldn't even go. I just can't think of any other reason why he wouldn't have tried to come back for us, unless he was dead."

Clark puts a gentle hand on my shoulder. "Or maybe he did try, and..."

"And it killed him?" My body shakes.

"Both you and I know there's no way to know any of this without finding the Grouping he joined out here. So I *do* think you need to go there, even if it's only to find out bad news. Then at least you know what happened."

"Okay, okay." I clench my hands, trying to stop the trembling. I can't freak out. I can't get all clingy. I've got to stay brave, but I just feel lost. "And what if I go there and he's already dead? Then what do I do?"

"That's easy," Clark says without hesitation. "Then you and that mongrel come back and live with me."

"Really?"

"Yes, really." He nods back at the dogs in the seat behind us. "Rachel wouldn't have it any other way."

"And you'd help me go back and save my mother?"

"What?" Clark shakes his head. "Oh, heck no. I never agreed to that. I don't ever intend to place a single foot inside Panopticus. I'm not like you. I run *away* from trouble. I don't run after it. I just thought maybe I could be like your super cool old dad or maybe your grandpa, and you could be"—Clark glances my way—"you could be my super stubborn, bull-headed daughter who's never going to give me any peace unless I help you go get your mom." He sighs and turns away. "You sure ask a lot from people you hardly know."

16

GOODBYE TO YOU

We drive on, the loud rumbling of the motor making it almost impossible to hold a conversation, which is probably for the best. Clark's right. I *do* ask too much. He's offered to take me in if I can't find my dad, and yet I still push for more. He's made it quite clear he wants to stay as far away as possible from Panopticus, so why did I go and ask him to do the very thing he said he couldn't do? What's wrong with me?

I turn to look at him—unkempt long gray hair, goofy sunglasses, faded clothes and all. He's focused on driving, sometimes throwing a protective glance back to check on the dogs. He catches my eye and smiles, but half-heartedly, then turns his gaze back to the road ahead. It worries me to leave him when I'm not sure what happens next. Do I find my dad, or do I come back? Will anyone help me get my mom out of Panopticus, or will I have to do it on my own with very little hope of success? Let's say I do manage to sneak back in undetected by the Suits. What happens then? What if Mom doesn't want to leave the city? The one thing she's really good at is the violin. She's rather ill-suited for living in the wilderness, and she's always hated exercise. She must have told me a hundred times how weird I was for liking to run so much. I can't imagine her building a home out here in the wild where there's no running water or concert halls.

Growing up inside Panopticus was unfair and frustrating—one dead end after another, and each one of them lonelier than the last. But so far life outside Panopticus isn't any easier. There's more freedom, for sure. More choices—too many, actually, because I don't have any practice making choices since everything has always been selected for me without much consideration for what I wanted. Or *any* consideration. My job, my clothes, and even the amount of food I was allowed was organized and determined by someone else. I just hope I'm doing the right thing by leaving Clark behind, because it sure doesn't feel right in my gut or my heart.

The scenery changes to beautiful bluff country. We haven't seen another vehicle—or another raccoon, for that matter—all day. The road is a little bumpy, which is to be expected since no one's maintaining it, but the breeze is nice and it's warm without being muggy.

Clark cuts the engine once we reach the Mississippi River. "Well now, here you are."

"Yeah." We've arrived at the bridge before I'm ready to cross it. "Time to figure out if my dad is still alive."

"You've got another seventy miles or so to go. Should only take you a couple more days if you use the highway for most of it."

I stare across the wide, empty bridge ahead. "You think it's safe to stay on the road?"

"Mostly safe." Clark nods. "But keep your ears and eyes peeled, of course. You could run into somebody you don't wish to, but on the other hand, you'd make much better time than floundering about in the woods with a compass. There's pluses and minuses to both routes."

"Right." All I can see is the bridge. "Just have to decide what risks to take."

Clark clears his throat. "At least you shouldn't have to worry about food and water anymore."

"You are the best, Clark." I turn toward him, trying very hard to look more determined than I feel. "You packed this thing so full it's bursting at the seams."

"Could've packed more if that big old jean jacket hadn't taken up so much space. Who is this 'property of Franco Harman' fella, anyway?"

"He's a friend of mine." My face flushes, and I realize I haven't even thought of him much the past twenty-four hours, which at one time would have been unthinkable. Back in Panopticus, Franco was on my mind constantly, distracting me with his confusing behaviors and multiple personalities.

"Is he a close friend?" Clark raises his eyebrows. "Because you didn't mention him last night. I heard all about how Gus is the most wonderful human being on earth, and your poor mom means well but drives you crazy. And, of course, we've talked a lot about your dad. But I don't remember the name Franco being mentioned."

I turn back to the bridge. "He and Liam were cousins. He helped us train for that race. He came to visit me that horrible day in the mortuary when Liam's body was brought in..."

"That poor boy." Clark doesn't say anything to fill the empty space when I can't talk for a moment, he just lets me take my time to recover while he scratches Rachel's ears.

"Franco saw Liam lying there." I shudder, reliving this awful memory. "He went nuts and ran off. Later, I went to his place to try and help him, but he was pretty drunk by then so it didn't go well. He kicked me out. Then I went home. I never saw him again."

"Because when you got home, the Suits took you away, right?"

"Yeah. I guess Franco tried to find me the next day and couldn't, so he told Gus. And Gus took it from there. I don't have any idea how Gus found me, but he did. And he got me out of there. I honestly don't know how he does half the stuff he does. He's like magic."

"I told you. That man is a legend out here."

"He saved my life." I clench my hands. "He needs to get out of there. Just because Ben's gone doesn't mean Gus should give up on having a better life. But sometimes I don't think he cares much about what happens to him anymore."

Clark sighs. "Sometimes you just exist and make the best out of what you've got."

"That's not good enough." I turn to him. "Don't you want more?"

"I used to." Clark gazes at the abandoned bridge. "But there doesn't seem much point to keep hoping for what is never going to happen."

"Why don't you come with us?" Here I go again, begging for him to join me, but he looks so sad and alone I can't stand it.

"I told you." Clark shakes his head. "I don't cross bridges. I stay home. Now it's time for you to go."

"Come on, Albert." I step down from the vehicle, hoisting the backpack over my shoulders.

Albert looks from Rachel to me, then back to Rachel. Oh no, he's not coming with me after all.

THE LADY IN RED

"Come on, Albert," I beg. *Please come with me. Don't make this even harder than it already is.*

"Go on, now." Clark gestures at Albert to join me. "We'll see you later, maybe."

Maybe.

After taking his sweet time deciding, Albert meanders down from the vehicle and makes his slow way over to me, throwing reluctant glances back at Rachel. Maybe I'm asking far too much from him too. Maybe he's given me enough already.

"Thanks, buddy." I pet him on the head. "I promise to do everything I can to make sure you get to see your girlfriend again."

"You be sure to do that, okay?" Clark drums his fingers on the steering wheel. "And feel free to stop by, anytime. I'd be happy to meet your mother. Might be fun to watch you two fight."

I smile. "Thanks for everything, Clark. I mean it. You've been so good to me."

"Okay, then." Clark waves us on, like we are not getting away from him fast enough. "I know you're in a hurry to see your father."

"Bye, Clark." I adjust the backpack straps and move away from the vehicle.

With a last longing look behind him, Albert follows.

"Thanks for everything." I turn away so he won't see the tears stinging my eyes. Behind me the engine roars and then fades. I glance back as Clark shrinks into the distance. It's just us two again. I hope it's not too mean to force Albert to come with me, but I don't think it's right to just ditch him with Clark, either. Not that he wouldn't take good care of him, just that it doesn't seem the responsible thing to do.

The bridge looms ahead, large and foreboding. Is Clark wise not to cross it, in case it falls apart when we are halfway across? No one maintains it, after all. How long are bridges like this safe on their own? The opposite shoreline looks so far away, with such a long expanse of open bridge between here and there. The time it takes to cross might seem like nothing much in a car, but walking across feels like I'm a worker ant undertaking a huge journey along an endless stretch of sidewalk. Albert and I are just two little dots out here in the big world. All alone again with no way to contact anyone. No phones. No way to message Clark if things don't go my way. It's all on me.

Soon we are halfway across, and despite my overall uneasiness I can't help but gaze at the breath-taking beauty around me. So much blue both far above and down below. The sky and water reflect and complement each other. The river goes on both ways forever. Birds swirl in lazy oblique circles, way up in the air. A light breeze caresses my face as I pause midway across. So far, I haven't heard any scary noises like the bridge could be crumbling underneath my feet.

"Albert, we're going to make it. We're going to be okay."

He eyeballs me. I'm pretty sure he's not real happy with me right now, and only following out of some sense of obligation.

"It's all right. I'll win you back."

We press on. I've never seen so much water before. This is even bigger than the lake in Madison, and full of possibility. What if you could ride in a boat up and down the river? You could go anywhere your heart desired. You could just take off and never come back again. You could leave everything behind that you didn't like. But you couldn't take everything you did like with you, either. Like my mom and dad. That is, if he's still alive. But I'll deal with that when I get there. Maybe he's waiting for me. Maybe it will be easy to convince him to go back and get my mom. After all, he loved my mom so much. Sometimes it was embarrassing to be around them, like I was just a third wheel.

I rub my eyes, blinking in the bright sunlight. Even though I'm in pretty good shape, this is still way more exercise than I'm used to even with all that race training.

Eight years have passed since that summer concert held in the park just before Dad disappeared, but I can still hear his voice.

"Don't fall asleep yet, hon, the next song is Mom's favorite. It's her big solo." Dad winks at me, making me feel so special in a soft red dress he made secretly for me with scraps from work. He puts his arm around me for support as the hour grows late.

Mom sits ramrod straight in first chair, her violin up and her hand poised and ready, the overhead lights shining on her smooth black hair.

"Doesn't she look beautiful?" Dad whispers in my ear, so quietly I can barely hear him over the music.

I nod, lost in a dreamy world of dangling lights over the musicians and twinkling stars in the sky, the melody diving and swirling in my ears, and the mesmerizing red velvet of my dress. How I loved the feel of it, the swish against my legs, the smooth softness under my fingers. I'd never worn anything like it before, and probably never would again. I cried when Mom told me I would have to give it up the next day. I wanted to keep it forever.

But in the end, I did get to keep it. Instead, I lost what I loved so much more. Dad vanished, and I was left to clean up the mess he left behind.

18

THE WAY YOU LOOK TONIGHT

I thought today would never end, but school is finally over. I rush home, passing everyone on the street. Adults warn me to slow down and be careful, but I don't listen. I want to get home. Next week's my mom's birthday, and Dad and I are working on top secret plans. My feet slap up the two flights of stairs leading to our floor, then I dash down the hallway to our apartment. Our door stands ajar. I pause a moment in surprise before giving it a slight push with the tips of my fingers. The door squeaks open as I peer eagerly inside, but no shoes stand guard in the front hall. Darn, I wanted chocolate.

A loud, unfamiliar female voice carries through the apartment. "And you're positive you'll have this done in time?"

Yuck. I don't like that annoying voice. I hope whoever she is doesn't stay long.

"Yes, you have my word." Dad's Fake Patient Voice responds.

I wish I had a Fake Patient Voice. My report cards always say "Silvia needs to work on her temper. Silvia bosses her classmates around. Silvia is the brightest girl in her class and bores easily."

"It's a very important government event. This gown must be perfect."

"Yes, ma'am."

"That's why I chose you for the job. I've heard you're very talented."

"Thank you, ma'am."

"I'm giving you a big chance here. If I'm pleased with this gown, I'll have you transferred to Government Level clothing production. I have the power to do this, and this promotion would be very good for your family."

"Yes, it would." Dad pauses. I wonder why. "Thank you for this opportunity."

I can't see what's going on, hanging out here in the front hallway. I'm so curious, but I don't want to get Dad in trouble. Using soft footsteps, I sneak closer and peek around the corner into the living room. There she is, some famous Representative I've seen on the overhead consoles, but I can't remember her name. Mom always comments on how glamorous she is. She's always dressed much fancier than anyone I know. The rest of us wear ordinary, plain clothes for everyday and special uniforms for work or school. I glance down at my government-issue blue shorts, red polo, and navy sweater. Always the same, we all dress the same.

But not her. Right now, she's dressed in some fancy black suit with a fuchsia blouse. She looks special—like a single bright peony in a field of plain grass.

"Come on in, honey." Dad beckons to me.

I ease down the hallway into the living room, embarrassed I got caught.

"This is my daughter." The pride in his voice makes me smile.

"She's charming," the Fancy Lady says.

I glance up, startled by the compliment, but she's focused on a small open notebook in her hand. I'm pretty sure she didn't even look at me. I turn to Dad, who shrugs and nods toward the most beautiful green fabric I've ever seen draped over the nearest chair.

I'm entranced by the color green. The Fancy Lady and my father move toward the door. She's in a hurry to leave, and he escorts her out.

When he comes back, I'm still gawking at the shiny emerald green fabric.

"I knew you'd like it." Dad smiles. "You can touch it as long as your hands are clean."

I race to the kitchen to dutifully wash and dry them and then return.

"Oh, Dad, it's beautiful. Look how shiny. And just feel it. It's so smooth and silky. I wish we could keep it."

"It's pretty fancy material, all right. A lot different than the stuff I usually work with."

"What's this?" Mom hovers in the hallway. We hadn't heard her come in.

"Yoshe!" Dad puts his arm around her, bringing her further into the room. "I've got some big news... Great opportunity... Could mean a promotion... Isn't this exciting?" He explains everything, but I'm too mesmerized by the buttery feel of the emerald fabric to listen.

I smooth my hands along the length of it, careful not to cause a wrinkle.

"Why you?" Mom stares at the material like it's criminal. "I mean, you make Basic Worker Level clothes."

"I know, but I could do more."

"Well, this is a lot different from what you're used to. Have you ever worked with this type of material? What kind of dress does she want? She's so famous and stylish. I'm sure she expects a lot."

"She told me to design it myself." Dad looks like a kid with a new toy.

"Seems like some sort of trick." Mom frets. "You'll have to be careful."

"Don't worry, Mom. Dad can do it. I know he can. And I can help." I race to my room, dig around in my art box, and yank out a big notebook before returning to my parents. "Hey, Dad, remember when we watched that one old movie, and you drew all those fancy ladies for our special Art Party?"

Dad's eyes light up. The page in my hands contains a dozen sketches of elegant ladies wearing fancy green dresses.

"Yes, I remember." Dad smiles. "You only let me draw green dresses, because you love that color. Which dress is your favorite? That's the one I'll do."

"Oh, Daniel." Mom gasps. "Do you think that's wise? She doesn't know anything about fashion. She's just a child."

"This one." I point to a gown which flows down to the floor, swirls around the waist, and has thin elegant straps over each shoulder.

"It's perfect." Dad nods, already deep in thought.

He gets to work at once, drawing out a plan, making a pattern, working every night after his other job is done. He barely sleeps. The Fancy Lady stops in once to approve the plan, but insists she's too busy to come back again until it's finished.

Dad frets, worried the dress won't fit right, ruining his chance for promotion.

"Don't worry, Daddy. Mom can be your model."

"What, me?"

"They're the same size, don't you think?" I reason, and Dad agrees, so Mom becomes Dad's muse, standing still on a wooden frame platform. They spend hours together, him pinning and sewing and creating.

When I get home after school on my mom's birthday, beautiful music greets me the second I enter the apartment. I drop my bag right next to the lone shoe standing in the middle of the hallway, signifying that this time there will be chocolate for supper. Eager to start the celebration, my steps pause when I hear hushed voices.

"You look amazing, birthday girl."

Mom laughs. "It's the dress."

"No, it's not. It's all you. You get all the credit."

"You're right, I should get a medal or something for standing still for hours while you fussed and fretted over this dress. I've been so patient with you."

Dad chuckles. "You're a saint, truly."

"I'm no saint, but wearing this sure makes me feel like royalty. I wish I could keep it."

"I'm sorry I can't give it to you for your birthday, but I'll get you anything else you want. What will it be, my queen?"

"Just this. Just us. Always."

"You got it. I'm yours forever."

Smiling, I hide just out of view, peeking into the living room. In a world of their own, my parents dance together, arms around each other, and eyes closed. I hold my breath, not wanting to make a sound.

Later on we play games, have chocolate cake for dessert, and laugh a million times. Mom spends the whole evening wearing the dress, careful not to get any food on it, because it belongs to the Fancy Lady for her Big Important Event held the very next day.

Birthdays at our house were always the best, until Dad made that stupid green gown that ruined everything and sent him away.

Now it's my job to bring him back home.

19

ALWAYS SOMETHING THERE TO REMIND ME

Preoccupied with memories of the past and how they all connect to each other, the miles pass by. Albert keeps up most of the time, but sometimes needs to be carried. We stop for water and food breaks. I keep checking the temps of both the road and the gravel next to it with my hand. We pass exit signs for ghost cities named Winona and Rushford. We might reach Rochester tomorrow or maybe the following day, but we're done for tonight.

"Come on, pooch. That's a good dog." I veer off the road to seek shelter in a nearby cluster of trees and shrubs where we can rest half hidden from view, not that we've spotted any signs of life today besides deer crossing the highway and birds flying overhead. I don't want to become careless, lost in daydreams about how my family used to be, but after talking to Clark and not seeing any signs of drones or helicopters or planes overhead this whole time, I'm starting to believe that once you're outside Panopticus itself, you're out of their clutches for good. Maybe they've got enough people to manipulate within the city limits, and they don't care about the deserters in the outlying territories.

Peeling the heavy backpack off my sweaty, tired back is a blessed relief. Clark sure crammed it full of food and water. Even if I don't find my dad right away, at least I won't have to worry so much about supplies the next few days. Glancing back the way I've come along the road, I feel torn in both directions. I want to find my father, but I also want to return to the quiet peace I found at Clark's place. I don't know why, but it felt like home to me. There wasn't anything posh or fancy about it, but it was perfect just the same.

"You hungry, little guy?" I dig around in the bag while Albert sits, drooling in anticipation. I tear a Clark sandwich into small pieces, and he digs in with relish, tail wagging.

After eating and drinking his fill, Albert curls up, ready for bed. I don't blame him. I really pushed the miles today, anxious to reach my dad or at least learn what happened to him. After pulling out the bug netting and repacking everything else, I lie down next to Albert and cover us both up. But I can't sleep, despite my exhaustion. It's not only my physical body that is fatigued. My heart and soul are weary too. I'm tired of missing my dad. All these years longing for just one more day spent with him, one more conversation, one more hug. So many of the terrible things that happened to me growing up seem connected to his absence. Mom falling apart, the Suits coming after me, my disappointment at testing into Mortuary Sciences—though that ended up being the very best place for me and also ended up saving my life.

Eight whole years have passed since the last time I saw my father. Eight birthdays, eight summers, eight Christmases my mother and I spent alone. My eyes scan the road for traffic, but all is silent. The world smells fresh and earthy. Summer is fading, and the ferns tucked between the trees show signs of withering. I love their arches and tendrils, probably because my dad always pointed them out in the park. Yawning, my fingers trace the delicate pattern of the closest fern, still green and alive despite the brown crispy fronds that surround it.

"Let's go, Sleepyhead! Time to rise and shine!" Dad jerks the curtains open, filling my room with bright sunlight.

"Ugh. No, Daddy, I'm cozy here."

"Oh, that's too bad. Guess I'll just eat your Special Breakfast while you stay here and drool on your pillow."

"I don't drool!" I hide under the covers, secretly wiping at my mouth until I smell something wonderful. "What's that? What's she making?"

"Your waffles are getting cold," Mom calls from the kitchen.

I gasp, throwing off my blankets. "Why didn't you tell me about the waffles?"

"There won't be any left for you if I get there first." Dad takes off at a sprint.

I follow close behind, or try to, but my foot gets trapped in a sheet and I fall to the ground with a loud bang.

"What's going on in there?" yells Mom. "Don't break the apartment already. We just moved in."

Dad ducks his head back in my room. "Are you okay?"

"No. I'm not." I struggle to get my foot released. "I'm injured and in mountains of pain, so you should give me your waffle."

"Not a chance." He takes off again.

The race begins, and he's winning until the last second when I surge ahead. We sit together at the counter, steam rising from the fresh waffles, one for each of us, with raspberries sprinkled on top. All my favorites, including time with my dad.

"I hear you two have big plans today." Mom takes small bites of her waffle in between tidying up the kitchen. She hates a mess, and Dad has a hard time getting her to just sit down and eat without completing all the other little jobs first.

"Yeah," I reply between bites. "Dad and I are going to the big Earth Day celebration. It's going to be awesome. We'll bring home a bunch of plants. You'll see. It will look just like a park in here."

"That will really brighten up the place." Mom glances around at this white-washed apartment which is still new to us and doesn't yet feel like home.

"The light in here will be great for plants." Dad waves his fork around. "This place is so much nicer than our last apartment."

"All thanks to your promotion to Government Level clothing production." Mom smiles.

Dad wags his finger at her. "Don't forget that you moved up two seats in the Orchestra. See, I told you. Together, we will go far."

"Maybe." Mom's smile disappears.

"Just trust me. Didn't I promise we can have everything we want?"

"I don't know." Mom sighs. "I feel like we always have to be so careful. There's always someone watching. It makes me nervous."

"Don't worry so much. I'll take care of everything. I promise." Dad gets up to put an arm around her, and she relaxes into his side. "As long as we've got each other, that's all we need... plus this nicer apartment and an endless supply of raspberries for our little girl." He grins at me, and I grin back. He's so good at cheering Mom up, and she's such a worrywart, not easy going like Dad.

"You ready, kid?"

"I'm ready, Dad."

"Thanks for cleaning up our mess, but if we don't get a move on, all the best plants will be taken. Bye!" He kisses her on the cheek.

"You got me all sticky with syrup!" She laughs and waves us off. "At least brush your teeth first."

We hurry to the bathroom, brush up, and head out the door. There are signs everywhere, mostly electrical, of course, to save on paper.

ON APRIL 22nd, COME CELEBRATE EARTH DAY WITH
PANOPTICUS! FREE PLANTS! SUPPLIES AND
INSTRUCTIONS INCLUDED!

The roads are crowded with walkers heading toward the park. Plant Production services hosts the whole event. Several important looking older men and women wearing long white lab coats over green scrubs circle the tables set up with trays of biodegradable planting pots, organic soil mixed with worm compost, and countless small plugs of ivy, fern, and jade plants. We hurry to get a good seat. A young intern comes up, introduces himself, and gives us instructions. I try to listen carefully, but I'm distracted trying to figure out how to nab all the pretty green plants I want to take home.

"Okay, then. Have at it." The intern finishes talking.

I reach out to grab my favorite plant, and Dad helps me carefully set it in a pot and add soil. I want to rush, but Dad slows me down, telling me to be careful. Once he's satisfied, we start over with a new plant. The intern said we can take as many as we want. He said the government wants us to have clean air and healthy lungs.

After we've got five gorgeous green plants all set in their pots, Dad stops me from reaching out to choose yet another.

"Listen, honey, we've already got as much as we can carry home."

I sigh, a little disappointed.

"Don't worry. We've got plenty, and your mom's going to love them. You did a great job potting them."

We load up our arms with plants and step away from the table. Dad takes most of them, only letting me carry one. I hold it with both hands, determined not to drop it. A few people I don't recognize stop to talk to Dad, which takes a long time.

"Can we go now?" I elbow him, careful not to drop the plant in my hands. "I'm bored."

"Give me a minute. Be patient." Dad talks a little longer.

I stare at him until he tells the strangers good-bye.

"Finally!" I say, eager to leave.

"One more thing."

"Now what?" This is taking forever.

"You need to say thank you."

"What? Why? They said it was free. Let's go already."

"Silvia. Don't be rude. We need to work on your manners. You need to learn how to be nice to people besides just your mother and me. Now go thank that young man who helped at our table. Do it now."

I hurry over, mumble a thank you, and turn away as fast as

possible, grumbling as I reach Dad's side. "I hate it when you make me do stuff like that."

"Don't pout," Dad whispers as we leave the park.

"Then stop embarrassing me," I whine.

"I'm not." His voice remains private and quiet, so only I can hear him. "But we need to work on your attitude in public places."

I sigh as loudly as possible. "I'm so tired of talking about my stupid report card. It's not my fault that none of my teachers like me."

"That's not true. Your science teacher said you're very bright."

"Oh, great. So one out of five teachers likes me, and the rest don't. And most of the kids in my class are stupid and mean too."

Dad sighs, then speaks quietly. "I need to teach you how to be what they want, so things go better for you at that school."

"You don't like me, either?" Tears sting my eyes. "You want me to be somebody else?"

"Oh, honey. That's not what I said." Dad tries to hug me, but the plants we are carrying get in the way. "I just want you to pretend. Nobody's their real self here. Be who you need to be at that school. Be your real self at home. It will make things easier on you."

"I can't believe you're saying this. I thought today was supposed to be fun."

"Listen to me. Be fake with everyone else and be real with me and your mom. We all have to work the system. It's like your mom said; there's always someone watching. We have to be careful what we say and do. That's the trick here. I know you can do it. You're my strong, brave girl, and I wouldn't ask you to change anything, except school is getting so hard for you. They won't let you have a good job if this continues, and I can't bear to see you fail. You're too smart for that, too talented. You're my wonderful girl."

"Sometimes I think no one likes me at that school."

"They don't matter." Dad stops and crouches down in front of me, so we can see eye to eye. "Life here in Panopticus is a game. Things will go a lot easier if you learn the rules."

"If I learn the rules, will school get better?" I huff, trying hard not to cry. "Because I kind of hate it there right now."

"Yes, I hope so." Dad talks so softly I know no one can hear but me. "I mean, you're just a kid. Your life shouldn't be so hard. You should be having fun."

"Why do they hate me? How come everything I do is wrong?"

Dad sets all the plants on the ground, then gives me the biggest hug. "Oh, Silvia, I'm sorry. I wish the world was a better place. I wish I could make it better for you. I love you just the way you are. The problem is that the world around us is so flawed that we have to modify who we are just to fit in. And until the world is made perfect, those of us who are already perfect will have trouble fitting in."

"But who's going to make the world perfect if everyone just keeps playing games to fit in and keep things just the crappy way they are?"

He kisses me on the head as he stands up. "Well, my brave, stubborn girl. Maybe it will be you."

20

WINTER

Dad and I were always bringing free plants home from various government sponsored festivals. They filled the apartment, crowding every open shelf. Dad tended them faithfully, watering and fertilizing them on a strict schedule, and rotating them in the sunlight filled windows. Until he left both us and them behind, and we got shoved into a much smaller, darker apartment with very little natural sunlight. Dad's precious plants withered and faded away, their brown leaves dropping onto the carpet. I tried to save them, but they just couldn't face life without my father. Neither could my mother. I've got to get back to her, but haven't even found my dad yet. I'm so tired. Why can't I fall asleep? Albert snores beside me, but my eyes remain open until consciousness slips away.

"Hurry up, Silvia. I've got a surprise for you," Mom calls from the kitchen. "I planned a big surprise for your birthday."

She slides over a bowl of organic oatmeal topped with raspberries. "I got us Park and Art passes today."

I start to eat, but Mom's voice from the front hall interrupts me. "Hurry up!"

We clamber down the brightly lit stairwell and push out into the swarms of people flooding the streets. So much traffic. So many bodies in blue scrubs or green overalls. Dozens of bikes whoosh close by. Red, white, and blue flags flap overhead. The noise is deafening. Every building looks the same. People shove on every side. I get pushed to the left then the right. My feet get trampled. My sides get elbowed. It feels like I'm drowning.

I've lost Mom. Where did she go?

I push against the crowd, but they push back. I can't breathe. I'm getting crushed. The crowd behind me presses forward.

Swinging my arms, I knock into first one, then another stranger. They fall to the ground and disappear into swirls of dark gray dust, like tiny tornados.

The road empties except for a small clustering of people ahead. I move closer, searching for Mom. Where is she?

There she is, shoving one of the Suits away and yelling at him, but I can't hear her voice. Tears stream down Mom's scared face, her mouth open in a scream. She backs away from the Suits and turns as if to run before doubling over in pain. In her moment of weakness, they surround her and drag her away.

I'm trying to reach her, but my feet won't move. I'm stuck, my arms flailing out in front of me. But nothing happens. I can't call out. I can't move. I can't see where they've taken her.

She's just gone.

🏃

I WAKE in daylight gasping for air. I couldn't save her. It was just a dream, but the scary reality is that it could become the truth. That's it. I'm going to reach Dad tonight, even if I have to carry Albert the whole way. I can't take this in-between time, this unknowing. We eat and drink and move out, thankful for the cloud cover overhead and cooler temps. We press on. The miles pass, and my mind wanders. Maybe if I focus on the good times, it will keep Mom and Dad both alive, at least until I can find them.

Dad loved Christmas. We were never allowed a real tree, because it was environmentally irresponsible. But making one from paper and putting it up on the wall was so much more fun and creative anyway.

One year, when I got home from school I found my Dad had cleared away everything in front of the far wall of the combo living/kitchen/dining room area and covered it with the most enormous green paper tree I had ever seen. It didn't matter that all the recycled greens didn't match. It didn't matter that the fake tree was so much fatter than it was tall.

I loved it. It was perfect. We spent hours decorating it with colored scraps cut into pretty shapes and glued up on the wall. We cut up shiny silver gum wrappers and my dad's old worn-out red socks and bright colored food allowance boxes. We cut out circles and squares and stars and spirals. We glued them in patterns and at random all over the tree.

Mom remained at orchestra practice until late evening. When she finally arrived to view our masterpiece, she was speechless.

"Isn't it beautiful?" I breathed, hands clasped together.

"Well, it's something all right." Mom had a tight, unsure smile.

"Don't tell me you hate it!" I pouted. "Dad and I spent hours on it. It's perfect!"

"All I'm going to say is, Dan, you're cleaning this up after the holidays are over. That's your job."

"You got it," he promised, holding a sprig of fake mistletoe over her head.

"You're ridiculous." She giggled, and I knew they were going to start kissing.

"I'm out of here!" I yelled, running for my room.

Later, they came to my bedroom to drag me outside. Soft snowflakes swirled around us, turning the quiet dark street into a magical snow globe.

Dad always knew how to make Mom laugh. Sure, they argued like any other couple, but any fights always ended with Mom laughing at something Dad said. And Dad seemed to understand me even better than I understood myself. My friends didn't get me. My teachers kept their distance. The only other people who knew me were Gus and maybe Franco, who somehow made me tell him so much more than I ever intended. But Franco didn't return the favor. I just found him confusing.

But maybe I didn't really know my dad. What were those secret meetings he attended? Was Gus there too? How about Franco and his Uncle Jack? I don't think Liam had a clue about any of this. He believed in the Panopticus government so much he talked me into running that race in order to get Chosen. I suppose it's a good thing he did, because it helps to be in shape when traveling all this way to find my father.

After stopping for lunch, we head out again. The next faded highway sign lists Rochester as an upcoming exit. We're getting closer.

21

HURT

Albert naps in my arms. He looked a little droopy at our last meal break, so I've been carrying him ever since. The signs counting how many miles to Rochester tick by, measuring our progress. I will make it there tonight even if I have to crawl. But how big is Rochester? Is it bigger than Madison? How will I find my father once I get there? I've only got Gus's big red dot and his scrawled "THIS is where you want to be" message as a guide. But at least I've made it this far. Without even Albert to talk to, my mind wanders again, this time far back to a memory I hadn't taken out and studied for a very long time. My one decent therapist told me not to dwell on my mother's miscarriages anymore. She said it wasn't healthy for either of us, and so I packed this memory in a tightly closed mental box and placed it deep inside.

Until now.

"Bye, Mom!" I wave, excited to join Dad on a short field trip.

She barely looks up, half asleep, curled in a blanket and wearing a big sweater.

"Mom's tired," whispers Dad, crouched down beside me. "Let her

be. We'll pick up the food allowance, then come home and make her a good meal."

"Yeah." I nod. "Maybe she'll eat something today."

Dad frowns, looking troubled. "Yes, she needs to build up her strength." We cross the street holding hands in the bright July sunshine.

"Daddy, am I always going to be an only child?"

He sighs. "I think so, honey."

"It's okay. I don't mind." I squint into the sun. "How come Mom's wearing a sweater when it's so hot outside? And how come she doesn't go to work anymore? She doesn't even clean, and she used to clean all the time. She hardly even moves from the couch, except when it's time for bed."

Dad gives me a worried smile. "It's just taking her a lot longer to recover this time. I don't know why. She refuses to go back to the doctor. She doesn't want to see anyone. She just wants to be left alone."

"Is that why you took me with you?"

He chuckles. "Nah. I just wanted to spend time with my best girl. Plus, I'm going to make you carry all the bags home."

"No way, buddy."

We get in line for our food allowance, then head home. I'm sweating by the time we get back, both from the heat and the two little bags Dad has me carry. He's got a lot more than me, all heavy, sturdy hemp bags, so nothing spills out. We reach our apartment door, laden down with groceries. Dad unlocks, then kicks the door open. After all the fresh air, the sick person smell hits me.

A low moan comes from the bathroom.

Dad drops the bags to the floor. Oranges roll across the front hallway. He rushes to the bathroom with me close behind, trying hard not to trip.

"Don't let her see!" Mom wails, her face pale and gaunt, her hair slicked back with sweat. She heaves toward the toilet and vomits, her hands gripping the seat.

Beneath her, the white floor tiles are smeared with blood.

Dad runs around trying to get help. Paramedics pour into the apartment, lift Mom onto a stretcher, and take her away, one arm draped limply over the side. Dad promises to come back soon. The nice old neighbor-lady first puts all our food away and then asks if I want to watch TV. I sit on our couch, faking interest, but stare instead at the framed picture of my parents clutched in my lap.

Once the old neighbor-lady falls asleep, I sneak away to clean the bathroom. But I'm not very good at it. My wet kitchen rag just smears the blood into red circles and stripes. When Dad finally does come home, he finds me on the bloodied bathroom floor and kneels down to give me a hug.

"Is she dead, Daddy?" I ask, gulping back tears.

He doesn't answer right away, just smooths my hair and helps me finish wiping up the mess.

"Let's get you cleaned up and go to the hospital to see your mother."

"Okay." I take one step toward my room before turning back. "But what are we going to do if she dies, Daddy?"

He shudders. "Don't say that. She can't die. I don't want to live in a world without her."

At the hospital, we sit at her bedside. Dad reads me books or we play games. Mom sleeps for hours and hours before coming to.

Dad takes her hand. "I won't let this happen again."

Mom opens her mouth to argue.

Dad kisses her hand in front of the tubing stuck into her vein. "I've already made the appointment."

Mom's last miscarriage could have killed her. She'd lost so much blood and had an infection. Later, I talked to Gus about it, but I never knew the full details. I was pretty little at the time and never wanted to push my mom to tell me about it once I got older. The only time she acknowledged her miscarriages was when she lit extra candles for them on my birthday, until the one therapist made her quit. She lit so many candles. I don't remember how many. I can't believe she went through this over and over. She wanted me to have a sister or a brother, but it wasn't meant to be. The same neighbor-lady watched TV with me while Dad went in for some injection. He said it made his arm sore but was worth it. He'd have to go back every two years, but he'd do anything to keep Mom safe.

Now I feel bad she had to stop lighting the candles. It's like she never got to mourn, or maybe never knew how to—just like she didn't know how to mourn the loss of my father. She'd been through so much even before he disappeared from our lives. No wonder she was a mess.

More time passes before I reach the actual exit to Rochester. I'm trembling, both from excitement and exhaustion. My legs and back ache. I'd give anything to quit and rest, but my mind won't let me. I need to find him. Passing by deserted buildings, I check every window for someone staring out at me. I never see anyone, and yet I still feel so on edge, like at any moment someone scary might come running at me. But it's all quiet, deserted, with every crack in the pavement crowded with opportunistic weeds.

I plod onward, one weary step after another until I reach a narrow path that follows a waterway. It seems reasonable to believe that any encampment would be positioned near water, so I follow it northeast, entering what looks like a park. I keep stumbling, my tired feet catching on the tiniest bumps in the road. Albert wakes up and wiggles until I let him down once we reach a small pond with ducks quacking in the center. I remove the backpack in relief and collapse on an old bench after testing it to make sure it won't fall apart beneath me. The sun sinks lower in the sky as my eyelids flutter. I'm just going to nap for a minute.

⚐

SHARP BARKING WAKES me with a jolt. Albert has deserted the ducks and instead barks incessantly at a clump of birch trees a short distance away.

"Come on, Albert." I get up with a groan and approach the trees. "What did you find, a squirrel or something?"

Albert emits a low growl.

The trees rustle as the sun's last rays hit their branches.

"Silvia Wood. Is it really you?" That voice is so familiar.

Albert goes wild as a man steps out from between the trees.

It's Franco.

22

OH FATHER

"Franco, I can't believe you're here! I was so worried about you! Is my mom here? How about Gus? Where is he? How'd you get here so fast? Did you get a ride?" I fight to step closer, but Albert blocks my way. "Come on, dog! Stop barking and get out of my way! Hey. Hold on. What... What happened to you, Franco? How'd you get so... old?"

"I look old, huh?" The man laughs. "Yes. Thank you for that. I feel old too. Sounds like maybe you're looking for my nephew."

"Oh, my gosh." I gape. "Are you Uncle Jack? I can't believe how much you look like Franco."

"Except for the occasional gray hair, right?" Jack smiles, pointing at his head.

"Right," I agree softly, coming to the awkward realization that in searching for my dad, I found poor Liam's father instead.

"So, tell me everything. How do you know Franco? And how's your mother? You look just like her, you know. That's how I knew who you were."

"Um. I'm pretty worried about Mom, actually. I don't know what happened after Gus helped me escape. And I met Franco because..."

My voice fades and I back away. I don't want to be the one who tells him his son is dead.

"Don't worry." His voice softens. "I won't hurt you."

"I know you won't." I nod. *But I'm going to hurt you, even though I don't want to.*

"You must be so tired."

"Yes." I can't even look at him. All I can see in my head is Liam's dead body on the cold, metal Mortuary table. My knees grow weak, and I stumble backwards, catching myself before I hit the ground.

"Are you okay? Here, let me help you." Jack extends a hand for support.

I raise my eyes to his. "Jack, is my dad here? Is he still alive?"

"Yes, of course, I should've told you that right away. He's close by. I'll take you to him right now. Here, let me carry your backpack. You look exhausted."

"Thank you," is all I can manage. My throat closes over any more devastating words. Albert trots after us, no longer barking, but keeping a close eye on Jack the whole time.

"It's not much farther," promises Jack.

My head swims as darkness falls and the air cools a bit. We travel a dirt path through many trees leading to a clearing up ahead with a campfire. The smell of cooking makes my stomach growl.

"Almost there," Jack chirps, then stops abruptly. "You know what. Why don't you rest here a minute? I'll go on ahead and tell your dad the good news before you see him. Ease the shock a little."

I'm not even listening to Jack, because I've already spotted my father's red hair in the campfire light. Dad. My dad. I found him at last. My breath catches in my chest. Tears blur my vision as I try to run to him, but my legs feel like worthless rubber bands that don't work right. They're weak and shaky after all these miles, but I've got just enough left in me to reach my father. Speechless, I hover behind him, gazing at his profile. I've never been more exhausted or hungry or sweaty before in my whole life.

And I've never felt this happy before in my whole life, either. My dad. He's alive and he's here right in front of me. Words catch in my throat when I try to say his name. My trembling hand reaches out for him.

I just wish he'd turn around and see me. Heart racing, I wait for him to notice me.

Instead he turns toward a tall woman to his right, brushes back her long blonde hair, and kisses her like he's done so a thousand times before.

23

THIS KISS

My father kissed my mother under the mistletoe, over a birthday cake, and next to our Christmas tree. He kissed her hand in the hospital bed, her head while they danced in the front hallway of our apartment, and pecked her cheek while stealing a chocolate chip cookie.

He kissed her all the time. He said he loved her, that he couldn't live without her.

Was any of that true?

Is this blonde the real reason he never came back for us? He just moved on when we never could, when we just kept living like ghosts of the past.

My hand which reached out for him drops to my side. I want to punch him, slap him, hit him. I want to hurt him as much as I hurt right now, to be as miserable as my mom was after he deserted her.

"Boy, you sure can run fast." Jack pants beside me. "Daniel, pay attention! Your daughter's here! Isn't this wonderful?"

When my father finally turns around, I notice a young boy cuddled in his lap and a little girl standing at his side. Both have his red hair.

I gasp, stepping away from them. This can't be true.

"Silvia..." his voice cracks.

I glare at the blonde next to him, their kids, and back at my dad. Why did I ever think he was so special?

"I came all this way to see you, *Dad*. I wanted your help to get Mom out of that awful city you ditched us in when you faked your own death. But now I don't know why I bothered. You never came back for us before. Why would you help me now when you've moved on with your *new* wife and your *new* kids? You have no idea how bad things were for us after you left. No idea at all."

"Silvia," he reaches out to me.

I back away. "I should've stayed with Clark, and *you* should've stayed *dead*."

I HATE MYSELF FOR LOVING YOU

I run away from the campfire and into the darkness.

I wish Gus was here right here beside me. He would know what to do now that I've learned the unthinkable. Mom and I idol-worshiped the memory of someone who didn't deserve it, someone who just moved on and started another family without us.

He finally got his multiple kid family. And they both have red hair, just like him.

The urge to go back and punch him is strong, but I won't do it in front of children. My hands tremble as I gulp in air, trying very hard not to hyperventilate. I sink to my knees as sharp jabs of pain spasm inside me as the world outside falls to pieces.

Everything I ever believed was a lie. For eight long years I missed Dad so much. Mom and I fought all the time. I even wished I'd been left with Dad instead of her. Mom knew it, too. I'm such a horrible, stupid person. I can't believe I treasured every little scrap of a memory I had of him like it was a precious stone or priceless jewel. What a fool I was! I'm so ashamed. But not anymore. I'm done with him and his new little family. I'll leave right now, head back to Clark, and live with him instead. I just need to find my dog first. Where did he go? Searching for Albert, I hear loud voices in the background. I don't want to even look at him, but my eyes draw straight to my father, in an argument with the blonde.

It makes me smile, glad I caused him trouble.

"Are you proud of what you've done, girl?"

I whirl around to find an older lady stirring something in a large pot over some coals, looking very much like a witch in a movie, except what she's cooking smells so delightful it can't possibly be a potion or spell.

"You like causing trouble, hey?" her wheezy voice asks.

I turn again to observe my father's distressed face, his eyes wide, his hands pleading and outstretched. The mysterious blonde wipes away tears, her kids clutching onto her legs.

"Is she nice?" I ask the pot stirrer. "The blonde, I mean."

"Oh, yes, she's very nice. She's a good person who's been through a lot, and I think you coming here just ruined what little is left of her life."

My temper flares. "You think this is all *my* fault? Until just a few days ago, I thought my father was dead. Every single day for eight long years I've missed him. Ever since I escaped, all I've done is search for him. But now it's *my* fault he doesn't want me? It's *my* fault he simply moved on and forgot all about us, like we never mattered at all, like our family was disposable, and it's no big deal for him to go out and get a new one?"

She listens to me rant until I run out of words. "You're hungry and tired. Neither of those things help this situation one bit. I might not be able to heal your broken heart, but I can fill your belly. Sit down."

I obediently sit where she points, and she hands me a wooden bowl full of steaming, delicious smelling soup. I scoop up a spoonful, blowing on it before tasting, when Albert runs up to me, begging for his share.

"There you are, boy. Where've you been?"

"This one's yours, eh?" The old lady grunts as she crouches down to dig in a bag at her feet. "I've got something for him too."

She fills a plate and sets it on the ground. "All right, now that your mouth is so full you can't talk back, let's get one thing straight, young lady. That father of yours didn't forget all about you. Nobody here ever does, they just try to survive and live day to day trying not to drown in their memories. Don't be so quick to judge what you don't yet understand."

I swallow fast in order to mutter. "He never came back for us."

"I realize that. I heard you loud and clear. Everyone here did. But let me tell you this—once you've actually extracted your mother from that city without getting either of you killed, then and only then can you sit there and judge the rest of us. Don't you think most everyone here misses somebody? Nobody chose to be here. We're all misfits, missing some parts and most of our hearts. We don't belong anywhere or to anyone anymore. We just exist."

Jack approaches, hands raised. "Silvia, could we talk?"

I nod, although this is certain to be a very uncomfortable conversation.

"I'm busy cooking here, you know," the older lady interjects. "Not a good time for me to wander off if you need privacy."

"Not to worry, Madeline, you can stay. I just want to have a little chat with Silvia here."

I frown. "Did Dad send you?"

"No, he didn't." Jack sighs as he sits down. "I came on my own. I want to apologize. I handled that situation very poorly. It was such a shock to see you and to hear Franco's name. I didn't think about how upsetting all of this would be to you until we already got to camp. I should've gotten your dad alone to see you, at least at first. I'm so sorry."

My shoulders soften. "I'm not upset with you. Yes, meeting Dad alone might have been better at first, but it wouldn't have changed much in the end. I can't believe he has a new family. I had braced myself for the possibility that he had died out here, but not this."

Madeline clucks. "Isn't this better than learning he had died?"

"Honestly, I'm not sure." I take a deep breath. "I'm used to him being dead, but I'm not used to him betraying our family. I just don't understand why he never came back for us."

"It's complicated," says Jack.

"Then try to explain it in a way I can understand. Your family adores you. Why didn't you go back for them? I don't get it at all."

Jack focuses on the ground in front of him. "Listen. Life out here isn't easy. Some winters we come close to starving. There's minimal medical care. Many women die in childbirth. I knew if my family remained in Panopticus at least they'd have food to eat, good medical care, and a warm place to sleep in the winter. Their basic needs would be met. I couldn't promise that out here."

"But the government tried to kill you. Weren't you worried about their safety?" I clamp my mouth shut, remembering Liam.

"I thought they'd be safer if I just stayed away." Jack shrugs, beaten already and I haven't even told him about his son.

"At least your family knew what happened. We didn't. We thought Dad was dead this whole time until Gus told me when he helped me escape."

"I'm not sure which way was better, but at least I had Franco on the inside to help take care of things, so that helped."

"Yes, he helps them a lot." I think about him sharing his food allowances and watching over his cousins. "He is a rock for them. But what about *his* parents? Where are they? Are they out here too?"

"No, I don't think so, or at least I've never found them. They just disappeared, first one then the other. We never knew why."

"Oh, my gosh. No *wonder* Franco's so paranoid, and no wonder he wants to tear Panopticus down. Can you blame him after all that?"

Jack grabs my arm, then releases it like he's embarrassed he touched me. "No, he can't try anything crazy. They'll kill him for that."

My eyebrows raise. I need to know everything. "What were those meetings you went to with my dad? What were you planning?"

He shrugs. "We never got very far, just idle talk about our frustrations and what we could do about it, which was very little. Nothing concrete was attempted or organized, but there are a lot of people who don't agree with the government there."

"And for that, you got on a hit list? All those people died in that big explosion because the government was worried about a few meetings?"

"I know." Jack hangs his head. "That's part of the reason I never returned. I thought it was just too dangerous. I thought if the rest of my family stayed low and quiet, they'd be safe."

"What about Franco? He's not a lay low kind of guy, is he?"

"Why do you say that? What did he do?" Jack's eyes widen. "Please tell me everything. How about my wife and kids? Do you know them? Do you know if they're okay?"

"I met your wife," I say, stalling for time. I don't want to be the one to tell him his son is dead.

"How is she?"

"Angry." I pause a moment at his shocked expression before rushing ahead. "Or maybe she just doesn't like me. I don't know."

"That doesn't sound like her, but maybe she was just being protective of Franco. Are you his girlfriend or something?"

I flush, avoiding his gaze. "Honestly, I'm not sure what we are, but I think your wife was worried about more than just Franco dating."

Jack stares at me until I turn to face him. "What is it you're so afraid to tell me?"

I'm rendered silent, digging my nails into the palms of my hands.

"Whatever it is, you can tell me." He already looks sad.

I'm about to make it so much worse.

"I'm so sorry," I squeak out. "I don't know how to say it. I've been dreading it ever since I realized who you were."

"Is it the girls? Are they okay?"

My voice wavers. "Both girls were fine when I left."

"Liam?" He whispers his name like a plea for mercy.

I can't take this. I set down the bowl and walk a few steps away to hide in the darkness, breathing hard.

"Tell me everything," he demands, his voice shaking. "Start at the beginning, so I can understand. I've been gone for so long."

"Okay, okay." I pace the edge of the small clearing. "I met Liam at the gym earlier this summer. He talked me into running this *stupid* race because he wanted so much to get Chosen. I only did it because my mom wanted me to get ahead in life. We trained together and became good friends. That's how I met Franco. He didn't want Liam to run and tried everything to talk him out of it. He said we shouldn't draw attention to ourselves."

Jack takes a shuddering breath. "Franco was right."

"But Liam was determined to make something of himself. He tried so hard. He did win the race, and they said he was getting transferred, promoted to some other Great City, but instead..." I halt.

"Instead, they killed him." He moans, covering his face with his hands.

"Yes, and I only know this because I work with Gus in Mortuary Science." Jack's shoulders silently shake as I continue with my damning words. "One day they brought him in. I think it was on purpose, because they came after me next, but I was lucky. Gus found me in the hospital and saved me."

"Does Franco know?" Jack lowers his hands to look at me, his face wet with tears.

"Yes. He was there that awful day in the Mortuary. He saw Liam and went crazy."

"And said he would tear everything down?"

I nod. "I don't know what happened next, because the Suits came for me, and Gus helped me escape, so I never saw Franco again. But I owe both of them my life."

Jack doesn't answer, lost in his own grief.

"Stir the pot for me, will you?" Madeline pats my shoulder as she passes by, then groans a bit when she sits next to Jack. She wraps her arm around him, whispering all the comforting words I failed to say.

I stare into the stew, stirring slowly. Even though I just ate, all I feel inside is emptiness. All the joy and love I've ever felt in my life have just been drained away.

Someone close by clears their throat, drawing me out of my reverie.

Oh, no. It's the blonde. "We need to talk."

THE WINNER TAKES IT ALL

I don't know what to say to her, but that's okay because she's apparently got a whole speech planned out.

"My name's Alice. I'm sure you hate me, but please hear me out. I met your father seven years ago. He got me out of a *terrible* situation, and I will never be able to repay him for his kindness. Yes, we are married. Yes, we have two children named Thomas and Serena. Is there anything else you want to ask me? I will tell you anything you want to know, and I'll tell you the truth. Because I have something very big to ask of you in return."

I mostly hate her, but a tiny sliver of me admires her for coming up to me and laying everything out on the table. But there are still things I need to know, and none of them are polite topics. "Yeah, I have a few questions. Like, did you know he was already married and already had a kid? Or doesn't he talk about us at all?"

She flinches, then braces herself. "Yes, I knew, but you were on the inside, and we were stuck out here."

"Stuck out here or trapped in there. What's the difference?" Did she really think I would make this easy for her? "What did he tell you about us? Does he miss us at all? Or did he just forget we ever existed?"

"No one forgets who they left behind," she speaks so softly I lean forward to hear her. "It's true I don't know much about you. Daniel can't bear to talk about the past, so I know very little. I try every day just to focus on the present, but it's so hard to go on living without my son..."

"What do you mean? I saw your son sitting in my father's lap. He's got red hair so he's hard to miss."

"That's Thomas." She takes a shuddering breath. "I meant *before* him. Back in Panopticus I have a son named Matthew." She chokes on his name as she wipes away tears.

"Matthew? What happened to him?"

"I don't know." The tears flow even harder. "I don't know! I haven't known what happened to him for *eight years* now. Every day I say a little prayer for him, hoping he's okay, but it's not enough."

"Then go and get him *out* of there." The solution is so obvious, why do I have to point it out to her?

She shakes and sputters. "I can't! I'm terrified! I'd fail. I know I would! What if I got him killed? I could never shoot a gun or plan an escape. I'm too scared to even travel back there. What if someone kidnaps me on the road? What would happen to Thomas and Serena if I got captured and never came back? Then I wouldn't be there for *any* of my kids. I just can't!"

"Kidnapped? By who? Honestly, I don't think anyone in Panopticus cares what happens to us once we are on the outside. I didn't see a single drone or anything. The roads seemed safe to me."

"Young lady, you have no idea what this woman has been through." Madeline shakes her head. "Her fears are very real indeed. There are dangers out here you're not aware of, and thankfully so."

Jack nods. "You got lucky. Traveling out there all on your own isn't safe."

"Then tell me. What's so dangerous out here? What is it? Wolves? Bears? Some other monster?"

"Sometimes the worst monsters wear a human form," says Madeline. "Sit down next to me, Alice dear."

Alice crumples onto the seat, leaning against the older woman for support. Now Madeline has two people to comfort.

Alice shudders, pausing before speaking again. "Eight years ago I found some hidden documents at work detailing horrible things, like stealing babies and organs. I thought it couldn't possibly be true and showed them to my supervisor. Nothing happened at first. I thought it was all just a fluke. But then one day Matthew never came home from school. I ran around, looking for him everywhere. I heard so many excuses that didn't make any sense, like he never came to school in the first place that day, or that someone came to check him out early. I was so confused, so I just went home, hoping he'd shown up there while I was out searching. But when I got close, the lights were on in my apartment, and I could see the Suits tearing through my things. So I ran off and hid out. I'd heard whispers of people having underground meetings against the government, and by word of mouth I found help. They searched for my son, but they couldn't find him anywhere. I had to leave without him, and I still don't know if he's alive, wondering where I am and thinking I deserted him, or if he's dead."

"So then you came straight here, and never went back to find out what happened to him?" I ask, wondering how that could be possible.

"Not exactly," Alice says quietly.

"Don't worry, dear, I'll tell it." Madeline's voice grows serious. "Alice got into some trouble on the road. You have to understand that some of the Groupings are rather unpleasant. It's not like all the good guys left the city and the woods is filled with lost heroes. Some of the people out here never were in the city at all. And some of them, I think, escaped Hell itself to come here and cause trouble for the rest of us."

Alice wraps her arms around herself.

"There was a rather nasty Grouping we sometimes traded with, mostly for ammunition," Madeline continues. "Several people here are pretty good at making cider or homemade wine or beer, and that's what they wanted in return. One year, Daniel went along to help with the trade, and that's where he met Alice. She was a kept woman, as in kept against her will and forced to do all their cooking and laundry and other services I'd rather not discuss."

Alice hangs her head.

"There's nothing to be ashamed of, my dear," Madeline says soothingly. "Long story short, your father traded everything we had to set Alice free. Maybe he wasn't the most popular person here in the Grouping upon his return, but he did the right thing."

"I'll never be able to repay him," Alice mumbles.

Madeline shakes her head. "I don't think he wants you to repay him, dear."

They both look up at me. I continue stirring the soup like it's the most important job in the world. They're trying to make my dad out to be some sort of hero, but it's a hard sell for me at the moment.

"So now do you understand why I can't go back?" asks Alice.

I shrug. "I'm sorry you had to live through that. I can see why you're scared."

She nods. "I have terrible nightmares about it all the time. It's either the dream where that Grouping recaptures me and I'm stuck with them forever, or else I dream that Matthew comes here and yells at me, angry that I never came back for him. That's the worst dream of all. And then you show up here and say those awful things to Daniel. All I could see was Mattie's face saying them to me instead. It was like my worst nightmare come true."

I'm rendered silent.

"Which brings me to that big favor I have to ask of you." Alice takes a deep breath.

"You want to ask me a favor?" I can't believe this. "What is it? You want me to leave you and my father alone? Or maybe you want me to apologize to him? I don't think so. I'm not ready to make any such deals."

"You've got me all wrong. This isn't about your father at all. This is about my son, my *eldest* son." She stands up. "You say you're going back for your mother, right?"

"Yes, that's right. And no one is going to stop me."

"I've no intention of stopping you." She takes a hesitant step toward me. "In fact, I want to make you a deal."

I stop stirring. "I'm listening."

She takes another step toward me. "Bring me back my son. When you go and get your mother, find him too. If you bring Matthew back to me, you win. I'll do whatever you want. I'll break up with your father. I'll move away with all the kids. Whatever you say, I'll do. I'll give you *anything* you ask of me if you bring back my son."

2 6

FEAR

"Alice, *please* don't talk to her like that." My father comes out of the shadows. I've no idea how long he's been hiding there. "That's not a fair deal. You'll get her killed. Is that what you want?"

"Who asked you, anyway?" I ditch my soup stirring job to confront my father. "I make my own decisions. I've been doing so now for *eight long years*. You weren't around to help me when I needed you most, and now that I don't need you anymore, your opinion doesn't matter."

"Silvia, please listen to me." He stares at me wide eyed—like I'm a mirage and not real. "All this talk about going back is just insanity. Don't you get it? It's dangerous. You won't get back out alive."

I glare at him. "Mom won't make it without me. She barely made it without you, and then only because I was there. I'm going back to get her. Don't you care about her anymore?"

He deflates. "Of course I do."

"You said you loved her. Over and over you said it."

"I do love her. I always will."

I can read in his face that he's telling the truth, and it upsets me even more. "You said you loved me. You said you'd always be there for us, and yet here you are."

"That wasn't my choice." His pleading eyes never leave mine. "You know that. I was forced out."

"But you never even attempted to come back and get us. You never even bothered to try."

"I thought you'd be safer if I stayed away." Dad gestures at Jack. "We talked about it a lot and decided together that was the right thing to do. Because at least you wouldn't starve, and we wouldn't get you killed in the attempt."

"Don't use Jack as an excuse. At least *his* family knew the truth. They knew he wasn't dead, just exiled. Why did you choose to leave us in the dark? So it would be easier to move on?" I gesture at Alice, then immediately regret doing so because now she's bawling and it isn't fair to her. I'm not angry at her for some reason, just my dad.

"Because I know you." Dad sighs again, rubbing a hand over his tired face. "I knew you'd risk your life coming for me."

"Of course I would have!"

"You were ten years old, Silvia! You would've died trying to escape!"

Instead of invoking any sympathy, the look of agony on his face infuriates me. I step closer to him and raise my arms to where he can view my scarred wrists. "I almost died trying to live without you, so not letting me know the truth only made things *worse*."

Dad's trembling fingers raise to touch my scars. I don't shrink away because I want him to realize how wrong he was and how much we suffered because of his poor decisions. He is speechless, but I'm not.

"Mom and I fight *all* the time. She drives me insane, and I do the same to her, but I'd *never* leave her there to feel so helpless and alone. I'm going back, and there's no way to stop me. You can't talk me out of it, so as I see it you've got just one decision to make. Are you going to help me, or are you going to stay out of my way? I don't need you anymore, so either way is fine with me."

"Please, Silvia," his voice comes out hushed, his hands cupping mine. "What you're undertaking is too dangerous. Don't do this just because you're mad at me."

"I'm not doing this because of *you*. I'm doing this because of *her*. I'll get Mom out of there, and why shouldn't I bring Matthew back with me at the same time? I can find him. I know I can. Why can't you just believe in me?"

"You don't even know what Matthew looks like, or where he is, or anything. How on Earth are you going to find him?"

Alice raises a tentative hand. "The pictures. I'll give you all my pictures if you want them. I've got them at home."

"But, Alice, that was years ago. You've no idea what he looks like now. They may have changed his name and everything."

"You don't understand." Alice stands, visibly shaking. "I can't live without him anymore. I just can't. I can't pretend anymore. I *need* him."

Dad pauses, then says gently, "You don't even know if he's still alive..."

Alice gasps, her breaths heaving. Madeline tries to calm her, but Alice brushes her off and runs away into the darkness.

"Nice job, Dad," I huff, yanking my hands out of his. "Looks like you're pretty good at driving all the women in your life crazy."

He just stands there looking helpless. Again, I don't feel sorry for him, just for everyone he's disappointed.

"Speaking of jobs," interjects Madeline returning to stir her pot. "You've neglected yours, Silvia."

"Yes, I'm sorry—"

"And I think you need to eat some more," she continues.

"What? Why? No, I'm fine."

"No, you're not." Madeline stirs then refills my empty bowl. "You need to eat some more to build up your strength if you're going back. Plus if your mouth is full, you can't say any more hateful things to your poor father."

"But—" I protest.

"Enough for one night. You need food, and you need rest. In that order." Madeline, I can tell, is used to being obeyed.

Dad nods. "Yeah, finish eating, then I'll take you home."

"Excuse me?" I take the offered refill of my bowl, but his words stop the spoon before it hits my mouth. "I'm not going anywhere with you."

"I'm your father. Your home is with me."

"Oh, I don't think so. Not anymore."

Dad clenches his hands. "Don't be ridiculous. You're acting like a child—"

"Of course she is," Madeline interjects. "And do you blame her? She came all this way to see her long, lost father and discovered that he's not the perfect icon she remembered." Madeline turns to me, seeing everything there is inside. "She discovered that he's only human and has many failings, just like the rest of us. And she learned that all those years apart has made the two of you strangers—strangers who care so much about each other that you're determined to drive each other away to avoid getting hurt all over again."

I remain silent, which seems wise since Madeline would only shush me anyway.

Dad's shoulders droop. "So what do you propose, Madeline?"

"The girl stays with me tonight. Both of you sleep as well as you can manage and start over in the morning."

I speak up. "It won't change anything. I'm still going back."

"Hush, now." Madeline swats at me with her spoon, spilling soup on the ground that Albert hurries over to lick up. "Haven't you heard a word I've said?"

"All right. I'll shut up and eat."

"Good girl." Madeline gives me a knowing smile. "Daniel, you go home and comfort poor Alice. She's had a bad shock."

"Okay, I'll go." Daniel nods. "Silvia..."

I look up at the same face I gazed upon each and every morning, his photo hanging up in the place of honor in my room.

"Welcome home." Dad sighs and walks away.

2 7

WE ARE FAMILY

I hold back my tears until Dad disappears into the night.

"There, there now." Madeline takes me into her comforting arms. "I wondered how long you'd last."

"I'm just so angry with him." I fiercely wipe at my wet face, annoyed at my own weakness.

"Yes, that's quite clear." Madeline pats my arm then bustles around her cook site, sorting leftover ingredients into bags and scooping the last of the soup into a small container. "Could you help me carry a few things? We just have to bring this leftover soup to a sick neighbor, and then you and your little dog can get some good rest at my place."

By the time we reach her front door, I can barely function.

She removes the rest of the bags from my weary arms, guides me to a little bedroom just across from the kitchen, and pulls back the bedsheets. "Just go to sleep now. Don't worry about anything more tonight. Let tomorrow take care of itself."

I kick off my shoes and collapse onto the soft bed, Albert curling up beside me.

I step outside the Incinerator, gazing at the purple and pink clouds staining the horizon. The colors fade and darkness follows until the overhead lights flicker on, one after the other, in each of the distant corners of the dirt parking lot.

As the last one sputters to life, I discover Mom half-hidden at the far edge of the parking lot surrounded by Suits yanking on her arms and shoving her forward. Showers of gold-colored sparks fly through the air, illuminating the scene as she stumbles and falls to her knees.

Incinerator alarms wail overhead as workers dash around me. Explosions boom across the sky, pouring forth silver and gold fire like a sparkling fountain.

"Are you going to help her or not?" Gus asks as he checks his watch. "Look at the time, Silvia. You'd better hurry."

But my mother has already disappeared from view.

I wake up confused, trying to figure out where I am. Dishes clink in the kitchen. "Mom?" I call out, rubbing my eyes.

The door to my room clicks open. "Sorry, hon. It's only me."

"Oh, of course." I shake my head. "I don't know what I was thinking. I'll be fine. I just need to wake up."

"You've slept the morning away, but no doubt that's just what you needed." Madeline glances down at Albert hanging around her ankles. "I let your little pooch out a couple hours ago when I heard him whine. We've been getting better acquainted."

"His name is Albert."

"It suits him. Well, Mr. Albert, do you think Silvia will like what we've made for lunch?"

"Ooh, what is it?" Yes, I'm hungry again.

"I don't provide breakfast in bed, or lunch, for that matter."

Madeline backs out of my room, eyebrows raised. "So you'll just have to pry yourself out of that bed to find out."

"You don't have to tell me twice." I fling aside the bed sheets. "I'm right behind you."

Over another scrumptious meal, I grill Madeline with questions. I'm so curious how this outer world works. How do they have enough food? How do they stay warm in winter? How do they manage electricity and water?

"Goodness, I just work in food supply, so I don't know everything, but here's what I do know. There's a huge garden up here in this condo complex, with multiple options. A group garden with rotating duties and another garden with plots separated by family. I prefer having my own plot, and I trade some of my surplus for meat. I don't hunt and I don't raise livestock, but others do. We use generators, some are solar and some run on fuel. A few clever folks around here have had luck experimenting with vegetable and waste-based oil fuels, but there's still a little diesel around if they search far enough. We've gotten to where the wells and water purification systems are quite reliable now. It's not like things used to be."

"How long have you lived here in this Grouping?" I've never eaten this much in my life, and Madeline keeps offering me more food. It feels so wasteful, but I'm like an empty pit. Must be all the exercise.

She shakes her head. "Longer than I care to remember. At first we holed up inside the caves down in the park, terrified of being discovered. Nowadays, we still use those caves for cold food storage, but most people now occupy the homes next to the park. I was lucky enough to snag one of these comfortable condos up here on top of this hill. I love the view of the city below, even if there aren't many homes with lights on at night."

"Do you always eat together?' I ask. "Seems like such a hassle to bring everything out into the woods if you've got your own kitchen and everything."

"You mean last night? Yes, it is a hassle. Believe me, I know. I'm the one who organized the whole thing. That party you crashed last night was for Harry's birthday, but you pretty much single handedly put an end to the celebration."

"Oh, crap. I'm sorry." I back away from the table, full to the brim. "Wait a minute. Did you say Harry? Like, Ben's brother Harry? That guy who sets off the fireworks every 4th of July near Panopticus to let Gus know he's still alive?"

"I don't know anything about all that." Madeline shrugs, then turns away to tidy up her kitchen. "Guess you'll have to ask him yourself. But first you need to go talk to your father, who has already knocked on my door twice this morning. I told him to let you sleep, but you can't put him off forever. You need to talk to him, and this time try to avoid a temper tantrum."

"Fine." I sigh, reluctant to leave, but she's probably right.

Following Madeline's directions, I head down the hill toward a charming one-story brick home. But I don't want to be charmed, so I pause in the middle of the empty, worn street, staring at it, waiting until I feel calm enough to approach the front door. Albert whimpers at my feet, wondering what's taking so long for me to make my next move.

"There she is!" The two little kids from last night gawk at me from their hiding spot in the side yard, whispering loudly to each other.

I wave, and they approach, wary eyed.

"I'm Thomas." The little boy narrows his eyes. "You yelled at my dad."

"Yes, I did." Oh, great. These kids are going to remember that forever. "But I was very angry."

"You made him so sad." The little girl frowns and crosses her arms.

"Yes, I suppose I did." I could at least apologize to my half-siblings, and if I figure out where Harry is, maybe I should apologize to him, too, for crashing his birthday dinner. But Dad's another story.

He's the one who needs to apologize. To me. And to my mom, eventually.

"You wanna play with us?" she asks like a command, bringing me out of my reverie.

"Yeah. Sure." Anything to avoid talking to my father.

"Good. I'm Serena." A sunny smile erupts across her face. She takes my hand to lead me and Albert right past the house and into the woods.

"I like your dog," says the boy. "I want one, but Dad says no."

We turn left onto a well-worn path, heading through tall grasses and over fallen logs and big roots before we reach their goal. Albert seems to love kids. He scampers from one to the other, keeping tabs on everyone.

"We skate up here in the winter." Thomas's eyes shine with memories of ice and snow on this muggy August day. After a sweaty uphill hike, we come to a sudden dramatic opening with limestone walls surrounding it. It's like a large room with no roof. "It's my favorite place in the whole world."

We explore, getting pretty dirty while we do—which is saying a lot, since I've traveled for days wearing the same old clothes. I sniff my shirt, trying not to be obvious.

"You don't smell very good," Serena informs me.

"Yeah," agrees Thomas. "Mom wouldn't let us go to bed smelling like that."

I immediately feel bad for Madeline, who I picture stripping down her whole bed right now to wash away my stink. "Well, I jumped in a lake a few days ago, but nothing since."

"You jumped in a lake?" Thomas gapes, impressed. "Dad won't let us do that."

"Well, I'm a lot older than you."

"No, you're not." Thomas sounds offended. "I'm six years old."

"No, you're not." Serena corrects him. "You're five, just like me."

"I keep telling you, we're *not* twins." Thomas's face gets red to match his hair. "In ten days I'll be six, and you'll still be five until next summer."

Serena scrunches her nose. "You're a fart face."

"No, *you're* a fart face." Thomas digs his grubby hand into the dirt to gather some sloppy mud. Things are getting serious. Clearly, this is a fight they have often.

"Okay, let's break this up. I'm eighteen, so I outrank both your ages added together." Now they both glare at me. Time to change the subject and the mood. "Listen, are there any raspberries out here?" I can't believe I'm asking for more food, but my trick works as their faces transform from crabbiness to excitement. "Albert loves raspberries."

"Yeah, let's go!" Thomas drops the mud and grabs my hand. "I'll show you."

"No, I wanna show her," whines Serena, following close behind. "I wanna feed the puppy some berries."

We scurry down a path. Thomas drops my hand right away, disappointed at my lack of speed and agility over this rough terrain. I can't believe how fast they can race along the rocky bed without falling down. They don't run like humans. They run like deer.

"Here they are!" exclaims Thomas in triumph, as he reaches the wild raspberry patch first, with Serena's little muscular legs following in hot pursuit. "Oh, hi, Dad."

"What on earth are you doing out here on your own?" Dad sounds upset. "You know it's not allowed. Your mother's searched for you everywhere."

"They're not alone." I bring up the rear, sweating again. "We were just playing."

My sudden appearance rattles him. He struggles to find something to say. "Silvia, you can't just barge in here and do whatever you want."

"Oh, I see. I'm barging in on your new life, am I? You don't want me to get to know my half-siblings? You want to keep your two families separate?"

Dad sighs. "That's not what I meant."

"What did you mean, then?" Any of the temporary calm I felt here in the woods evaporates. I'm right back to fury, and we're right back to fighting.

Both kids gape at us, wide eyed and scared.

Dad raises both hands. "Okay, okay. I don't want to argue with you right now. Let's just get the kids home. Alice is beside herself with worry. She always thinks they're going to disappear on her, taken away just like Matthew."

"Okay." I nod, recognizing how much Alice must live in fear every day of her life.

"We should talk privately later, but Alice asked to talk to you first before I, uh, piss you off again."

Serena giggles. "You said 'piss,' Daddy."

"Piss, piss, piss," Thomas repeats under his breath.

Dad rolls his eyes. "This is why we need to talk in private."

"Agreed." For just a moment, we're on the same side. "Let's just get them home."

The kids feed Albert some berries before grabbing a few handfuls for the hike home. With the state of their hands, I'm not sure if they're eating more dirt or fruit. After they finish eating, they scurry ahead of us, Albert scampering alongside them, begging for more fruit the whole time.

Dad glances at me. "Alice wants to talk to you about Matthew again."

"Yeah, I figured."

He takes a deep breath. "You don't have to say yes, you know."

"I don't think you know me very well."

Dad sighs. "That's the problem. I think I do know you, and that's what worries me."

My eyes narrow, because he shouldn't assume he knows anything about me anymore, which puts us right back where we started and two sentences away from another big argument.

PICTURES OF YOU

Alice paces the backyard, clutching at her hair. The kids glance at each other with unsurprised, but worried faces. Clearly, this situation has happened before.

"Let me talk to her first," Dad whispers, touching my arm.

Too troubled by Alice's fragile state of mind, this time I don't flinch or pull away. After I nod in silent agreement, he ushers the kids forward into Alice's view. She exclaims and races to meet them, arms outstretched. She draws them close, murmuring in their ears. As I approach, I hear the kids comforting her instead of the other way around.

"Everything's okay, Mom." Thomas gives her a weak smile. "Don't be sad."

"Mommy?" Serena smooths Alice's hair. "Please don't cry."

My next step crunches a loud stick, and everyone turns around to look at me, including my dog.

Thomas waves me closer. "Look, Mom. Silvia's here. You said she could fix everything so you won't be sad anymore. And here she is."

Alice turns to me, face flushed and eyes blood shot. She wasn't faking anything yesterday, and it's obvious she's always terrified something bad will happen to her kids, both the ones here in front of her and the older son she left behind.

"Hello, Alice," I say softly. "I should've told you I took the kids into the woods to play. I'm so sorry. I wasn't thinking."

"Please don't apologize." She stands, adjusting her hair and clothes, attempting to smooth away the signs of distress. "I just worry about the children is all, even though I know I'm overreacting. It's not your fault."

I glance at my father's strained face, his eyes watching Alice's every move, analyzing each word.

"Are you hungry?" She looks so eager to please. "Can I get you anything?"

"No, thanks. I'm full. I stayed with Madeline last night, and she really likes to feed people."

Alice turns to my father. "You promised I could show her Matthew's pictures, remember? You promised you wouldn't stop me."

Dad winces, but doesn't argue the point. "Come on, kids. Let's play some ball and leave the ladies to it. The dog can stay outside with us."

Alice gestures for me to follow, and we go inside. The house looks so normal, with older furniture and well-loved toys scattered across the floor. Alice leads me down a hallway to an end room on the far right. She pauses at the closed door, one hand outstretched but unmoving.

"Are you okay?" I touch her shoulder. "Do you feel faint? Do you need to sit down, or should I get you some water or something?"

"No, it's not that." She pauses. "It's just that once I show you this, Daniel says you're going to think I'm crazy. But I'm not. Promise me you won't think I'm losing my mind."

"Don't worry about what Dad said. I'm perfectly capable of forming my own opinions."

She nods, giving me a tiny, tight smile. "Okay. Have a look." She opens the door with a slow creak, letting me walk through first. Two bright windows fill the small room with light. The only furniture in the space is a single wooden chair next to two worn card tables pushed together. Mismatched crayons and colored pencils overflow from tubs lining the far edge of the tables, the shiny linoleum floor below littered with stacks of papers of every size. But what takes my breath away are the hundreds of hand drawn pictures crowding every surface. The walls have eyes, far too many eyes, all staring out of the same face. Over and over, the same young boy, sometimes smiling, sometimes crying, sometimes grim or vacant. His hair short, his hair long, wearing a hat, wearing a colored shirt, wearing a school uniform. Every color used, drawn from every possible angle, and always watching. Alice hovers in the doorway. It must have taken her forever to draw all this. Hours and hours and days upon days of obsessing over every detail, for each image is hauntingly beautiful and perfect.

"Is it hard for you to come in here?" I ask.

"Sometimes. Yeah, sometimes I can't bear to see him, and I'll stay away for days. But then all of a sudden I just have to see him again, and I'll sit here alone in the silence, making up a conversation we might have, pretending he's here with me."

I turn counter-clockwise, taking it all in.

"You think I'm crazy now, don't you? I guess Daniel was right."

I turn to face Alice. "The first thing I saw waking up each morning was a big picture of my father hanging on the wall opposite my bed. I'm pretty sure Franco thought that was a little crazy or self-destructive or something, but I needed him there every morning. It helped me, having him there."

She nods. "So you understand?"

"Yes, I do."

"And you'll try to find Matthew for me?"

"Yes, I will." I turn back to the drawings on the walls. "But I'll need more information. Like, what did his father look like? And is his father alive? Any idea what you think he'd have tested into to try to find him that way? Or any names of people I should question?"

"His father's gone too. And not disappeared, he died of a heart attack. He was so young. And he was tall with dark hair. Matthew looked just like him as a kid, so maybe..."

Alice brushes past me to sit down, slaps a piece of paper on the closest table, and selects a few crayons and pencils out of the buckets. "In case you're wondering where I get all this, I've been scavenging art supplies for ages. Crayons and pencils don't dry out and go bad like paints and markers do."

"Makes sense." I stare in wonder as her hands race around the sheet.

She works so quickly, I'm rendered silent. First one eye, then the other, the nose, the mouth, dark bushy eyebrows and hair, a jawline and the neck. Within minutes, a man's face comes to life. Alice continues to shape and shadow while I stare over her shoulder.

"You're amazing," I say, breathless with wonder. "I don't know how to draw like that."

She finishes, holding up the page for my closer inspection, then grabs another sheet and begins to scribble names and places.

"I'm not sure where he is or if any of these people will talk to you, but it's worth a shot."

"Right." I scan her writing. "Gotta start somewhere."

"I can't believe you're doing this for me."

"I haven't found him yet, and I can't promise I will even if I try."

"I know, but you're willing to try. That's what counts." Alice slowly puts away each crayon and pencil. "Silvia, I want you to know I'm so sorry if I had anything to do with your father not going back to get you and your mother. I didn't mean to get in the way. I just... I'm sorry."

"I don't blame you, Alice. I really don't."

"Why not?" She turns to face me. "I told you I knew he was married."

I shrug. "I'm not sure why I don't. I just don't."

"But you're still mad at your father, aren't you?"

"Yes."

"You have to forgive him. You won't find peace until you do. I know you still love him, even if you're angry with him. He's your father. You just told me you looked at his picture every morning when you woke up. You must've loved him a lot."

"I did." I take a deep breath. "I think I just don't understand why he never came for us. That's what's hard for me to forgive."

Alice shudders. "Do you think that's the way my son feels about me?"

"I don't know." I feel bad saying this to her, but it's the truth. "But maybe if he talked to you, he'd understand."

"I think you should take your own advice." Alice stands up, moving away from the art table. "Go talk to your father. Ask him your questions, and don't interrupt him when he answers, and don't walk away when you get mad. Give him permission to tell you the truth, even if it hurts. Otherwise you'll never understand each other, and you'll just keep fighting. Go and make your peace with him. Do it right now."

I hesitate. "I'm not sure that right now is the best time to be doing this."

"Why not? I'll take the kids out of your way, so don't worry about them."

"Well...we've already had one argument today."

"But you just got here! What happened this time?"

I shrug. "Dad was mad that I went into the woods with the kids without telling you, so then I got upset and accused him of a couple things. But after getting back here and seeing how things are, I realize that I was in the wrong this time. And I'm sorry. I won't do it again."

She leads us into the hallway, closing the door behind us before speaking again. "So you're fighting about me again."

"Alice, it's not your—"

"Yeah, I don't need to hear that. It's not like this whole situation is all going to be just one person's fault anyway. It's so many people's faults I can't even count that high. It's everyone who turned Panopticus from a haven into a hellhole. It's the good people who helped first your father escape, then me, and now you. It's your father's fault for saving me from the prison I was living in, but it's more those devils' faults for kidnapping me in the first place and keeping me their slave for a year. It's everyone's fault and it's no one's fault, all at the same time. Things happen, and there isn't always somebody specific to blame. You can blame the whole world, or just me and your father, or no one at all. It's your choice."

"Well, anyway," I follow Alice down the hallway into the dining room, "I just don't know if now is the best time for a real heart to heart with my dad."

"What's this?" Dad's in the kitchen, making sandwiches for the kids and feeding bits of bread to the ever begging Albert. "What'd you say about me?"

"Hey there." Alice glances back at me while approaching my father. "I didn't hear you come in. Goodness, you kids are filthy! You must have had fun out there! Come over here to the sink, and let's get you cleaned up before you have lunch."

Dad and I exchange silent glances while Alice scrubs the squirming Thomas and Serena with damp cloths. After Alice sets the kids down at the kitchen table with their meal and something to drink, she turns to watch us eye-ball each other.

"Okay, you two. Time to take a walk in the woods. But I've got a couple ground rules you need to follow."

Dad raises his eyebrows, and I keep my mouth shut.

"First, only one of you has got red hair, but you've both got the matching temper. So try your best to control yourselves. Second, you need to be honest with each other."

"I am honest," protests my father.

Alice points a finger at him. "True honesty means talking about things you don't want to talk about."

Dad frowns.

"And thirdly, take turns talking." Alice looks at me. "That means, when Daniel takes five years to answer something he really doesn't want to talk about, you have to give him the five years. Don't just run him over with your words because you're better at expressing yourself than he is."

I exhale. "Yes, ma'am."

"Last thing," she turns to my father. "Don't make her so mad she runs off. Keep your cool and bite your tongue before you say something stupid."

"Okay." He looks like a little boy being reprimanded by the teacher.

"Got it?" Alice puts her hands on her hips. "No running each other over, and no pushing each other away."

Dad cups his hand over his mouth and stage whispers to me, "Watch out. She can be super bossy when she wants to."

Alice rolls her eyes. "Now get out of here and behave yourselves."

Dad smiles at her and the kids, and we head outside into the sunshine with Albert at our heels.

"Was this your idea or hers?" he asks. "Us having this big talk, I mean."

"Her idea. I told her I didn't think this was a good time."

He sighs. "But will there ever be a good time to explain the impossible?"

I shrug.

"So what do you want to know?"

"Everything."

"Okay." He sighs again. "Then I'll start at the beginning."

29

FATHER FIGURE

"First off, you need to know that I loved your mother very much."

I raise my eyebrows but hold my tongue for Alice's sake.

"And I loved *you*. I wanted everything in the world for you. I tried my best to get promoted in my line of work so we could get a better apartment and more provisions. I encouraged your mother to do the same in the orchestra. We were a good team, but we had our problems."

I tense, not sure I'm ready for what he'll say next, even if I asked to hear it.

"Your mother wanted kids so badly. We should've stopped long before that last miscarriage. You were too young to remember, but she was so hard on herself, trying over and over and losing so many babies. When you were born healthy, it took her a long time to accept it as real. I'd find her in the middle of the night hovering at your crib, staring at you. I'd lead her back to bed, and once morning came she never remembered what she'd done."

"She never told me any of this." I gaze at the woodland trail beneath my feet. There were so many things I didn't know about my own life.

"She didn't want you to be an only child. I told her you were fine, but she couldn't accept it. She wanted more for you. I don't know if you remember her last miscarriage—"

"I remember," I whisper.

"When she stopped eating, I should've forced her to go to the doctor, but you know your mother..."

"I remember all the blood on the floor, and that I thought she would die."

"She almost did." Dad avoids my eyes. "I blame myself. I should've brought her to the hospital earlier. She was too weak and muddled to be expected to make rational decisions. She refused to talk to any more doctors, and she wanted to hide her illness from you."

"I knew anyway."

"I know." Dad looks at me with sad, distant eyes. "I found you cleaning up the bathroom afterwards. Do you remember doing that?"

"I can still smell it." I shudder, attempting to push away the memory by watching Albert stick his nose into a rotting tree stump.

"That poor old neighbor-lady. She was nice, but she always fell asleep when she was supposed to be watching you, so I never trusted her completely. But she tried her best."

I stare at my father, reliving old memories in his head. But his memories are different than mine.

"When I asked if Mom was going to die, you said she couldn't die because you couldn't live in a world without her. Do you remember saying that?"

He looks like a hurt child. "I remember feeling it."

"Then how could you go off and marry someone else?" I'm glad Alice isn't here to hear me. "You probably don't want to talk about it, but you have to explain to me how this happened. Instead of coming and getting us, you married someone else. It's that simple."

"Nothing out here is simple." Dad shakes his head. "You should know a lot of stuff happened in between those two events. You act like five minutes after I left you, I moved on to someone else when that's so very far from the truth."

"Then tell me the truth, starting with all those secret meetings you went to. The ones where you had me cover for you so Mom didn't know."

He raises his eyebrows. "You remember that, do you? Well, I wish I'd never gone to those stupid meetings. It's where I met Jack Harman and his nephew Franco. I understand you know Franco. You're... friends or something, right? Jack told me."

"Right. Yes, I met his whole family."

"Jack also told me what happened to Liam."

I close my eyes, wishing I could stop seeing his corpse on the cold metal gurney, but it's burned into my brain and won't leave me alone.

"So you know how dangerous it is in Panopticus, and why I don't want you to go back there?"

I glare at him. "And you know that Mom's still in danger staying there—maybe even more so now that I've escaped—which is why I *have* to get her out?"

"I want you to stay here where you're safe."

"I'm not staying, and you can't make me." I pause. "But since Alice told us not to fight, let's change the subject back to you telling me more about the meetings."

"Okay." Dad runs a hand through his red hair. "I only went to the meetings in the first place because I wanted to make things better for our family. Life in Panopticus seemed unfair to most people. Unless you were a politician, I mean. They had everything handed to them."

"But I thought you and Mom got promoted, and life was good. At least I thought life was good. I thought everything was great until you went away. We had that wonderful apartment with all the sunshine, and we had so much fun together, and you and Mom seemed so very much in love."

Dad sighs, avoiding my gaze.

"You made Mom so happy. But she fell apart after you left."

Dad turns toward the trees, the sky, anything to avoid looking at me.

"Was she happy?" I wonder aloud. "Or am I remembering everything all wrong and not how it was at all?"

He finally looks at me. "Sometimes she was happy, but she never got over losing all those babies."

"I know. She lit candles for them on my birthday."

He shakes his head. "What?"

"Until that one psychiatrist made her stop."

"What psychiatrist?" he asks.

I hold up my scarred wrists, and he flinches.

"I never should've gone to those meetings." He stares at my old wounds. "I ruined everything for the both of you."

I shrug, dropping my arms back down to my sides. "Even if you hadn't gone to the meetings but other people in your department did, you might have died in that fire anyway. So many people did, and they didn't all go to your meetings."

"I've thought about that possibility too." Dad watches me. "Somehow Gus always eludes detection, and he's done more crazy things than I can imagine. He got Jack and me out and now you, plus countless others. How does he get away with it all?"

"Probably because he's a genius."

"That's right. You worked for him, didn't you? You must have known him pretty well."

"Yes. He understood me better than anyone else." I smile, because thinking of Gus always makes me happy. Except when it doesn't. "And I hope you're right that he always gets away with everything, because I'm terrified something happened to him after I left. What if someone does catch on? What if they figure out what he did to save me, so they go after him?"

"Silvia, calm down." Dad tries to put a hand on my shoulder, but I pull back. "Don't upset yourself over something you can't do anything about."

"I hate being told to calm down. I'm upset for good reason. Gus is the most wonderful man in the world, and I can't bear to think that someone would harm him because of what he did for me. And I *can* do something about it. I can go back and get him out of there."

Dad takes a shaky breath. "How many people are you planning to save, Silvia? How are you going to work this miracle? Do you even know how to use a gun?"

I stop short. "No, I don't. But you're right. That's a great idea. Will you teach me?"

"That's not what I meant."

"Of course not." I rush ahead, pulling away from him on the path. "Of course you don't want to teach me. Doesn't matter. I'll just ask Jack instead, so I can go back and help Franco."

"Silvia, please." He hurries after me. "Please slow down. Let's just talk this over."

I stop to face him, almost stepping on Albert in the process. "You didn't take Mom to the doctor fast enough, and you regret it. Then you went to anti-government meetings, and you regret it. Then you came out here and married someone else and had more kids, and now do you regret that too, because I found out?"

"You really know how to take some cheap shots, don't you?"

"Actually, after listening to Alice and Madeline and Jack and everyone else, I *do* kind of get it. Here's what I think happened. You shut me and Mom up in a tiny box and put us out of reach, so thinking about us couldn't hurt you anymore. Then you found Alice, and she needed your help. So that's what you did. That's what you're still doing. And she does need you. She's scared out here, and with good reason after being kidnapped by that nasty Grouping that treated her like trash. I'm sure you are her hero, just like you used to be mine."

Dad watches me with fearful eyes, like he's afraid of what I might say next.

"Clark was right. I *don't* recognize you anymore. You don't act like my dad. You don't even care about what happens to Mom." I examine him from head to toe, scowling at what I see. "You don't even look like my dad anymore, with your old T-shirts and those stupid leather beaded bracelets. Everything about you is all wrong now."

Dad takes a deep breath. "I'm sorry to be such a disappointment to you."

"You're even more of a disappointment to Alice, though, aren't you? Because you can't provide what she really needs, can you, Dad? What she needs more than anything else is her son, Matthew. I'm willing to go get him, and I've just met the woman. Why aren't *you* willing? Honestly, you should've done this years ago."

He hangs his head. "Because I know when I've been beaten."

"Fine. Then at least promise me you won't get in my way." I turn to leave. I've had enough of this conversation.

"I don't make promises anymore." He whispers at first, as if he's only talking to himself. "I've learned not to. I promised both of you I'd always take care of you, and then I didn't."

Slowly, I turn back without a word.

"I failed both you and Yoshe. And I know you're angry. I don't blame you. Sometimes I hate myself, but I can't change what happened. I'm so sorry for everything that happened to you. I'm sorry I wasn't there to help. I'm sorry I wasn't able to save you. I'm sorry I failed you and your mother."

My eyes fill with tears that I fight against. I don't want to feel any of these feelings. I need to be strong, not weak.

"And I'm sorry I don't want you to go back there. I don't want you to risk your life doing this, and I will do everything in my power to stop you."

"And I will do everything in my power to make sure you don't succeed."

We stare at each other, both stubborn enough to be certain we are in the right. I can feel Albert watching us warily.

Dad narrows his eyes. "You're about ready to run off again, aren't you?"

I clench my hands. "Yes, because everything with you is too

much. It's too intense. I missed you so much. I wanted you back in my life, but I thought it would be different than this. I thought it would be like it was before."

He sighs. "I think your memories of *before* are a little brighter than mine."

This knocks the wind out of me. "You mean you didn't like our life? You didn't want to be with us? That you're happy to have something else?"

"That's not what I meant at all." He pauses, carefully choosing his words. "I meant you were a kid. We tried to shelter you the best we could."

"I'm not a kid anymore."

"Yes, I can see that." He shifts uneasily. "I think the image you've held tight to all these years of me is… a bit glamorized. I'm not the hero you expect me to be. I don't have it in me."

"Well, I've got it in me." I step away from him and from all these unwelcome, overwhelming emotions. "I'm going to do everything I said I would, and you can't stop me."

"Please don't leave."

"I think this conversation is over." I move further away, Albert close by my side.

"Please don't do this to Alice."

That makes me pause. "Just tell her that it's all my fault."

"She won't buy that." He shakes his head. "Alice thinks you can do no wrong."

"Why? Because I'm willing to go get Matthew? Just so you don't think I'm irrational, I did warn her I might not be able to find him. But at least I'm willing to try."

"And I've warned her that your chances of getting killed increase drastically if you do try to find him."

"And what did she say about that?"

"She just wants her son." He shrugs. "It's not that she wants anything bad to happen to you, of course. She's not that kind of person. She's just so focused on getting Matthew back that she can't think of anything else."

"No, I get it. I saw that room. His absence is a huge, gaping hole in her heart."

Dad steps closer. "Just like I was for you."

"You were *everything* to us. It's like we were your plants, and you were our sun. After you were gone and Mom stopped playing violin, we got demoted to a much smaller apartment where all the windows faced north and we never got any direct sunlight, and every single one of your plants withered and died."

Dad looks stricken. "Yoshe doesn't play violin anymore?"

"Actually, she just started up again recently, but before that she didn't play for years. She said she didn't have anything left inside her to give. She just sat there for the longest time, like it was after that last miscarriage, but without all the blood."

"But who took care of you?"

"Who do you think?" I shrug. "I did. I fed myself and got myself to the school and the library. Well, I stopped going to the library after the Suits kept bothering me there."

He pales. "Why would the Suits go after a child?"

"They asked me all sorts of questions about you, of course. They must have known about the meetings. They said you caused the explosion. I didn't believe them. And don't worry. I didn't tell them anything."

"When did this happen?"

"On my birthday. Always on my birthday."

He rubs both hands across his face, as if he could wipe away the past. "This is why you can't go back," he insists. "They'll just come after you again. You're a target already."

"No, they stopped after a while. I'm not afraid of them, anyway."

"You should be." He raises his eyebrows. "But you were a tough kid, and clearly self-sufficient. Maybe you're not capable of being afraid."

"Well, you're wrong there." I pace the beaten dirt path. "I'm terrified of lots of things, but going back isn't one of them. I'm afraid Franco's gone and done something foolish and gotten himself killed. When Liam died, he went nuts."

"Poor Jack."

"I'm so scared someone found out that Gus helped me and then hurt him. I'd never forgive myself."

"Gus knows what he's doing, and you said he's a genius."

"Yeah, but anyone can make a mistake. And I worked with him, he knew me. What if that puts him on their radar?"

Dad frowns. "I don't know what to say. I'm not going to fill you full of false hope."

"Most of all I'm afraid about Mom. What if she goes all catatonic again and there's no one there to help her? What if she's just sitting in that dark apartment with no one there to make her eat?"

Dad grimaces. "It got that bad?"

"Yeah, it did." I turn to the east and point. "I wish I knew what she was doing right this minute. I wonder if it would make me feel any better, or if it would make things even worse."

"I used to play that game." Dad averts his gaze. "You know, wonder what you were doing on your birthday, or at Christmas, or even just any day, nothing in particular. I'd make up these little stories, and in my mind you were doing so well. Yoshe in first chair and you as the head of your class with many friends."

"That's pretty much the complete opposite of how it really was."

He sighs. "Then I'm glad I never knew."

"If you'd known how bad it was, would you have come and gotten us?"

Dad takes a sharp breath as if I'd punched him in the gut. "Silvia, things weren't any better for me out here than for you. Jack and I traveled together, and we argued a lot about where to go and what to do. Days went by without proper food or water. Sometimes I thought we'd die out here, lost in the woods. I didn't want to drag you through that. Eventually, we settled out here, but I just was so angry all the time that my life had gotten destroyed. I was a failure and no good to anyone. I was just your troubled past, and you were better off without me."

"How could you ever think that?"

"It got worse before it got better, believe me." Dad turns away, averting his gaze. "I became an expert at making wine and cider and excelled at drinking it. I started most of my days with a liquid breakfast and kept it up from there. There were whole days where I didn't remember a thing that happened. I just wanted to die and hoped that would speed things along."

"Are you freaking kidding me?" I grab his arms, wanting to shake him. "When did it stop? You seem sober now."

"Yeah, I am." He nods. "Completely sober for years now. It stopped when I traded all the booze for Alice."

"Alice?" I release my grip on him.

"Yeah. She helped me through withdrawal, and she cleaned me up, got me back together. She wouldn't take no for an answer. She stayed by my side the whole time."

I glance back toward where I imagine their house to be past all the trees. "Then she's stronger than she appears."

He nods. "She's much stronger than she believes."

"So you were too *drunk* to come get us?"

"Too drunk and too scared and pretty much just a complete failure in general."

"Then what's your excuse now?" I level my gaze at him. "Come with me. Leave Alice with the kids. Jack will help her while you and I go and get Mom and the others. Let's do this together. You and me. We'll figure it out. We can do this."

"I don't know, Silvia. I don't know if just wanting this to work is enough. The odds are stacked against us."

"Look, if nothing else, you *owe* Mom this much."

"Not if I get you killed. Yoshe wouldn't want that."

I throw my hands in the air. "Why can't I get you to understand?"

"Oh, Silvia, I *do* understand." He pauses. "I just don't agree."

"Come on, Dad," I beg. "I could really use your help with this, you know."

Eyes downcast, he turns away in silence. Tree branches dance on a light breeze as birds sing overhead. While my insides twist in turmoil, everything around us remains calm and peaceful.

Until we hear distant shouting. "Daniel! Silvia! Where are you?"

"What is it, Jack?" Dad calls out, hurrying down the hill toward the voice, Albert scurrying after him. "We're up here!"

"Oh, good, I finally found you." Jack rushes up to us, panting. "Daniel, you've got to get home right away. The kids are scared. Alice is in a real bad way."

30

YOU CAN'T ALWAYS GET WHAT
YOU WANT

All four of us, dog included, race down the trails to reach Alice and the kids. Despite all my training, Dad takes the lead, desperate to reach her.

As we near the house, Jack puts a gentle hand on my arm. "What do you say we give them a little privacy?"

I stop in my tracks, watching my dad rush into the backyard, pausing to crouch down next to his younger kids and listen to them. Both point at the house, urging him inside. He nods and disappears through the back door.

"I suppose you're right." I turn to Jack, and once again I'm a bit thrown by how much he resembles Franco. "I'll just make myself scarce."

Jack raises his eyebrows. "You going anywhere special?"

I shrug. "Albert and I can just go hang out at Madeline's again. At least I think she's expecting us. I left my backpack there and everything, anyway."

He nods. "I'm sure she'll be fine with it. She likes company."

"Hey, wait a minute. Could you do me a big favor?" I hope Jack's the right person to ask. "Do you think you could teach me how to use a gun?"

Jack glances at my dad's house then back at me. "Mind if I ask why?"

"Don't be ridiculous. I'm not going to shoot my dad. I know we fight a lot, but it's not like that. I need to learn how to protect myself so I can go back into Panopticus and get my mom."

"Ah, I see. An activity which your father isn't too keen for you to do."

"If it makes any difference to you, my mother isn't the only person I plan to get out of there." I'm losing my patience with these passive people. "Franco's on the top of my list as well. I don't think it's safe for him to stay there, and I'm pretty sure you want him out of there before something horrible happens."

"You make a good point." Jack nods. "Sure I'll teach you. How about tomorrow?"

"Tomorrow works for me." I turn back to Alice and Dad's house. "I should go, right? Or do you think I should stay with the kids? I don't know what to do here."

"Please don't take this personally." Jack looks worried, and all I can see is Franco's face when he wanted me and Liam to stop racing. "I don't mean this as any sort of insult, but I think you being here has pushed Alice into another setback. She's been pretty stable for a while now, but all this talk about Matthew has set her off again. Don't worry about the kids. I can hang out here for a while."

"Okay, then. We'll go. Come on, dog."

Albert and I head up the hill toward Madeline's condo. No one else is outside on this street. I'm not sure which of these houses are inhabited by members of this Grouping, and which ones are deserted, because none of them look that run down. Maybe people are staring at me from inside, reluctant to come out and meet me because of all the trouble I've made for their friends.

I don't want to cause Alice more pain than she's already endured. Maybe I wasn't thrilled with the idea of her at first, but none of this is exactly black and white or right and wrong. It's much more complicated than that, and I pretty much feel like I'm in the way here. Glancing back down the hill, I can't see the backyard of their house anymore. Too bad Jack couldn't somehow teach me how to shoot a gun today. Actually, I've no idea how long it takes to learn what I need to know. Maybe it takes a long time, much longer than a day, which is longer than I have to sit around and wait. I need to get back to Panopticus and get the people I care about out now, not a month or a year from now. I need to hurry.

Maybe it would be best for all involved if I head back to Clark's right away. He could always give me shooting lessons, and maybe he would give me a ride at least part of the way back on the highway. I don't want to run into any of those horrible people Madeline mentioned that hurt Alice. It might take more than one trip into Panopticus to get everyone out. If I can get Franco on board, he could help me. Gus might be the hardest one to convince to leave, which is ridiculous, but he's stubborn when he wants to be.

Pausing my steps, I glance back down the road towards my dad's house. My hanging around here now isn't doing anyone any good. I feel like Dad and I have talked most things out, and with Alice so upset now, he's got too much going on here to come with me, so I'll just do things on my own. That's fine. It's not what I wanted, but it's like that old Rolling Stones song Gus used to play for me when I'd complain about my mom. It's childish to think you can always get what you want, and I'm no longer a child. Like Dad said, I'm clearly self-sufficient. That means I can do this on my own, and I will.

Once I reach Madeline's front door, I knock and Albert lets out a sharp bark, but no one answers. I try the knob, but it's locked so I wander around to the backside. There she is with some guy with a cane, chatting as she hangs out laundry. My laundry, actually. My backpack is on the line, along with Franco's jean jacket and the few other clothes that were crammed inside.

"Hello?" I approach the clotheslines flapping in the summer breeze. So much for my plans of high tailing it out of here right away.

"Hey, Silvia!" Madeline brushes loose hairs out of her face. "As you can see, I washed all your stuff for you. With this wind it's almost dry."

"Yeah. I can see that."

"Don't look so ungrateful. So what if I'm a nosy busy-body for digging through your bag? We were looking for Harry's letter." Madeline shrugs, gesturing to the man standing beside her.

"You're Ben's brother, Harry?" I step closer, trying to find familiarity in his face based on the picture Gus kept in his office.

Harry raises his eyebrows. "You knew Ben?"

"No, but I wish I had. I've heard so much about him from both Gus and Franco."

"Did you work with Gus?" He watches me closely, wincing a little as he leans on his cane.

"Yes, in Mortuary Services." I rush my words. "Gus is like my best friend in the whole world. He's so brilliant. He taught me everything I know. And then he saved me."

Harry pauses before speaking. "Then you're the girl who was supposed to set him free, but now you're here instead."

His words silence me, partly because I've thought them already myself.

"So where's my letter?" Harry holds out a hand.

"I don't know what you're talking about." I glance from his open hand to his disappointed face. "Gus didn't mention any letter, and I never found one in the pack."

"But he always sends me a letter," Harry insists.

"Maybe he didn't have time," Madeline guesses.

"That's it." I nod, sure she is right. "He found me last minute drugged in the hospital and hid me in between the bodies going out to the Incinerator. I'm sure he didn't have time to write. But he knew you were out here yet because of the fireworks we saw out by the Incinerator on the Fourth of July."

My words falter as I glance back at his cane.

Harry nods. "You're right. It wasn't me this time. Had to beg someone else to do it. My knee has been giving me heck this past year, and I just can't make the trip anymore."

"I'm sorry," I say, because what else is there to say?

"I worry that Gus will never leave Panopticus." Harry shakes his head. "Even after everything that's happened."

"Sure, he will. He just doesn't know it yet." I level my gaze at Harry. "I'm going back for both him and my mom."

He chuckles. "I'll believe it when I see it. I may not have seen him for years, but even I know Gus is as stubborn as you can get."

"Don't worry. I'm sure Silvia here can give him a run for his money in the stubbornness department." Madeline smiles. "Say now, didn't you promise to apologize to Harry for ruining his birthday party?"

"Oh, right." I blush. "Sorry about that."

"No worries. Everyone's got their own problems to work through." He stretches out his sore leg, wincing. "But listen. If you can actually bring Gus here to see me one more time, that would be the best birthday present I can think of. Well now, I'd better head on home. The wife is waiting."

"Good night, Harry." Madeline waves as we watch him limp away.

"How long has he been like that?" I ask.

"He's been a lot worse this past year, and around here there's not a lot of treatment options available."

"One of the few benefits of living in Panopticus, I suppose." My gaze wanders back to the clotheslines. "Did you keep all my food? Because I'm going to need it."

"Of course I did, silly." She shakes her head at me. "I've got it all piled up on the kitchen counter. Cleaned up everything nice and neat for you. Soon as this dries, you'll be all set."

"Good. And thanks." It wouldn't hurt me to be more grateful to this nice woman. "Because I'd better head out soon. I don't think my being here is good for Alice or her kids or my dad."

Madeline raises her eyebrows. "Isn't this a change of tune?

Sounds like maybe you've matured a lot in the last twenty-four hours. Must be my good influence."

"Well, you've been so good to me, and you were right. Talking to him did help clear up a lot of things. I talked to Alice too."

Madeline pauses, clothespin in hand. "And what did Alice tell you about Matthew?"

I take a deep breath. "She brought me into his room."

Madeline nods emphatically. Clearly she knows what I'm talking about.

"I gotta find him. It's as simple as that."

"Simple? Is that what you think?" Madeline looks away, her eyes watering. "Fixing someone's destroyed life is just a simple thing? No problem. Easy-peasy."

"Well, finding him would be a good place to start, anyway."

"Finding him will be next to impossible."

"Why is everyone here always so pessimistic?"

"Because he could be dead."

"I know that." I brace my shoulders. "My mom could be dead already, too, but that won't stop me."

Madeline finishes hanging everything on her line, shaking a couple items straighter before she's satisfied. I look down on the valley below. She's right about the amazing view. So many single houses close by, leading to tall buildings across what looks like a narrow river. This is a real town, or at least it used to be before the war. Before everyone moved into identical tall apartments and lived the life, worked the job, and ate the food determined for them by others. And sometimes got killed just because they had the right set of lungs or a healthy uterus. Franco's right. Panopticus needs to come tumbling down. That's the only way this will all end.

Madeline moves into my line of view. "What are you planning? You've got a dangerous look on your face, my dear."

"Madeline, I know you don't really know me. And you might not have a good reason to believe half of what I say. But I'm going to get the people I care about out of that awful city, and then I'm going to go back and destroy it and let everyone start over. Not just the people I care about. All the people. And I know you think it's dangerous, but I think I'm dangerous too."

Madeline takes my face in her old, worn hands, and gives me a sad but proud smile. "Then this is a dead girl in front of me, a dead girl fighting against the whole world."

MILLION REASONS

"Isn't there anyone around here who could just believe in me?" I shake my head, releasing a sigh. "I know I can do this."

Madeline tilts her head to the side. "At least take a shower or something while I reorganize your pack. I'll make sure you have everything you need for your trip."

"Are you kidding me?"

"Not about the shower, I'm not. You'd smell a lot better." She pats her kitchen counter, turning serious. "You don't have any food allergies or sensitivities, do you?"

"No."

"Okay, good." She bustles around, flinging open cupboards and grabbing containers.

I hesitate. "You mean you're not going to argue with me, or tell me what to do, or try to talk me out of leaving?"

She turns to face me. "Here's how I see it. I could give you a million reasons why you shouldn't risk your precious life, especially after your friends risked their own to save yours. But you've got your mind made up, and if everyone keeps bugging you about it, you're just going to run off in a hurry, unprepared. I'd rather make sure that at least you don't go hungry. The rest is up to you, including that shower."

"Thank you." I head for the bathroom knowing there's limited water, but I'm used to short showers back in Panopticus. I just can't believe that for once someone is on my side. "Thank you so much."

I clean up in a hurry, then nudge a napping Albert off the pile of fresh clothes Madeline washed for me so I can wear them.

She grabs my dirty clothes. "I'll just launder these up quick right now. They should be dry by morning. It's windy out there on the line."

I nod. "I'll leave first thing, before anyone can stop me."

"I'll make you a good supper. The best one you've ever had." She turns away quickly, but not before I see the unspoken words in her eyes: *and maybe the last.*

Over her promised delicious meal, she grills me for details. "I can't help but notice you don't have much for weapons in your pack. How do you plan to protect yourself?"

"I asked Jack to show me how to shoot a gun." I shrug. "He was going to teach me tomorrow, but I guess that's not going to happen now."

"Right, and I can't help you much with that, I'm afraid. I just know how to cook the meat, not how to hunt for it."

"Maybe Clark can teach me. I'm sure he'll give me whatever I need."

"You do seem to have that effect on people." Madeline gets up to bring me seconds.

I dig in, savoring each fresh mouthful while I can. "Well, I can't tell you how much I appreciate all this good food."

"Ha. You better. It's dried tack from here on out." Madeline glances down. "For both you and your pooch. You know, part of me wants you to leave him with me since I've grown rather fond of the little guy, but I know you'll be safer with him watching out for you. You never know when a second set of eyes and ears could save you. Plus, I'm sure he's good company."

"Yeah, having someone to talk to out there helps make the miles pass by." I smile down at him. "Even if he can't talk back."

Madeline chuckles. "That makes him even better company. At least he won't argue with you. Oh, and by the way, I know it might seem a bit bulky, but I stuck a bolt cutter in your pack."

"A bolt cutter?"

She nods. "You'll need a way through all that perimeter fencing."

"Right." I set down my fork. "I suppose I could plan for a year and still not know what I'm up against. I'll have to wing it no matter what."

"Well, a little planning wouldn't hurt. You've got more than enough time on the road to think about it. I'd recommend getting in and out as fast as possible. Make a mental map in your head. Where do you think your mom would be? Find her as fast as you can, and then get the heck out of there for good."

"You're right."

"Got your scrubs all cleaned up and dried for you already. That should help you blend in. From what I hear, everyone in there wears scrubs of some color or other, right?" Madeline grunts as she attempts to drag the full backpack across the room.

"Right. Gus gave me those. Oh, here, let me do that. You've done so much for me, and this thing is pretty heavy." I lean it next to the front door.

"Yes, I don't know how your little body is going to carry all that food plus supplies." Madeline places a gentle hand on my cheek. "What I do know is that you'd better get yourself some sleep. Morning will be here before you know it."

"You're right again. Off to bed I go. Come on, Albert."

Albert starts to follow me into the bedroom, but pauses with one front paw held in the air before crossing the threshold. He cocks his ears for a moment to listen. At first, I don't hear a thing, but Albert does. He turns and races back to the front door, barking his head off.

Somebody starts knocking.

"Oh, crap. Don't let them in." I point at the backpack. "It's probably my dad. He can't know I'm leaving tomorrow. He'll try to stop me, and I don't want to argue with him about it anymore."

Whoever it is keeps knocking, and Albert continues to sound the alarm.

Madeline winces. "Okay, okay. I'll have to answer it or they'll never leave, but I'll try to keep them outside."

"Who is it?" she calls in a fake, cheery voice.

No answer except for the continued knocking, not that we can hear much over Albert's shrill vocalizations.

"Too bad you don't have a peephole," I whisper.

Madeline's hand pauses at the lock. "Why won't they say who they are?" Finally, she unlocks the door, and before Madeline can step out, Alice shoves her way in.

"Oh, I found you." Alice's eyes are red rimmed, her face pale. "I need to tell you something. It's important, and you can't say no."

She notices the full backpack waiting right next to the door. "You're leaving now," she states rather than questions.

I nod. "Tomorrow morning, and you can't tell my father."

"I won't tell him, because I'm not going back home." She grabs my hand. "I'm coming with you instead."

3 2

STILL THE NIGHT

"You're doing *what?*" I can't have heard her correctly.

Alice nods, her face aglow with excitement or frenzy, I'm not sure which. "You heard me. I'm coming with you. We're going to find Matthew together and bring him back here where he will be safe."

Madeline's hand flutters to her heart. "Now, Alice. Are you sure about this?"

She drops my hand and turns to the older woman. "I've never been *more* sure."

Madeline pauses. "Because you've got two kids here at home who depend on you."

"Don't you think I know that?" Alice frowns. "But I know I would be a much better mother if Matthew were here."

"Oh, come now," Madeline says kindly. "You're an excellent mother."

Alice shakes her head. "Not when they have to babysit *me* instead of the other way around. Not when I hide in Matthew's room for hours staring at his face and crying. It's not right, and I'm not going to do it anymore."

Madeline turns to me. "Silvia, you've been quiet so far. What do you think?"

I cringe. "I can't believe I'm asking this question, but does my father know about this?"

Alice evades my gaze. "Yeah, I told him...of course I did...and he said, um...to go ahead and do this if it's the only way I can be happy."

"That doesn't sound much like him," I have to say.

"Okay, you're right." Alice frowns. "I didn't tell him face to face. I left him a note."

"What do you mean you left him a note? Where is he?"

"He's asleep with the kids. I know that deep down he will understand." Alice straightens her back as if in defiance. "He'll know I had to go, just to find some peace."

"I don't know, Alice. It's one thing for me to argue with my dad and not do what he says, and it's a whole other thing entirely for me to take his current wife, the mother of his other kids, along with me."

Alice's eyes flash. "If you don't let me come with you, then I'll just set out on my own. I don't care anymore. And if you don't want me, I'm still going. I've always been scared of going out on my own because of Eddy and his Grouping, but I'm pretty sure they're all dead by now anyway."

"Wait." I interrupt her ramblings. "Who's Eddy?"

Alice shudders, and Madeline hurries to answer. "Eddy was part of that no-good miserable drunken Grouping your father traded all our supplies to in order to free Alice all those years ago."

"But I'm sure he's dead," Alice says, maybe to convince herself. "He must be. No one can live like that forever. Someone must have killed him by now. He was always looking for trouble. I'm sure he found it."

"I'm sure he's gone, dear." Madeline smiles reassuringly at Alice, then turns to me. "So what is it, Silvia? Can Alice join you, or are you going to make her travel alone?"

"Are you sure?" I ask Alice. "I can't promise we'll find Matthew. I can't promise we won't starve or run out of water. I can't control the weather, and I don't have a plan on how to break into Panopticus. It's all up in the air at this point. I'm just going to do my best to try and figure it out as I go along."

Alice clenches her hands prayerfully. "Please, please take me. I promise I won't be a bother. I don't want to be afraid anymore. I want to be strong like you. Just being with you will help make me brave."

I hesitate. "I'm not sure I should do this, but it would be even worse to make you go on your own, so I guess you can come with me."

"Thank you so much!" Alice hugs me. "When do we leave?"

"I'm sorry to say this," Madeline grimaces. "Because I know neither of you are well rested, so it's not ideal. But you two had better leave right now if you don't want Daniel to stop you. There's no time to waste."

Alice looks between Madeline and me. "Let's go."

Madeline digs through closets and cabinets, shoving supplies into a rainbow colored backpack she hands to Alice once it's plump and full. "You two had better hurry."

I glance at the worn, faded purple tennis shoes Alice is wearing. "Are those shoes comfortable? They look kind of old, and we need to cover a lot of miles."

She brushes away my concerns with a wave of her delicate hands. "They're fine. Don't you worry. I'm good to go."

Once we're standing at the front door ready to embark on yet another cross country adventure, I hesitate again.

"Honey, if you're going to go, the time is now," prods Madeline.

Alice nods, her eyes a little too bright and her lips held a little too tight.

Albert waits at my feet expectantly. I know he's tired, and I wish both he and I had gotten a good night's sleep before we left. This is the wrong way to start this long and treacherous trip. I'm so torn and feel a little bit manipulated by Alice into leaving before I'm ready. But what else can I do? I can't let her go on her own. She needs my help.

"Well, then. This is good-bye, at least for now. Thanks, Madeline, for everything." I pat her on the shoulder before she drags me into a warm hug.

"I wish you both the best of luck." She breaks the hug and turns to clasp Alice into her arms. After a long moment she stands back, looking very much like she's debating saying more, but remains silent.

"Okay, then." I open the door.

Alice turns to Madeline. "Please take care of my family. You will, won't you?"

Madeline nods. "Of course I will. Now, hurry there and hurry back. Don't take too long and make me miss the two of you."

"Thank you." Alice joins me.

The three of us head off, our eyes adjusting to the starlit night. Albert trots between us but with less than his usual amount of pep. I shouldn't be making him do this, not without letting him rest. This isn't how I wanted to leave. Not in a rush, not in the middle of the night, and not with a traveling companion who might flake out on me at any moment. She might decide tomorrow or the next day or even later tonight that she already misses her kids too much and wants to go back home. So many things could go wrong, even though right now she seems so sure of her plans. And despite how he's let me down in so many ways, this isn't how I should treat my dad. Disappearing in the middle of the night with Alice feels a little bit like I'm doing this to get revenge. To show Dad what he should've done so many years ago. To show him how he failed both me and my mom. But I no longer feel righteous, I just feel dirty and wrong. My stomach knots at the thought of him having to explain to little Thomas and Serena that their mother has gone without saying goodbye, and maybe gone forever.

"Would you really have gone on your own, or were you just bluffing?" My words sound ruder than I intended, but I want to know the truth. I feel trapped into this decision, and I'm regretting it already.

Alice chooses her words carefully. "Yes, I would've. Or at least I would've tried to, but I know I'm not strong like you. You're so brave and sure of yourself. I'm just copying you now. Whatever you do, I'll do, and *that's* what's going to help me survive this."

My steps falter. I glance back at Madeline's house lights.

Alice tugs on my sleeve. "I need you. I need my son. I'd get lost and most likely starve without you. Please don't change your mind. Let's do this together."

"Okay, fine. We'd better figure out where we're going and how to not get lost in the dark. We don't want to end up going in circles. Tonight we need to get far out of reach in case anyone tries to come after us to stop us."

"You mean Daniel, right?"

"Yes." I can't help but wince. "He's going to be so pissed at me for taking you along."

"Oh, I hadn't thought about that. I don't know that he'll be angry. I just think he'll be sad. Hopefully not too sad. I don't want him to go back to how he was before."

"You're worried he'll start drinking again?" This gives me pause. "Now I feel even worse. I would hate for him to do that to the kids. I don't even know how you stayed with him through that. It must've been awful."

Alice shakes her head. "No, you've got it all wrong. He wasn't a mean drunk. He was just sad. And I owed a debt to him for setting me free."

"You mean you don't love him? You're just with him out of—I don't know what—a sense of obligation?"

Alice shakes her head. "No, that's not true. At first, I stayed with him to help him get clean, but I grew to love him, and now we're a family."

"So you're not angry with him for not getting Matthew?"

"It's not as simple as that." Alice shakes her head. "Like I've said, I don't think I'll ever be able to repay him for what he did for me by saving me from Eddy. Of course, running off on him like this isn't the best way to show my gratitude, but there is one thing I can do for him while we're out here together. I'm going to convince you to forgive him."

"Are you sure you want to get into this conversation?"

"Yes, because you need to forgive your father for marrying me instead of coming back for both of you. I could see how much of a betrayal it was for you to see our kids."

"It does put a whole different spin on everything I grew up believing about him. I idolized him. And then there's my mom. If you think I'm not good at forgiving people, you should meet her. She might rip your hair out."

Alice nods. "She'll probably hate me, but it won't stop me from helping you find her."

"We'll just deal with that uncomfortable situation when we get there, but for right now I just hope you know your way around here at night, because I'm feeling a little lost."

"Don't worry. I know my way around this park by heart, and there's plenty of starlight. Just go left here and this path will take us all the way to the old highway on the other side. We can't get lost after that, because you brought all those maps, right?"

"Yeah, I've got them." I adjust the straps on my heavy backpack. This isn't going to be an easy night, but we'll make it through.

"Listen..." Alice sighs. "I know I messed up your plans and forced you to bring me along."

She falls silent for so long I realize she's waiting for me to respond. "I don't know what to say, Alice. I can't deny that this situation you've put me in isn't ideal."

Even in the dark, I can see Alice wince. "I know that, but ever since you showed up at the bonfire that night, I've known I can't go on any longer without my son. This is what I must do, and you're the only one who can help me."

"Because my dad won't go back, you mean."

Alice shrugs. "It's not just him. It's everybody here, or at least everybody who's still around. There've been a couple people who've said they're going back to get someone, but we never hear from them again, so who knows what happened to them?"

I shudder. "That makes what we're attempting to do sound like suicide."

"I know that, and I accept that risk."

"Even if it means you never see Thomas or Serena again?"

Alice gasps. "Please don't talk like that. I feel like I'm forced to choose between my kids, and I can't do that anymore. So I'm going to at least try to help them all. I don't expect you to understand."

"I do understand. I'm not just going back for my mom. I want Gus and Franco too. And I'm sure Franco wants the rest of his family, and so on. I don't know how far this will go. And I don't know if I'm attempting the impossible. I just know I have to try."

"Then we're the same, you and me."

"Not quite. And maybe I should've told you this from the start. You see, you're just interested in escaping Panopticus, and I'm planning to *destroy* it."

Alice halts. "I did not sign up for that. I'm only interested in my son. Nothing else."

"I know."

She glances back where we came from.

"If you're already thinking about going back home, now is a way better time than fifty miles down the road. So you better tell me right now if you're in or out."

She squares her shoulders and turns back to me. "You're not being fair. I told you *exactly* what I wanted. I didn't know you had other plans. But I still want to find my son. I'm all in, but I'm not sticking around afterwards to fight the system or something. I don't care one bit about that business. I just want my son. That's all I care about."

"Yeah, I know."

"So then, will you be okay if I grab him and go? You won't be mad at me, or try to rope me into anything more? Because it's taking all the strength I have in me just to do this much. Can you respect that?"

"Yes, I can respect that. I only wish that years ago my dad had done for me what you're doing now for your kid."

She shakes her head. "I'm sorry I can't say the same, because if he had gone back to rescue you, he couldn't have saved me."

"Even though I'm still mad he didn't come get us, I am glad that you're okay. I hate to think of you stuck with those awful men. That was a thoughtless thing for me to say to you about my dad. You've suffered enough."

"It wasn't that thoughtless. Not really. You and I have both suffered, just in different ways. But what's done is done. We should just focus on what comes next. And maybe that means you should just focus on the people you care about, instead of the government you hate. Don't sacrifice one thing for the other, especially when it might not do any good, and you might get yourself and those around you killed because of it."

Albert whines so I pick him up to carry him for a while. "I don't know exactly what I'm going to do about Panopticus itself, but I promise to get everyone I can out of there first, including your son if we can find him."

"We will find him, and I'm going to hold you to that promise." Alice glances over at me. "And I'm going to try my hardest to talk you into coming straight back with us. It's the least I can do for Daniel after all he's done for me."

"Fair enough."

"Let me know if your arms get tired carrying the dog. My pack is lighter than yours. I can carry him for a while whenever you want. Just let me know."

"Thanks. I'm good for now."

We hurry on through the night noises, stars overhead, and insects buzzing. Something scuffles nearby, and Albert rouses himself awake enough to growl from the protection of my arms before falling back asleep. My back begins to ache, but I don't hand him over. My mind swirls with one far-fetched plan after the other. I need to find a way to get inside undetected, then find Mom and Gus and Franco, and get them out of there without getting caught. After that, do I really want to go back inside and fight some more? Or do I just want to cut my losses and run away again? Alice might be right. Maybe I need to decide what's most important to me and focus just on that. It's not like I'm a superhero or a miracle worker. I'm just one person who's pissed off about what's going on in there and wants it to end for everybody, not just those I care about. Would it be wise or selfish just to do the bare minimum? Of course, the bare minimum is still going to be quite difficult. I'll stop by Clark's place and have him teach me how to shoot a gun before we go any further. It would be stupid of me not to have some form of protection with us when we re-enter Panopticus. I'm sure I could learn quickly, and it might save us in the end.

Hours pass by in mutual silence. It's after midnight by now, but the morning light is still a long way off. Alice stumbles and catches herself, her shoes scuffling on the ground.

"Are you okay?" I reach out a hand to steady her.

"Yeah, I'm fine." She stretches her arms. "Actually, I'd better be honest with you. I think I'm too tired to go on. Do you think we could rest now?"

"I'm worried we haven't gotten far enough away, but maybe we'll just take a quick nap and start again at daylight."

We lean against a big tree at the side of the highway, Albert nestled between us. I'm so exhausted I don't remember anything more until I wake in the daylight to Albert's low growl.

"Well, look what we have here," sneers a tall man in dirty jeans and a T-shirt.

Alice clenches my hand so hard it hurts.

"Who are you?" I ask.

Without taking her eyes off him, Alice whispers, "That's Eddy."

33

CREEP

"You're looking *good*, Alice," leers Eddy, his beady eyes examining every inch of her. "Makes you *almost* worth the wait."

"Leave me alone," she begs, cringing away.

"Oh no, can't do that." Eddy never averts his lewd gaze. "Not when I've been such a patient man, and it's finally paid off. I've been waiting for years for you to leave those two brats of yours and come back to me."

Alice gasps. "How do you know about my kids?"

Eddy chuckles. "Don't you worry. I've been checking in from time to time, watching you in that little house with your little husband, cooking his meals and doing his laundry when you should be doing mine. Because you're mine, and you know it."

"She doesn't belong to you, asshole!" I struggle to my feet, Albert barking and bearing his teeth.

"Sit yourself right back down, little lady." He points at me with an ugly scowl.

"Don't tell me what to do," I retort as Albert lunges forward, snapping.

"Make that lousy dog of yours back down." Eddy pulls out a gun and aims it. "Or I'll put him down *permanently*."

I grab at Albert, trying to restrain him, but he's furious and keeps slipping away.

"Get that damn dog away from me." Eddy cocks the gun, his eyes narrowing in on Albert's head.

"Eddy, don't!" Alice screams. "He's just a little dog. Leave him alone!"

"Maybe I will." Eddy's gaze flicks to Alice. "If you tell me how happy you are to see me."

Alice sobs wordlessly.

"Well, now, that's not very convincing." Eddy holds out a hand toward Alice. "Why don't you get on over here and *show* me how much you've missed me?"

Grasping the frantic Albert in my arms, I whisper to Alice, "Just ditch the bags and run for it."

"Oh, I don't think so." Eddy steps up and grabs Alice by the hair, dragging her down toward the road where an open top vehicle is parked, waiting.

"Leave her alone!" I yell, scrambling after them.

He points his gun at me. Alice flails her arms, trying to grab for the weapon. "Stop that, bitch!" He slaps her hard in the face. Blood streams from her nose as she cries out in pain.

"Nooooo!" I scream.

He smirks at me, as if abuse is just a joke to him.

"Why do you even want a woman who doesn't want you?" I ask him, wanting to humiliate him but knowing I'll just piss him off even more. How I wish I had a gun and knew how to use it. I should've stayed at least one more day and forced Jack to teach me. Then we wouldn't be in this situation.

Eddy growls, "Oh, she'll want what's coming. Trust me."

Tears stream down Alice's terrified bloody face.

I clench my hands, wanting to rip his eyes out. I glance up and down the road. If I take off now, I might be able to run for help, but he'll just drive off who knows where and we'll never find Alice again.

"Where are you taking her?" I demand.

"Oh, yeah, like I'm going to tell you." Eddy yanks on Alice's hair once again, pulling her toward the vehicle. "Why? You wanna come along?"

"My dad's going to *kill* you." The words fly out of my mouth without thinking.

"Wait a minute." Eddy jerks back around to face me. "Your father is that same red-headed bastard who stole my woman? How interesting. Now you'd better come with me."

We never should've left on our own. That's clear now.

"Get in the jeep," he snarls. "Both of you."

I hesitate, again searching the road north and south for help that doesn't come.

He gestures at me with the gun. "No funny business now. Grab your bags. I don't need anyone finding them, plus whatever you got in there is mine now."

I nod, my mind scrambling for a good plan as I leisurely go back for the packs.

"Hurry it up," Eddy yells. "And if you're thinking about running, I'll shoot you both. *Her* first."

I turn back to see the gun pressed up against Alice's forehead.

3 4

NEVER GONNA LET YOU GO

Eddy narrows his eyes. "Those little muscular legs of yours aren't fast enough to outrun bullets, are they?"

I glare back, again wishing I had a weapon.

"I think you'll find that I'm a generous man," Eddy continues, pulling the gun slightly away from Alice's head. "All I want is my wife here, but if I can't have what's rightfully mine, then I'll collect that little daughter of yours—"

Alice gasps.

"I know where she plays in the woods." Eddy sneers at her terrified face. "I've *watched* her many times."

Alice shudders.

"Then I'll go after your son." Eddy turns from Alice to me. "And, finally, I'll shoot that red-headed fool you both care so much about. It's about time I finished him off, anyway."

"You leave him alone," I growl.

He gestures with the gun. "Shut up and get in. You don't have a choice. And no funny business. I'm warning you."

"Fine. You win. For the *moment*." I slide the backpacks over one shoulder, shift Albert to the other arm, warning him to stay quiet, and hoist everything into the back seat of the ATV.

Eddy spins the vehicle around, jerking us to the right before speeding south down the highway. With each mile that passes, help seems further away. My mind races with impossibilities. I imagine grabbing the gun out of his hands and using it on him. Staring at the back of his head, I wonder if Alice could take over driving if I tried to choke him with my bare hands. I turn to my backpack, wondering what item inside I could use against him. Would he notice if I dug out the bolt cutter and smacked him over the head with it?

The wind blows Alice's hair around in the seat in front of me, her shoulders slumped. She's given up already. But not me. I don't give up this easily.

We head east in menacing silence except for the loud motor. Eddy turns to look at Alice every so often, but she never raises her head. An hour passes while I feverishly try to plan an escape, but every idea I start with ends up with Eddy shooting us both dead, just as he promised. We travel on, crossing the Mississippi River on the huge bridge Clark doesn't trust. Once we reach Wisconsin, I scan both sides of the road hoping for a glimpse of him, but Clark has long since gone back home.

"Where are you taking us?" I demand. His silence is torture.

"Wouldn't you like to know?" he calls back over his shoulder. He jerks the vehicle off the highway onto a gravel backroad, again yanking us sideways in our seats.

Albert growls as I lurch to keep the backpacks from toppling out of the vehicle.

"Remember what I told you. You either shut that dog up, or I will," Eddy warns.

There's only one of him and two of us (three if you count the dog). But I don't relish the idea of fighting him on his territory, where he knows the layout and where all his weapons are located. And I can't count on Alice to help me, not when she acts like there's no fight left in her.

He slows down to a crawl. "We're almost there, ladies. Now, this is a nice Grouping. They like me here. There's no reason why you two can't settle in just fine. Just go along with everything I say. If either of you try to run, I'll be back in Minnesota after your family within the hour. And I guarantee I'll get there before you do. Okay?"

"Okay," Alice whispers, her voice sad and quiet. "Whatever you say."

"And you, girlie in the back. What do you have to say?"

"I'll do whatever I can to protect my family."

"And that means doing what I say. You got that?"

I remain silent.

He slams on the brakes, jerking the vehicle to a complete stop, and whips around to glare at me. "Answer me right now. You got this or not?"

"Yes," I reply through gritted teeth. "I've got this."

He grabs Alice's chin. "You look like crap. Better clean up that pretty face of yours." He hands her a somewhat soiled towel from one of his pockets.

Her hands shake as she wipes her face to hide the signs of his temper and abuse.

After a few minutes of watching her, he grabs the cloth away again. "That's enough." He drives on, tapping his fingers on the steering wheel and humming to himself. Soon afterwards, he pulls into a small collection of cabin-like houses. It's cleaner and more organized than I expected. There are clothes hanging on lines, sturdy wooden chairs surrounding a spent campfire, and one more vehicle to the side of where Eddy parks his.

A few people mill about, turning to watch our approach.

"I'm back!" Eddy calls out joyfully, as if we were all on a fun family vacation together. "And I've got a big surprise for you. I've brought home my long lost wife!"

A middle-aged woman frowns, looking at the two of us. I can't tell if she doesn't like us or if she doesn't like Eddy.

"Man, you're going to be in trouble," mutters a young man who looks a bit familiar, sauntering up to the vehicle and patting its side.

"I'm not in trouble for anything," Eddy scoffs. "And you should learn to respect your elders, kid."

The young man shakes his head. "You're not supposed to take the vehicles without asking. I sure learned my lesson."

Now I remember who he is. He's the kid who hit the deer on the road who got lectured by someone named Nate who fed Albert some scraps instead of hurting him. This gives me an idea. I just hope it works. But it must be timed perfectly.

"Get out of my way." Eddy waves the young man off. "My wife here needs to lie down for a moment. The long trip tired her out."

Alice stiffens. I know she doesn't want to be left alone with him, but that's what must happen for my plan to work.

"You stay *right here*." Eddy points a grubby finger at me. "You hear me, girl?"

I nod, attempting to look meek and obedient when I really want to punch him in the face.

He saunters away, one arm around the limp Alice, leading her off to the smallest shack furthest to the right in this Grouping here in the woods.

As soon as he's out of earshot, I turn to the young nameless man with urgency. "I need to talk to Nate *right* now."

EVERYBODY HURTS

"You know Nate?" The young man seems surprised at first, then turns suspicious. "Who are you, anyway?"

"The more important question is if that poor woman is really Eddy's wife," mutters the frowning middle-aged woman, staring right at me.

"She isn't his wife, and even if she was she wouldn't want to be."

"That's what I thought." She shakes her head. "I never wanted that man to join our Grouping anyway. Let's find Nate. He's got company right now, but he won't mind."

She leads the way along a worn footpath around the small homes. Laughter travels back to us on the wind. Albert sniffs the air and tears off ahead.

"Be careful!" I warn, but he chooses not to listen, flying ahead on his four little feet, his tail spinning in crazy circles. He disappears, then returns moments later with Rachel at his side. Their joy in meeting again lifts my heart, because now I know help is at hand.

"Clark is here?" I exclaim.

"You sure know everybody," mumbles the young man beside me.

I rush around the corner to find Clark and Nate sitting together, looking very relaxed.

Until Clark spots me, jumps out of his chair, and rushes to my side. "Hey, kid, did you find your dad?"

"Uh, yeah, but we can talk about that later. I need your help right now. There's some creep named Eddy—"

At this, Nate groans. "What is it this time?"

"I warned you about accepting him into your Grouping." Clark shakes his head. "Like I said, kid, not everyone out here is worth knowing."

I nod, my words spilling out on top of each other. "Eddy kidnapped Alice again, and he's got her in his cabin, and he told her that if she doesn't cooperate he'll hurt her kids."

"Wait a minute." Nate grimaces, running a hurried hand through his dark hair. "Who's Alice?"

Clark's already loading up his gun. "I think I've heard enough, but you can finish explaining while we head over."

"Okay," I hurry, out of breath. "So, my dad married Alice after finding her held like a prisoner in whatever Grouping Eddy was in at the time. I hope it wasn't this one…"

Nate shakes his head. "Nope. He's only been with us a few months."

"Good. Anyway, Dad traded a bunch of booze for her, but I guess Eddy's been stalking her ever since, and when we left to go back to Panopticus together, he saw his chance and took it. And he told us if we tried to run, he'd go after the kids and my dad."

"Let me get this straight," says Clark, striding across the clearing. "Your dad remarried, had more kids, and now you and the new wife are going back to get your mom, the old wife?"

I shrug. "Kind of."

"You're something else, kid." He pats me on the shoulder. "Too bad you got kidnapped along the way. Although it's great to see you."

I smile at him, and for just a moment I feel Gus's presence—like I don't have to worry, because someone who cares about me will help me and protect Alice.

"All right, then. Let's get this over with." Clark steps up to Eddy's cabin and bangs on the door.

"I'm busy!" growls Eddy from inside.

Muffled crying comes from behind the door.

"I'll bet you are," grumbles Clark under his breath. "Get your sorry ass out here! Oh, sorry, Nate. Should've let you say that."

Nate shrugs, then raises his voice. "Come on, Eddy. Like the man said, get your sorry ass out here."

Nate steps back as Eddy comes to the door, a rifle in his hands. "I'm going to ask you real nice and polite for a little privacy while I welcome home my little wife here."

Alice sobs in the background while my hands shake in fury.

"Come on out, and let's talk this through peacefully," offers Nate, gesturing for Eddy to step closer.

Eddy shakes his head. "You've always had it in for me. You think you're so great. The big man in charge. You're a joke, Nate. And everyone here knows it."

Alice continues to cry until Eddy turns to yell at her. "Keep it down in there!"

The moment his head is turned, I lunge for his gun without any plan what to do with it once I've got it. All I know is I hate him, and I don't want him to hurt Alice anymore.

"Bitch, are you insane?" he yells, pulling back on the gun.

But I've got a firm grip, and I'm not letting go. Unfortunately, neither is he, and the loaded rifle swings back and forth, endangering everyone around me.

"Watch out!"

"Duck!" Voices and movements from the crowd blend and blur around me.

"Let go!" Eddy growls, then yelps in pain.

Glancing down, I see Albert has latched onto his ankle and won't be shaken off. Eddy's grip loosens on the gun, and I fall back with it in my lap.

Clark gestures toward me while keeping his eyes on Eddy. "Someone who actually knows something about guns, please take that away from her before anyone gets hurt."

Face flushing, I hand the rifle off to the middle-aged woman, who gives me a small smile.

"Let's move over here." Nate nods to the side, and Eddy follows, grumbling under his breath.

"Go get your friend," Clark says to me before following Nate.

I rush inside to Alice, tears and blood running down her face.

The middle-aged woman follows behind me. "A loaded gun is a dangerous weapon in the hands of someone who doesn't know what they're doing."

"I'm sorry," I mumble.

"You're also very brave," she says before turning to Alice. "My name's Sarah. You're safe now."

We adjust Alice's clothes, then walk her outside the cabin, Sarah taking the gun with her.

"Let's bring her to my place," Sarah instructs, pointing to a cute little home surrounded by flowers and an herb garden.

I glance back at Clark and Nate still arguing with Eddy.

"What's going to happen?" I ask.

"Pretty sure he'll get banished. It's about time. I never trusted him. There's something wrong with his eyes and the way he looks at a woman."

"What happens if he's banished?" I ask. "They can't just set him free. He threatened to go after Alice's kids and my dad."

Alice grips our arms. "I can stay with him if it means he'll leave Thomas and Serena alone. I can do that. I can manage."

"That shouldn't be necessary." Sarah glances back at the men. "Why don't you let me take care of your friend here, and you go on over and tell them what you just told me?"

I nod and head over.

Eddy's lip curls when he spots me. "I knew you were trouble. Should've left you behind with that stupid dog of yours."

"Oh, I don't know about that." Clark gives me a reassuring smile. "Seems like a pretty smart dog to me. He sure recognizes trash when he sees it."

Eddy spits at him.

"Don't worry about your dog," Clark says to me. "He's gone off somewhere with Rachel. Nate's just banished Eddy here, so he won't cause you any more trouble as long as you're with us."

"But he threatened to go after Alice's kids and their—my—dad. How do we stop him from doing that?"

"Well, Eddy will be leaving with what he brought here," Nate explains. "Just his hat and his clothes. No weapons. No vehicles. That all belongs to the Grouping."

"You're a jerk." Eddy sneers. "You think you're so tough."

Nate cocks his head to the side. "Maybe if you talk nice to me I'll get you some food for your travels."

"You can kiss my ass," grumbles Eddy. "I'm strong and a hard worker. You're going to miss me when I'm gone."

"Actually, I don't think we will." Nate gestures toward the little cabin. "Pack your stuff and go. You're done here."

Clark takes me aside. "We can get someone to go over and warn your father to keep an extra eye on those kids."

"That's just a temporary solution. I don't think he's ever going to stop coming after Alice. He's been following her for years now."

Clark sighs. "Then there's only one solution, but nobody here is going to be willing to do that."

"I'm willing."

Clark chuckles. "I hope I never get on your bad side."

"I mean it, Clark. I need you to teach me how to use a gun. We need weapons if we're going to be safe out here."

"I can teach you all the technical aspects, but you also have to be emotionally ready." Clark turns serious. "Any time you hold a gun, you have to recognize it can take a life."

"I know that."

"It changes you." Clark's voice grows distant. "Permanently."

EARLY THE NEXT MORNING, Clark starts my gun training lessons.

"Okay, here we go." Clark sets three different guns on the picnic table in front of me. "You're gonna need something lightweight and easy to carry."

I reach for the closest gun, eager to begin training.

Clark brushes my impatient hand aside. "Hold your horses, young lady. We need to establish some ground rules first. I don't want anyone's head to get blown off."

"Yes, master." I bow, smirking.

"Could you be serious, please?" Clark sighs. "As I was saying, you're traveling many miles, and you need a way to hide your weapon once you get back inside, so for both of those reasons, a rifle is definitely out. Just remember, you'll have to be a lot closer to your target with the smaller options in front of you."

"So I have to be right in their face when I shoot them?" This sobers me up a little.

"Well, it's not like we have time to train you to be a sharpshooter." Clark nods. "Closer is better for accuracy, but of course, it's harder psychologically."

"What happened to you? What did you mean earlier when you said any time you hold a gun, it can change you permanently?"

Clark pauses. "You don't want to hear about that."

"Actually, I do."

He avoids my gaze for a long moment, until I think I've pushed him too far. Then he takes a shallow breath and speaks. "You were lucky."

"Lucky? I've just been kidnapped. I don't think that's very lucky."

He shakes his head. "I mean before that. You were still in pretty good shape when I found you near the lake in Madison. A little skinny, of course, but otherwise intact."

"Intact? What do you mean? I didn't have any pieces missing?"

He nods, his voice a whisper. "Sometimes, the people who escape from there are so sick. They have big surgical looking scars. I think parts were cut out of them. Things were removed. I don't exactly understand it."

"I do." We lock eyes. "I worked in Mortuary Services. I know they took organs like lungs and kidneys. And they stole babies."

He nods like he had already guessed all this but was hoping he was wrong anyway.

"A few years back, my Rachel sniffed out a young lady who had fainted in the snow. I brought her home, warmed her up, and tried to revive her. But everything I did brought her more pain. She cried and moaned in agony. Her skin was so cold and yellow. Her eyes were yellow. Her nails were yellow. It was such torture watching her suffer when there was nothing I could do to fix it."

"Sounds like jaundice." I remember what Gus taught me about this. "Maybe something happened to her liver?"

"There was a long, ugly incision across her abdomen. I wondered if they took parts of her, then dumped her. I don't know how she got as far as she did. Just sheer desperation, I suppose." Clark pushes back from the table and takes a few steps away, pulling his hands through his hair. "One night when I thought she was sleeping, I cleaned my guns beside her..." He sighs. "She reached out and pulled the pistol to her head."

I hold my breath, waiting for him to continue.

"I tried to talk her out of it." Clark's voice cracks. "I promised I'd make her better, to give it time, to just hold on a little bit longer." His eyes remain unfocused, rewatching a nightmare from his past. "But she was in so much pain, and she knew better than me. She knew it would never end, that she would never get better. That they had stolen her life and discarded her like garbage."

Clark shakes his head, like he's trying to get rid of the memory. "I couldn't do it. I couldn't do what she asked of me. So she grabbed my pistol and shot herself right there on my couch. She ended her own pain while I just sat there and watched her do it."

I reach out my own hand to cover his. "You're a kind man."

"Am I? Maybe I should've let her die out there in the snow. Maybe I just prolonged her suffering. Maybe I just made things worse for her."

"You gave her a safe place to rest. That's the best you could do given the awful circumstances."

"Maybe there's more I could do." Clark takes a deep breath. "Ever since I met you, I've felt restless and bored with my normal life. I can't settle down. That's why you found me here. I don't think I want to be alone anymore. I want to be brave like you."

"I'd be a lot braver if I knew how to use a gun," I point out.

Clark smiles. "Then let's get started."

3 6

TAKE ME WITH U

For hours, Clark drills me in every detail. He instructs me how to load, aim, and shoot a gun properly. He warns me to always be aware of where my gun is pointed, even when it's not loaded.

"Best to get in the habit of not aiming it at anyone unless you mean it."

He takes me to a makeshift shooting range, balances old metal cans on a crooked wooden fence in an empty field, and guides my aim.

"Remember to use your sights and aim at the bottom third of the can to get the bullet to pierce the middle."

At first, I can't hit a thing. But with Clark coaxing me along, by the end of the afternoon, I can knock down every can in the row.

"Don't get too cocky, now," he cautions.

"I want to do it again."

He cocks his head. "I think you've used up enough ammo for one day. It's not the easiest thing to come by, you know. Even if I do know how to make my own."

"You're right. I don't want to waste supplies."

He pats my shoulder. "There's a lot more I could teach you, but you don't have the time."

"You've taught me so much already. I can't tell you how much I appreciate this. I'll feel a lot safer now."

He glances down at the treasured Smith and Wesson .38 special resting in my hand. "This baby will be easy for you to carry during your trip to Panopticus and small enough to hide once you get inside."

"Really, Clark? You're giving me your favorite gun?"

"No, I'm not. Silvia, this is just on loan. You gotta bring it back to me. I need this gun. It's precious to me. I'm counting on you to return it." He holds my gaze so I know he's not just talking about the weapon.

"I'll do my best to bring it back to you in one piece," I promise.

"And preferably unused, but do what you must while you're out there. This is a dangerous stunt you're trying to pull. Don't let your guard down for a single second."

"I won't," I assure him.

He stares at me for another long moment, then breaks it off, gesturing again at the gun and giving me more pointers. "Now, don't forget, this one's a double action."

"I know. It doesn't have one of those safety features with a red dot, but it's harder to pull on the trigger, so it shouldn't just go off while it's hidden inside my belt or something. There are five bullets in the cylinder when it's fully loaded. And if I need to shoot someone or something, I must be close, not far away."

"Sounds like you were listening." Clark smiles sadly.

I gaze at the gun. If only I'd had this in my hand when Eddy showed up, then I could've protected Alice better.

"Alice!" I come out of my reverie. "I need to check on her. I haven't seen her for a while."

Clark nods. "Pretty sure she's with Sarah."

We walk together, Clark gazing off in the distance, preoccupied. I just let him be. He seems to be the kind of person who needs to work through things on his own before discussing them with others. He'll let me know when he's ready to talk.

Nate hurries up to us. "Okay, Silvia, I've already sent someone off to inform your father about Eddy's threats, so they should get there soon. Oh, and another thing. I want to have a full Grouping meeting tonight to discuss your plans about getting back into Panopticus."

"Thank you. You've been so helpful. Not everyone I've met here has wanted to help me get back in. In fact, most people told me not to."

Nate raises his eyebrows. "Don't get your hopes up, because most people here aren't going to support you going back, either."

"Oh." I frown. "Then why have the meeting? I could just leave quietly."

"The meeting's for me." Nate smiles, but I'm not sure why. "I want to know your plans."

"Oh. Okay. Well, I could just tell you now." I'd rather talk to him in private, not a big group setting, especially when he's acting so funny. Is he hiding something?

Nate waves me off. "Let's wait for the whole Grouping. Best to be open and clear about what's going on. Now, I've got a bunch of wood to chop and stack. I'll be back for the meeting tonight. See you then."

"I don't know what to think about that." I watch Nate jog away. He always seems to be in a hurry to get somewhere fast. "Why hold a whole meeting? It's my business, not any of theirs. I don't know why he wants to do this."

"I don't, either," Clark muses. "But I'm sure he has his reasons."

We find Alice and Sarah kneeling on cushions weeding the huge garden together. Sarah spots us first and hurries over to have a private word with us.

"She's doing better." Sarah nods and waves back at Alice, speaking low so her voice doesn't carry. "Of course, she's been through an awful scare, but as I've always said, gardening is good for the soul."

"And good for my appetite," chuckles Clark. "Which reminds me. I'll need some more of your cooking spices before I go home."

"You got it." Sarah turns to me. "I heard about the big meeting tonight. You're going to give a speech or something?"

"A what?" I glance at Clark, who just shrugs. "I haven't prepared a speech."

"Well…" She wipes her dirty hands on her clothes. "Sounds like you'd better."

Alice reaches us in time to hear about the meeting. "I don't have to say anything, right? Because I don't want to." Her eyes widen.

Seeing her pale, worried face makes me want to do anything I can to decrease her fear. "Don't worry, Alice. I've got this. No problem." I reach out to squeeze her shoulder, and she smiles in relief.

"You're so good to me, despite everything." She smiles hesitantly. "Your father would be so proud of you."

The guilt hits me. "I should've figured out a way to stop Eddy sooner. I wasn't fast enough."

"Don't say that. You got help and stopped him as soon as you could. And I know your father can take care of himself and the kids back at home. We can just go on to Panopticus from here and finish what we started. We'll get both your mom and my son, and then we'll head home. Together. And if Eddy shows up again, I'm sure your dad will take care of him."

"I don't ever want to see his ugly face again." I shake my head. "And I don't want him anywhere near you."

She shudders. "Could we talk about something else, please?"

"Yes, of course. You don't have to talk tonight, but maybe you can help me write a speech." My vision catches on her bracelets as she plucks at the leather straps in agitation. "You and Dad have the same jewelry."

She nods. "I taught the kids how to make them. We found some beads, and someone gave us the leather strips. We gotta get creative for birthday and holiday presents, you know. Once we get back home, I'm sure they'll make you some of your own. I can tell they like you already. You'll be a great big sis—" She stops talking, a hand covering her mouth, the bracelets dangling. "Never mind. I promised I'd leave you and your mother alone if you helped me get my son. And I keep my promises. I won't bother you anymore once we get back home. I mean it."

She hurries off before I can say a word.

"You keep saying that this is just about you, but that isn't really true, now, is it?" A Grouping member points her finger at me. "If they think you're dead, and you show up back in there, they might start wondering about the rest of us they assumed were dead and come after us. We can't risk that."

Murmurs of agreement follow. Arguments bubble to the surface.

"Your friends risked their lives to save you. Going back is just throwing that away."

"You should listen to your father. He finally has you in his life again. He doesn't want to lose you twice."

"You're only thinking of yourself. Don't be so selfish."

My detailed, practiced speech has failed. As I explained how my father went into hiding, how the Suits came after me, how I trained for the Race for Citizen Glory not knowing the competition was yet another way for the government to target their next victims, how Gus helped me escape, how I found my father, and how I wish to return and free my mother I watched their eyes glass over and their faces stiffen.

"Okay. I give up. I can see there's no convincing you. Just forget I was ever here. I'll be out of your hair in no time. Just forget I ever said anything."

"Do you promise not to go back?" another stranger asks.

Clearly, this Grouping is too busy surviving day to day out here to bother worrying about life back in Panopticus. I shrug, not wanting to talk about it anymore. Worried at what I might see, I sneak a glance at Nate who has so far remained silent and expressionless during my entire speech. He's in charge of this Grouping, but so far hasn't said a word. Even now, he remains still and unreadable as stone. I have no clue what he's thinking.

"No! You can't give up!" Forced out of her silence, Alice bursts forth to stand by my side, tears in her eyes. "We *have* to find my son! I can't go on without him! How can you not understand? Haven't you all lost someone you love?"

Alice deserts me, pushing her way through the crowd. She stops in front of a young woman whose long black hair hid her face while I spoke.

Alice places a gentle hand on the woman's slender shoulder. "If you could be given one wish in this life, what would that be?"

Slowly, the dark eyes raise to meet Alice's fierce gaze. "I want my little sister back."

"And where is she?"

The dark haired young woman breathes rapidly, almost hyperventilating. "She's inside! She's stuck inside! I'm out here, and I didn't save her! I feel terrible, because I haven't done anything to save her all this time!"

She stands on shaky legs and points to the crowd. "How *dare* you call Silvia selfish when she's the only one willing to do something about this! We are all cowards."

Silence hovers as Alice moves on to an older gentleman.

"Oh, don't ask me," he begs, his hand fluttering across his face.

"Who do you have left inside?" Alice will not hold back.

He sighs and wipes his cheek. "My wife. Don't know if she's dead or alive. It's been ten years. She doesn't know what happened to me."

Alice nods and moves on, allowing the gentleman to compose himself.

"Sarah, how about you?" Alice approaches her gardening partner.

"Oh, you're a tricky one, aren't you?" Sarah's shaking hand

brushes loose hairs away from her flushed face. "At first, you seem so fragile, like everyone should protect you from the world. But there's more to you than that, isn't there? You're braver than I thought."

"Who is it?" Alice stares her down.

"Oh, fine." Sarah sighs. "I have grandchildren, or had grandchildren. Who knows anymore? They don't know who I am. Maybe now I wouldn't recognize them if they walked right by me. I don't know if it even matters anymore. Maybe you've just got to accept what little life gives you."

Alice persists. "But your life is less full for the lack of them, right?"

Sarah throws up her hands, exasperated. "Oh, what do you think? Of course I want them. I want everything I lost when I escaped, but does that give me the right to risk the lives of others to get what I want? I just don't know..."

Grumblings follow, but more muted and solemn than before. Hands wipe away tears. Not a stern look remains in the place. Alice has made everyone grieve. Alice has made everyone cry. She returns to my side, and I grab her hand and squeeze it in solidarity.

Nate approaches, raising his arms to the crowd. "I think we can all agree that our visitors have given us a great deal to think about tonight. We all look out for each other here in the Grouping. We share food, protection, chores, companionship. We have a good life here. Maybe the winters are long and bitter, but we endure."

Nate turns to me. He's about to say something big, something important, but I can't tell if he's for or against me, and that leaves me vulnerable. He's in charge here. Everyone listens to him. If he's against me, I'll have trouble.

I strike first, leaning in to whisper: "I'm doing this. You can't stop me."

He looks at me, his face unreadable. Then he turns back to his Grouping and raises his voice. "I have no intention of stopping you, Silvia. In fact, what I want most is to join you."

37

HOLD ON, I'M COMING

"I'm coming too." Clark pushes through the noisy crowd spilling out from the meeting to reach my side.

"Are you, really?" Overcome with emotion, I hug him.

"Don't get too excited." He holds still for maybe a second before he wiggles out of my embrace. "I think you have the wrong idea. I'm not coming inside. No way. I'm only driving you there so you can save your strength for the fight ahead."

"Thank you, Clark." I glance around for Nate, who has been detained by concerned members of the Grouping.

Clark shakes his head. "I don't envy him the job of calming everyone down. He'll have to set up everything before he goes, just in case he doesn't make it back. They all count on him so much."

I set my shoulders. "Then we just have to bring him back."

"Just like you're bringing back my gun," adds Clark.

"That's right." I gesture for Alice to join us instead of hanging back. "Alice, you're my hero. You know that? I tanked in there, and you rescued me."

She smiles slightly. "We're really doing this now, aren't we? I'm going to see my Matthew again."

"That's the plan."

She takes a breath. "Will he even recognize me?"

"I recognized my dad, remember?" I offer.

Alice grimaces. "Yeah, you did. And you were so angry with him. I hope Matthew doesn't yell at me like that. I don't think I could take it."

Clark puts a hand on her shoulder. "Let's just cross that bridge when we come to it. You've got enough troubles ahead. Don't add more by worrying about things out of your control."

Glancing back, I watch Nate talking his way through a long line of Grouping members.

Sarah approaches us. "Ever since Nate wandered in about five years ago, he's been everything this Grouping needed, even if we didn't know it at the time. He's our most accurate hunter, he's fair during quarrels, and he's never once asked for or done anything for himself. It's all been what's best for the group. Until now."

The members disperse off to their own homes for the night, and Nate joins us.

"Sarah, you're in charge of any of the harvesting I'll miss on my trip. You know what to do and when to do it."

"Yes, I do." She smiles at him, shaking his hand like a business transaction, but then neglects to let go. "I look forward to meeting your little sister."

"You remembered?" His brown eyes turn sad, then quickly revert back to neutral.

"Well, you never talked much about her, except the one time you overindulged on my good apple cider, and you wouldn't stop talking all night."

He smiles. "That's dangerously good tasting cider."

"And a bit of a truth serum to boot," she responds. "Now, you tell me what you want, and I'll spend the night preparing and packing it. I want you to have everything you need. I'll do the work prep. You all should get some sleep."

THE NEXT MORNING dawns cool and clear, perfect traveling weather. Clark fusses with the vehicle while a very tired Sarah helps Alice and me arrange the backpacks. Nate takes the longest to be ready to leave. Everyone wants to ask him something quick before we go. Finally, it's time. Clark drives off, Nate waving from the front passenger seat, and Alice and I huddled with Albert and Rachel in the back.

"Okay, here's the plan," begins Nate. "I brought wire cutters so we can slip through the fencing, scrubs so we can blend in from there, and enough weapons to cause as much trouble as needed."

"But we don't know where to look for my son and your sister," Alice interjects. "We can't just walk up and down the streets calling out their names."

"Right." Nate nods. "We'll need computer access to school records to find the kids."

"I'm sure Gus could figure it out, once we reach him." I say this because it's true, but also because I need him to be a priority in this rescue.

"Silvia," Clark calls back. "I know you won't like this, but I think you'd better leave Albert with me. Having a dog follow you around in there will make you stick out like a sore thumb."

I reach out a hand to rub Albert's floppy golden ears. He leans in, and a low moan escapes. "I'm going to miss you, buddy, but Clark's right, and this will help keep you safe."

"Rachel and I will take good care of him. I swear."

"I know you will." Leaving Albert behind will not be easy. None of this will be easy. I change the subject. "Where do you think Eddy went?"

Alice tenses beside me, making me wish I hadn't asked, or didn't have to ask.

"Honestly, I don't much care, as long as he stays away from both our Grouping and yours," Nate replies. "I guess I felt bad for him and wanted to give him a chance when he showed up a few months ago. But he's been trouble from the start, pitching people against each other, making up stories, and causing fights. But I'm not worried about letting him go. I've got plenty of folks on guard making sure he doesn't step foot in the Grouping while I'm gone, and we've already told your family."

"Daniel *hates* him," mumbles Alice, fidgeting again with her bracelets.

"I do too." I reach over to squeeze her hand. "But let's not worry about him now. I'm sorry I brought it up. We've got enough other things to discuss."

"And plenty of time to discuss them before we get to the drop off point," Clark says. "Nate and I talked some of this through last night."

We fly across the state. It will take a few hours to get to the drop off point, where we will eat a small meal with Clark before saying good-bye to him and the dogs. Then the three of us will hike to the outskirts of Panopticus, planning to sneak in under the darkness of night. Nate used to work in Surveillance Sciences when he lived inside, so he's in charge of evading detection as we enter the city. I'm in charge of finding Gus's place. Once we reach him, I trust his mad computer skills will help us find Alice's son and Nate's sister. After that, I know he'll help me get my mom out of there.

I must find Gus. Everything else will follow. Everything else will be all right. I'll get them out safely. They just need to hold on a little bit longer. We're on our way at last. I'm coming for them. It's really happening, and this time I've got help.

Clark slams on the brakes. Tires squeal.

"What's going on?" Alice yelps, slamming into my side.

"What are you doing? Trying to kill us?" I struggle to hang onto Albert.

"Hold on! Hold on!" Clark leans over to peer down an embankment. "There's a kid down there!"

"A kid?" I ask. "Are you sure it's not just another raccoon?"

"No, it's a kid," whispers Clark, horrified. "And I think he's dead."

38

BURNING DOWN THE HOUSE

Nate grabs his rifle, scanning every direction for trouble. We spill out of the vehicle, Albert barking and careening down the embankment, me following close behind, trying not to fall head-over-heels.

"Be careful!" Alice calls.

Albert gets there first, stops barking, and starts rooting around the child's head and neck. To my immense relief, the child stirs.

"You're alive?" Small rocks scatter from under my feet as I get closer to the child.

He shrinks away from me. "Are you going to hurt us?"

"Why would I hurt you?" I wish he didn't look so scared. "See, even my dog, Albert, likes you."

"So we're safe now?" The young boy's initial fear gives way to giggles as Albert licks clean his dirty face.

"Yes." I glance around. "But you're all alone. Why do you keep saying 'we'?"

He stands up and calls toward the woods. "You can come out now!"

Two more little kids—another boy and a girl— wander out from between the trees, each one filthier than the last. Mud-covered faces, torn clothes, and leaves stuck in their hair.

"Is this all of you?" I ask, searching the edge of the woods for more kids.

They nod.

"Then let's get you all up to the vehicle and figure out what to do next. What are you doing out here alone? Where are your parents?"

They shrug, all staring at me without offering up any more information.

"Where were you heading?" I try again.

The little girl tugs at my clothing. "I want to go home, but my home's gone."

We trudge back up to the road, Albert leading the way.

Nate shakes his head. "There's nothing around. I've looked everywhere."

"I don't know where these kids belong, but they say their home is gone."

"I'll bet you're hungry." Alice kneels in front of them, unzipping her backpack and handing out snacks. "Here you go."

"Do you often find kids alone out here on the roads?" I ask Nate.

"Never." Nate shakes his head. "Something very weird is going on."

"What do we do now?" I ask. "We can't just leave them here, but we've got to get to Panopticus."

"We'll take them with us, of course." Alice settles the small girl in her lap.

"Bringing three kids with us will make it a little more difficult to sneak back inside," I remind her.

"Don't be silly," Alice corrects me. "That's not what I meant. They'll just ride on our laps until we get to the drop off point, then Clark can take them back to the Grouping. Won't that work? I know Sarah would take them in."

"Works for me," Clark agrees.

After feeding the hungry kids and asking them more questions they don't know the answers to, we load back up. Twenty more miles down the road, we come across discarded items resting along the roadside: piles of books, pictures, even the occasional potted plant.

"What's going on here?" Clark wonders aloud, slowing down to gape.

Every eye trained on the road ahead, all passengers fall silent at the sight of a small crowd growing bigger as we approach.

"Do you think they're dangerous?" I lean forward to whisper to Nate as the crowd grows near.

"I don't know. Clark, watch my back." He grabs his rifle, passes a kid back to me, and jumps out of the vehicle as it slows to a halt. "Hello there! What's going on here?"

One of the little boys starts to struggle, trying to escape. "I see my mom!"

"You do? Are you sure?" Alice's eyes grow wide. "Here, Silvia, you go with him. I've got the other two."

I help the boy down. He takes off immediately, me racing after him. We pass Nate talking to a small group. The boy darts and turns, and just when I start to believe he was mistaken, a woman cries out and falls to her knees to collect him in her arms.

"Mommy, I found you! I thought I'd never see you again!"

I turn away, because it reminds me of how much I wanted this exact scene to happen to me as a kid.

"Thank you so much for finding him and bringing him to me!" The mother hugs him tight, tears in her eyes. "We got separated, and I was so worried."

"I'm glad we found you." I scan the small crowd stranded on the road. There must be two dozen of them, at least. "But what's going on? Where are you all coming from? Are you from some Grouping?"

"What's a Grouping?" She shakes her head. "Can you help us? We don't know where to go out here."

I pause, wondering how much to tell her, but forge ahead. "We're going back to Panopticus to get my mom and some other people out."

"Oh, no! You can't go in there. We escaped just in time. Everyone's gone insane. Panopticus is burning."

39

IT ONLY HURTS WHEN I'M
BREATHING

"Panopticus is burning?" I repeat in disbelief, searching the surroundings as if somehow my mother will magically come into view.

The woman caresses her son's hair. "If you keep heading in that direction, you'll soon smell the smoke. Trust me. You don't want to go back in there."

"I'm glad you've got your son back, but I've got to go now." I hurry off to find Nate.

Gentle Alice searches the rest of the small crowd with the other children in tow, seeking their relatives without any success.

Nate paces in front of our all-terrain vehicle. "Oh good, you're here, Silvia. I don't know what to do. There are so many of them. They say there are even more down the road. I don't want to overwhelm my Grouping when I'm not there to help, but these people all need food and housing. I don't know what to do. What do you think?"

"Being in charge isn't always the most fun thing, is it?"

He shakes his head. "A lot of times there's no winning. No matter what you do, somebody's got to lose or at least think they've lost and be upset about it."

"Then you just gotta do what you think is the right thing for right now," I advise, not sure if this is good advice or not.

He sighs. "The right thing right now might be the *wrong* thing in the long term. We've only got so much food, but I think...I think I'll have Clark taxi them back to the Grouping. We'll go on foot from here. Maybe we give away half the food in our packs and hope we can find berries in the woods, and I can hunt game."

"Okay," I agree, wondering if his generosity will get us into trouble.

"And we'd better hurry. Panopticus sounds like a war zone. I don't know what we'll find."

"I think I'm finally afraid," I admit.

"Sometimes it's smart to be afraid."

We turn to discuss the plan with Clark, who is already in the process of loading up his vehicle with two elderly women, three children, and the two dogs. He shrugs as we approach. "I'm sorry. I didn't know what else to do. Can you make it the rest of the way on foot? I know that wasn't the game plan. I thought I'd take them to Sarah."

Alice comes back with the two kids still searching for their families. "What should we do with them? We can't bring them back into the city."

"And who knows where their parents are now." Nate runs a hand through his dark hair, while bending down to them. "This nice man, Clark, can give you a ride to somewhere safe where you can rest and eat until we find your families. Do you want to go with him?"

The little girl takes a moment to respond, frowning slightly. "Can I sit with the doggies?"

"Yes, you may, sweetheart." Clark hoists her up first, followed by the boy.

Alice whispers. "Oh, it's so sad. They look so lost."

"You've got a full load there," says Nate. "You take care."

"I know. I'll drive slow." Clark pauses just before getting in the vehicle, then rushes over to grab both my arms. "You come back now, you hear?"

Before I can even answer, Clark rushes back to the vehicle and starts the engine. The small crowd clears, and he turns to go, all without looking my way again. Only Albert watches me as his sweet little face shrinks into the distance. Nate and Alice give away a good portion of our food supplies to those who remain while I can't rip my eyes away from the departing vehicle.

"We can move faster with lighter packs." Nate nudges me. "Okay. Time to go."

I turn away, placing one step after the other, my head in a fog. I wanted to burn Panopticus down myself, but now it's happened before I got a chance to light the match. On the road, we meet people all heading the opposite way. We give out advice and food until we don't have enough of either left for ourselves. Sometimes one person walks alone. Other times, small groups huddle together. All are lost, many are scared. Some are angry. Others have already given up, just sitting forlornly on the side of the road. Every step we take brings us closer to the original goal, no matter how the plan may have changed. Each group we pass, I scan the faces, hoping to find Gus or Franco leading my mother away from trouble. But it's always strangers and never them.

My stomach rumbling, I dig out Franco's edible plants book, searching for items still in season we might find near the side of the road. "Okay. There are still blackberries and raspberries to eat. Maybe we should search for some before it gets too dark. I'm getting hungry. Aren't you?"

"Sounds good," Alice agrees, searching the faces of some children running around us in circles on the road. "Oh, I hope that's not trouble ahead."

A woman yells, "No, you're wrong! It can't be! It's not true!"

"Wait a minute," I say. "I might recognize that voice."

"You don't look like you like that voice," mutters Alice as Liam's little sisters drag their mother toward me.

"See! We told you!" Lydia and Lucy hop up and down, pointing at me, their eyes shining in excitement.

Linda and I stare at each other, her mouth open in shock. Perhaps mine is too. I'm not sure either of us is pleased to see the other. She's always made me feel unwelcome, unwanted, and uncomfortable. This was even before she lost her golden boy, Liam. So now I suppose I'm just a painful reminder. No wonder she acts like she doesn't want to see me.

Gaping at me, she doesn't say a word. I guess it's up to me.

I clear my throat before babbling nervously. "You got out okay. That's a relief. I met Jack. He's doing well, but he misses you. He'll be so happy to see you. He's in Minnesota now. I've got a map you can have. I already know how to get there. It's called Rochester, or it used to be." I drop my pack to get her the map, but she stops me with a shaking hand.

"You're *alive?*" She asks me, even though I'm standing right in front of her.

"Yeah." I nod. "So far."

She just stares at me.

"Where's Franco? Is he with you?" My heart leaps with hope as I search past her, looking for him.

"You're alive," she whispers, her shaking hand rising to cover her mouth. "Of course you are. They *lied* to him."

"What are you talking about?"

"They had pictures and everything..." She looks away, her eyes unfocused.

I grab her shoulders. "Tell me what's going on with Franco! Right now!"

She snaps to attention. "He wouldn't come with us. He thinks you're dead, so he's burning it all down."

"He wouldn't save himself?" The words catch in my throat.

"No." Her voice turns cold. "A few nights ago, some Suits came to our house, bringing Franco pictures of you dead on a gurney."

My head swirls with memories of the Suits surrounding me in the library, then dragging me across the floor.

"Franco killed them. The Suits. Right in front of the kids. Then he helped us escape. I thought he was coming with us, but he turned back. He left us on our own!" Linda screams in my face. "And it's all *your* fault, because you were *dead,* and now you're not..."

Linda sinks to her knees, sobbing uncontrollably.

The world pauses and grows still. Franco's gone crazy. My mom's probably gone crazy. If the Suits showed Franco pictures of me on a gurney, they might have figured out what Gus did to save me and killed him too. My Gus. What if I finally make it back and everyone I love is already dead? What will I do then? All of this will have been for nothing.

But what if they're alive? And I can help them escape?

My tears and vision clear as I kneel next to Linda. "Do you know anything about my mom?"

"No," she gulps through her tears. "I haven't heard a thing."

"Okay, then. Here's the deal." I wait until she looks right at me, so I know she's listening. "I'm going back for Franco right now, and I'll do everything in my power to bring him back to you alive, okay? But I've got one condition."

She shakes her head. "You're too late."

"Don't tell me that. You don't know that."

"Fine. What's your stupid condition?"

"You're going to stop being such a bitch to me. This ends right now. Maybe you don't like me much now, but if I bring Franco back to you alive, you're going to find space in that cold, dark heart of yours to start being decent to me."

Linda takes several deep breaths before shaking her head and answering me. "You don't know what you're asking. I'm out of practice. I stopped being nice eight years ago when I lost my husband. I wouldn't even know where to start."

"Start with finding Jack in Minnesota. Then I'll know where to find you." I dig in my backpack for the map. "Here's Gus's map. Do you know anything about him? Is Gus okay?"

Linda frowns. "No, he's not okay. He got shot in an uprising and couldn't risk going to the hospital because he thinks they figured out he helped you escape. And he refused to come with us because he's injured and didn't want to slow us down."

"Oh, Gus." I hide my face in my hands.

"I'm sorry, Silvia, but Gus is dying."

40

HERO

Runners wait in the starting corral as Representatives give speeches on overhead screens.

Liam elbows me. "Are they seriously going to make us listen to this right before we take off? What a killjoy."

I shut out everything but the announcer's voice. "On your mark, get set, GO!"

We're off with the thunder of feet. People everywhere, both in the road and lining the streets. I've got to get away from the crowd.

Liam follows my lead.

First mile. Second mile. I grab a sports drink, swallow, and toss.

We pass more runners, picking them off, one by one. Once I can see we're in the top ten, I settle in to ride it out. Let them reel me in.

Miles three and four. Liam races beside me.

Miles five and six. We're in the top pack.

"Go, Silvia!" Mom screams. "And Liam, you too!"

"Mom, come back!" I yell, but she's already gone from view.

We press on through mile seven.

My dad and Alice push through the crowd alongside the road as if searching for something or someone.

"Dad? Alice? I'm over here!"

They didn't hear me and turn away, still searching.

Miles eight and nine are history.

Mile ten. Another water stop. As I reach down for a cup, the table transforms into a gurney carrying Gus, his body coated in blood.

He waves me on. "Keep going. Don't stop now."

"What? You're hurt," I argue. "I can't just leave you here."

Liam pushes me forward. "Come on, let's go."

"Gus, I'm coming back for you!" I yell into the wind as it steals my hat.

Miles eleven and twelve go by in a blur. We're near the end. I'm almost there.

"And our winner is... Silvia Wood!" The announcement blares over the loudspeaker.

I spin around to find Liam, but he's disappeared into the crowd.

"Where's Liam?" My eyes fill with tears. "And where's Gus? And my mom? And Dad and Alice? Where is everybody?"

Representative Waters-Royce scoffs. "She's in shock. Take her to the medical tent, immediately."

"Come with me, please." Franco swoops in to haul me away.

"I don't want to go to the medical tent," I argue.

"Do you want to find Gus or not?" Franco asks. "People who get shot go to the medical tent."

Once we reach the tent, the Suits swarm me, pushing me onto a bed and inserting an IV.

"Where's Gus?" I flail, trying to push them away, but there's too many of them. I can't even see Franco's face anymore. "Where is he? What did you do to him? If you hurt him, I swear I'm gonna—"

"Silvia, wake up." Nate shoves me hard enough to disperse the bad dream. "Good grief. I've never known anyone to talk so much in their sleep."

"Sorry," I mumble. "I'm just so worried about Gus and Franco and my mom and everything."

"I know," Nate whispers, sounding exhausted. "But we're getting closer, so get some rest. And whatever you do, please don't wake Alice. She's struggling enough to keep up as it is."

"I know." I sigh. "I'll try."

After we left Linda and the girls on the road, we pushed on for hours, anxious to reach Panopticus as soon as possible. Alice never complained but was dragging by the end. We'd barely eaten anything, just dropped down close to each other a ways off the road to rest.

Too wired and anxious to fall back asleep, I watch the darkness of night melt into dawn. Everything smells like smoke. Birds chirp, but not enough to wake my two companions slumbering nearby. As soon as it gets light enough to see, I stretch and rise, careful not to disturb them. I might as well gather some food to supplement our meager supplies. There should be some berries close by.

All I bring with me is Clark's gun and a bag for the berries. It takes some searching to find the first small patch, but after that I find a lot more. We won't be lacking calories today, thank goodness. We need the energy to keep moving forward. Pretty soon my bag hangs heavy with juicy fruit. Carefully, I trace my path back to our resting site. Shadows stretch across the forest floor as the morning light grows brighter with each passing second.

Branches shake on my right. I freeze, hearing a low rumble. Is that a man's voice or a bear's growl? I can't tell. Slowly, I set the bulging bag of berries on the ground next to me and rest my hand on my weapon, knowing this little gun would only irritate a bear, not kill it.

I back away, leaving the bag behind. If a bear wants my berries, it can have them. But I'm not sure it's a bear. Could it be Eddy? No, he wouldn't follow us all this way, would he? I see a flash of red between the leaves, and a young man pushes his way through the branches and steps into the clearing, brushing cobwebs from his hair.

I stare at him, realizing I've seen his face a hundred times before.

"Matthew?" I ask, not wanting to scare him. "Is your name Matthew?"

"Yeah, I'm Matthew. Who are you?" he glances behind him as a man follows him into the clearing. A man with red hair.

"Dad!" I yelp, sprinting to throw myself into his arms. "You came!"

41

I WILL REMEMBER YOU

Dad hesitates before returning the hug. "So you're happy to see me? I wasn't sure how you'd react."

"Of *course*, I'm happy to see you!" I give him one more squeeze before stepping back. "How did you find Matthew?"

"Well, it wasn't easy, but I had plenty of help." Dad glances behind him. "Jack's here too. I don't know what's taking him so long."

Jack eventually emerges between the leaves, startled to have three people gawking at him. "Good grief. Can't a man relieve his bladder in private without the whole world knowing about it? Hey, Silvia, we've been looking all over for you! Where's Alice?"

"Alice, she's..." I turn to Matthew trying so hard to be patient, but there's no need to make him wait any longer. "Let's go find her."

We take off running together, ducking around tree branches and over roots. I've wandered farther picking berries than I realized. We're both breathing hard by the time we reach our temporary campsite. Nate's already awake, rummaging through his backpack. I hold a finger to my lips motioning him to stay quiet.

"Your mom's still sleeping," I whisper to Matthew. "Why don't you go surprise her?"

Matthew rushes over to her sleeping form, then kneels at her side. "M-mom?"

She listlessly waves her hand, her eyes still closed, her voice muffled. "Just let Mommy sleep a few more minutes, okay? I'll get you breakfast in a minute, kids."

"Mom?" Now he sounds confused, and maybe a little hurt, his voice louder than before.

Alice wakes with a gasp, flings herself up to sitting, then pulls Matthew into her arms with such force they almost topple over. "I can't believe it! Let me have a look at you!" She holds him out to examine for two seconds, then yanks him back into her arms like she can't get enough. "You've grown so much! Do you even remember me?"

"Of course, I remember you," Matthew says softly. "I just can't believe you're alive."

"But, Matthew, how did you find me?" Alice spots my father, her mouth falling open in shock. "Daniel? How did you get here ahead of us? Did *you* find Matthew? Who's watching the kids?"

Alice and I share a knowing glance. Dad must not know about Eddy yet.

"Madeline took them in," Dad explained. "She felt bad about how upset I was when you both left."

"Which means your father manipulated her into staying with the kids until we get back." Jack raises his eyebrows as he digs into my bag of berries. "Hey, Silvia, thanks for the snack."

"Those were meant for everybody, by the way," I remind him.

Jack laughs and passes around the bag. The berries are delicious and stain everyone's fingers purple and pink.

"Tell me how you found Matthew," Alice begs, still holding him tight as if she'll never let him go.

"We left as soon as I could make arrangements for the kids," Dad begins. "We headed straight to Panopticus, hoping to catch up with you somewhere on the road."

Alice and I share another look.

"It was easier than I expected to get inside the city." Dad shakes his head. "Returning to Panopticus was not at all what I expected. Everyone's gone crazy in there. It's not just the Suits and the Government. Even just regular people are armed and dangerous."

"People are protesting," Jack continues. "Windows are smashed, and the greenhouses have been bombed."

I gasp. "Did you find Franco?"

Jack turns serious. "Couldn't find him anywhere. No sign of him or the kids or Linda."

"Linda and the girls got out okay," I tell him. "We just saw them on the road yesterday. They're fine, but Franco refused to leave with them."

"That doesn't sound like him," Jack puzzles.

I take a deep breath. "It does to me."

"You're right." He sighs. "I don't know my family anymore."

"Linda and the girls are headed to Nate's Grouping," I explain. "Maybe you could catch up with them there."

"And you're Nate?" My dad moves to shake his hand. "I'm Silvia's father, Daniel. How do you fit into all this? I'm confused."

"Yeah, I'm a little confused too." Nate smiles. "I joined these two after—"

"Yeah, Dad, we met with some trouble on the road," I interrupt Nate. "But maybe we should talk about it later or privately or something."

"No, it's okay," Alice decides. "Matthew can know. I don't want to have any more secrets, and he'll need to be careful too."

"What's going on?" Daniel demands.

"Eddy's been watching us this whole time." Alice shudders. "He found us the first day out and forced us to come with him to Nate's Grouping. He told them I was his wife, but Silvia got me help right away, and Nate kicked Eddy out of the Grouping. But he threatened to come after you and the kids. And I believe him, so I'm worried about the kids staying with Madeline when you're not there to protect them."

Nate interjects. "I sent someone to tell your Grouping about Eddy right away, so I'm sure they're on high alert, but I had assumed you were still there. Daniel, I'm sorry. I didn't realize..."

Dad's eyes widen in terror. "I've got to get back there right away."

"But what about mom?" I protest. "I thought you being here meant you'd help me find her."

Dad grimaces. "Silvia, I'm so sorry. I tried to find Yoshe, but didn't know where you moved. I started at the old apartment, but no one there even remembered who she was. And Gus hadn't seen her in days. He didn't know where she'd gone, but he knew several places where kids were being held, so we focused on trying to find Matthew instead. Then things got crazy, so we just hightailed it out of there to avoid getting killed in the crossfire."

I seize Dad's arm. "Why didn't you bring Gus with you?"

"He refused." Dad shrugs. "Says he's going down with the ship or some such nonsense."

Jack winces. "I think he's hurting a lot more than he admits and can't manage the trip."

I turn to Jack. "Gus didn't know how to find Franco?"

"No, he hadn't seen him for days, but suspected he was responsible for what happened at the greenhouses. Do you think that's even possible?"

I shake my head. "We just gotta find him and get him *out* of there." How could Franco destroy everything he cherished and worked for?

"Silvia." Dad grabs my hands. "I want to stay and help you find your mom, but I also need to get Alice home and protect the kids from Eddy. I'm torn in too many directions at once."

"You're leaving right away?" I pull away and step back. He came for Alice's son, but never for me. He'll protect Alice, but not my mom. I know how awful Eddy is, but part of me can't help but be jealous and angry. That part of me wants to argue with him, but instead I take a deep breath and let it go. "I guess I understand. I hate Eddy. I just wish he was out of our lives for good."

"Listen, Nate—it's Nate, right?" Jack asks. "You've got somebody in there, right? You didn't come along to just chaperone, I'll bet."

Nate nods. "Yeah, my little sister, Edwina."

"Okay then, let's divide up tasks in a way that makes sense," Jack directs. "Nate, you go with Silvia. And, Daniel, why don't I take Alice and Matthew back to Minnesota while you stay and help your daughter? We'll get there as fast as we can to protect your kids."

"Okay." Dad looks like a little lost boy needing someone else to tell him what to do. "If you think that's best."

"Yeah." Jack nods. "I think so. This way, I can find Linda and the girls. And, Silvia, I believe I can count on you to get Franco out of there in one piece, right? Gus made it sound like you two were close. Maybe you can talk some sense into him. You probably understand him better than I do now."

"I'll do my best." Everything he ever said to me all runs together in my mind.

I find it useful that no one really knows who I am. If I lost someone I loved, I'd hide or destroy every picture. I don't think I could bear seeing them at all if that was all that was left for me. Please wear this jacket. I need to know you made it out alive.

🏃

"TAKE good care of your mother while I'm away." My father ruffles Matthew's hair. "I'll be home soon, and then we can all be together..." Dad stumbles for words, glancing between me and Alice. What does he plan to do once he has *two* wives living together in the same place?

"We'll figure it out once you get back." Alice holds my gaze while my father hugs her good-bye. "No need to worry about it now. Just go get Silvia's mother and everyone else she needs out of that horrible place. Focus on that. Go on, now. You should hurry."

Dad looks from me to Nate and back again, clearly wanting one of us to take the lead.

"I'll just grab my bag. Won't take a minute." Once I've got it swung up in position, I hurry to Alice's side and whisper in her ear. "Don't you *dare* run off while we are gone. Don't you disappear on him just because you promised me. I want you to forget all about that nonsense with Eddy out there still on the hunt. I need you and the kids to be safe. You gotta promise me…"

She nods with tears in her eyes. Matthew watches as I move to stand between Nate and my father. Words fail, and everyone stares at each other. We all need to go our separate ways, but none of us know when or if we will see each other again.

Nate clears his throat, breaking the quiet. "Well, there's only so much daylight. We need to take advantage of that to cover as much ground as we can in both directions."

Jack nods. "I'm anxious to see my family. So if it's okay with you, Alice and Matthew, I'd appreciate leaving as soon as possible."

"I'll hurry." Alice gathers her supplies. "That is, if you're not too tired, Matthew?"

"I'm not tired." Matthew straightens his back.

"Thank you, Daniel, for finding my son." Alice fights back tears.

Nate pats her on the shoulder. "Don't worry. We've already got one job done. Matthew's out safely. There's no reason to think the same won't be true for the others."

"What about Gus, who refuses to leave?" I can't help but mutter.

Nate chuckles. "Really, Silvia. No one else seems to be able to say no to you. Why should *he* be any different?"

We separate, three heading away from Panopticus and three of us rushing toward the city as fast as we can.

"So, Dad, you need to tell us everything you learned about what's going on inside the city. Starting with how you found Matthew. We need specifics."

He nods. "I didn't think we would find him, actually. The computers are down, so Gus couldn't track him. Plus, he's injured and in hiding, so he doesn't have a lot of access to info anymore, but he'd heard of several schools where students were being housed since the fighting broke out. We went to one after the other, and at the fifth school we visited we finally found Matthew."

"You mean you just walked up and took him away without anyone noticing?" Nate asks.

Dad shrugs. "There were just a bunch of kids milling around. Sometimes we saw an adult, but none of them wanted to be in charge. They acted like they were afraid *we* would hurt *them*. Once Matthew told them he wanted to leave with us, they had no problem with it."

"How did you get Matthew to agree to come with you?" I ask. "It's not like he knows you."

"I brought one of Alice's self-portraits with me," Dad explains. "That's all the convincing he needed."

"I'm glad he remembered her." I kick a small rock further down the road.

"You remembered me." Dad looks at me, then shrugs. "You recognized me at once, and it had been eight years for you, too."

Nate sighs. "I haven't seen my sister in five years. She'd be thirteen now. I just don't know if they hurt her or eliminated her or used her for something."

"Let's not fret unless we have to," I suggest. "Fear isn't our friend."

Nate smiles at me. "Good advice from the girl who frets even more than I do."

"Guilty as charged." I shrug. "Let's just get there as fast as we can."

We pass more people on the road heading the opposite way. They all have so many questions, often begging us for information we do not have.

"We need to save time," says Nate. "What do you think about getting off this road?"

"I don't want to get lost," I argue.

Nate points to black smoke curling on the horizon. "I don't think that's going to be a problem anymore."

I sigh. "We gotta get Mom *out* of there."

Dad nods but seems preoccupied. Maybe it took eight years for him to come back for my mother, but now he's at my side. But what about Gus? What if I can't convince him to leave the city? What if he's too injured to travel? He's sacrificed so much already and been burdened with so many secrets. How many people had Gus set free through the Incinerator sewer drain? He might be willing to die on his own, but I refuse to let it happen. Not without a fight.

I just hope Nate is right that no one can tell me no. Not even Gus.

IF I CLOSE MY EYES FOREVER

The closer we get, the more my mind and heart race. Clouds of smoke clog the sky. The whole world is burning, and we are stubbornly, and perhaps foolishly, heading right into the heart of the fire. The three of us are well-matched physically, with no signs of anyone waning after so many miles. We will be there soon. Darkness is almost upon us, as the sun sets into the hazy horizon.

Dad breaks the silence. "If we don't stop to rest, we might be able to make it to Gus's hideout before the sun rises."

"Let's do it," I decide, and no one argues with me.

Night falls, which slows our progress considerably. I can't get to Gus's side fast enough and resent every root and stick in my way. Every moment we spend outside the city limits weighs on my mind.

"We're almost there," Nate whispers as we creep closer.

Trying not to cough or choke on the smoke, we hover just outside the tree line.

"Electricity must be spotty because it's not lit up like usual, but I can still tell that's the Incinerator over there." I point at the building where Gus helped me escape into the wilderness with a backpack full of supplies and the firm belief I would never return. "We'd better change into the scrubs now. Hey, Dad, did you bring any with you?"

Dad nods. "Yeah, Madeline gave me some. They helped us blend in last time."

We creep forward after switching clothes and repacking. The open space between the trees and the fence line seems endless. Stillness hangs heavy in the air until we reach the fence line.

"Over here," Dad whispers, waving us over. He peels back a heavy sheet of metal fencing, making a loud creaking sound. We crouch down instantly and freeze in place, waiting for trouble, which doesn't arrive.

"Someone already cut this open," Nate observes. "Is this how you got in last time?"

"Yes, right by the Incinerator and Greenhouses. We're on the very edge of town."

"Right." I groan. "Ten miles out from the last stop on the monorail."

"Don't worry." Dad places a warm hand on my shoulder. "I know a shortcut."

We follow him through this endless night, racing across open gaps between buildings, peeking around corners to search our surroundings before making another dash for safe cover. I forget what hunger is. Will we ever again see the sun or breathe in fresh air? There's smoke everywhere, which might help us hide but is hard on the throat and lungs. It feels like my insides have been scrubbed with sandpaper. Every breath is rough and harsh. Hours pass with few words and little light. Once we get close enough to town that we aren't the only people around, we must be even more careful. No one can be trusted. It's not just the Suits and the Government who might harm us now. Panic and terror have transformed some Citizens into monsters of their own making.

"We're almost to where I last saw Gus." Dad breathes the words into my ear, trying to make as little noise as possible. "You want to go to his place first, right? Or do you want to check on your mother instead?"

I lean against the nearest building. Who needs me more right this second—Gus or Mom? Or maybe the more important question is: who can help me find the other? Mom won't be any help whatsoever. We might have to carry or drag her out, she'll be so weak and confused by now. But Gus might know something that can help find my mother and Franco and Nate's little sister. He'll at least have his wits about him. Mom will be a helpless mess, just like last time.

"Gus's place first," I agree, feeling guilty that Mom will have to hold on a tiny bit longer. I hope I am making the right choice.

"Okay, follow me." Dad leads, and again Nate and I follow in between shadows and the few streetlamps still working.

Covering my mouth to suppress the coughing, we press forward, curling around dark corners and dashing down poorly lit streets. Sweat runs down my neck and back. Ash sticks to my arms. We pass fires in the streets. Chairs and tables are piled haphazardly together and set ablaze. Glass from broken windows and bottles crunches underfoot. Screams and gunfire echo in the distance. This is not the Panopticus I remember. Before, the fear was hidden, suppressed, unspoken. Now it's out in the open. I'm not sure which is more dangerous.

"Go in here." Dad opens a door I didn't notice and grabs my shoulder to keep me from forging ahead. "Be careful on the stairs."

Using my hands on both sides of the walls to guide and balance myself, one slow step at a time I proceed into the darkness. Nate follows, holding aloft a burning chair leg he must have grabbed from the nearest fire, illuminating the stairs below. I let out a sigh of relief. This is much better, but still tricky. We reach a series of underground tunnels where Dad once again takes the lead, turning left and right, ducking under pipelines, and finding hidden doors where there seems to be none.

"How do you know all this?" I ask.

Dad turns back with a finger to his lips.

We pass by blinking red lights overhead. Nate's chair leg is shrinking. The fire creeps toward his hand. We won't be able to use it much longer to light the way. The air around us cools slightly.

"In here," Dad whispers before disappearing through another almost-hidden passageway.

We enter a dank, dimly lit room, passing by people sleeping huddled together on the floor.

"I'm *hungry,*" a child cries nearby, the sounds muffled but heartbreaking.

"Where are we?" I grab my father's shirt, demanding an answer.

His face, half hidden in shadows, is wretched. "I didn't want to tell you how bad it was down here. I knew you'd have to see it for yourself."

"Where's Gus?"

Dad points to a makeshift bed pushed against the far wall. The smell of urine hits me the closer I get. People moan in the other corners of the room, but silence presses in on me as I approach.

This can't be Gus. A soiled bed sheet covers a still body. I stare intently, waiting for him to take a breath, but nothing happens.

His bedding reeks of old blood and a dirty wound.

"Bring me the light!" I insist, and Nate rushes to my side. The very last flickers of flame fall over Gus's pale, slumped face.

"He's not breathing!" Tears blind my vision as I reach to shake him.

His eyes are closed. His skin is cool to the touch. His limbs are limp, not yet stiffened in place. I hold a hand over his mouth and don't feel any breath.

"He can't be dead! Gus, wake up! Please, wake up!" I shake him hard.

He doesn't respond. His eyes remain closed. He can't be dead.

Nate's light flickers once more and dies.

43

STAYIN' ALIVE

"We can't stay here." Dad tugs me away from Gus's side. "It isn't safe."

I yank my arm out of his grip and wipe my wet eyes.

"Silvia." Nate speaks calmly. "Gus did everything he could to keep you safe. He was a great man. He sacrificed himself for others, including you. We should respect his memory and leave him in peace."

I turn toward the two of them. "Leave him in peace? You call this *peaceful?* This place is a hell hole, and he shouldn't have died in here alone!"

A hand weakly pats my wrist.

"I came back for him. He deserves so much *better* than this! I'm not *ready* to say good-bye to the best friend I'll ever have!"

The hand keeps tapping, and I push it away. "Stop touching me! I said I'm not ready to leave yet!"

I gasp, realizing that Nate and Dad are both standing in front of me, and the hand is coming from behind.

Whirling around, I grab Gus's cool hand.

"Best friend, eh?" Gus's breathless voice croaks with effort.

"Don't let your mother hear that. You know she doesn't approve of me." A burst of wet coughing follows.

"Gus? You're alive! I thought you were dead!"

"I will be soon, no doubt." Wheezing interrupts his words.

"No, Gus, you can't die. I won't allow it."

"Still so bossy." Gus struggles into a sitting position, making him cough even more. "What on earth are you doing back here? Don't you ever listen to me?"

"Of course I listen to you, Gus, but I can't *agree* with anyone who won't save themselves. Why didn't you leave with Dad when he asked you to?"

Gus laughs, and the sound is awful, like a frog's croak. "Silvia, my dear, there's nothing to save here. I'm just a burden. No one would get out alive if they had to carry me along, and I refuse to be a death sentence for anyone other than myself."

I rub his hands to warm them. "You're coming with us. No arguing allowed."

"You're not listening, and you're not seeing reason. I'm done for. And I didn't get you out of this city just for you to turn around and come right back and get killed at my side on some fool's errand to save me. I'm old. I've lived my life."

"Perhaps you've forgotten how stubborn I am."

Gus chuckles, interrupted by coughing. "Not a chance. I remember everything about you, every flaw and every perfection. You're my brave, foolish girl, and I sure hope you didn't come back just for me. You have a mother out there who needs you. Leave me be and go get her out of here instead."

"I came back for *both* of you. And Franco, too, of course. Have you seen them?"

He shakes his head. "Not for days."

"Wait a minute. Why aren't you surprised I'm still alive?"

"Why wouldn't you be alive? I got you out of here in time, which *was* one of my most ingenious rescues—that is, until you decided to come back."

"When I saw Linda and the girls on the road outside, they said the Suits told Franco I was dead. That's why he wouldn't leave Pantopticus with them, and he's still stuck inside."

Gus remains silent for a long moment. "Your poor mother."

"What about her?"

"Franco must have told her. He was spending every waking moment with her last I knew."

"He was taking care of her?" The degree to which I adored Franco before, now blossoms a hundred-fold. "Was she a mess again? Like last time?"

Gus meets my eyes, but I can't read them in the darkness. "She came to visit me to ask in person what happened. She had to hear it for herself that you were okay. She refused to take Franco's word for it. But if later on Franco told her otherwise, I don't know what she'd do."

Fear sinks my stomach. "I'll find her."

"Yes," Gus urges. "Go do that now. Forget about me."

"That's impossible." I straighten to assess him more closely. "Can you stand and walk?"

"Not very well," Gus admits. "Listen, I think your mother needs you more than me."

"Stop arguing and focus your energy on getting out of that stupid bed."

"And where are you going to take me? Do you plan on carrying me piggy-back style while you search the town for your mother? Don't you see how pointless this is?"

"I've got to get you out of *here* at least."

Gus shrugs. "I've nowhere to go."

"What about your apartment? Is that still intact? How far is it from here?"

Gus sighs. "It's not far. It's just more out in the open, but I suppose if someone shoots me now, they might do a better job of it this time and finally give me some peace."

"I don't appreciate your negative chain of thought, but let's at least get you out of this dump and into the sunlight."

"You're wasting your time," Gus grumbles as I help him to his feet. He wheezes and shakes while trying to stand.

Nate rushes in to support him. "Lean on me."

Gus groans in pain. "Who are you? And why are you in on this ill-fated escape plan?"

"I'm Nate." He smiles. "And I may not have known Silvia long, but I've already learned that nobody can tell her no."

"You've got that right," grumbles Gus, wincing as he takes another step.

We shuffle away from the bed, my father hovering the whole time, anxious and jumpy as a mouse. "Daylight is coming," he warns in my ear.

"We'll be fine. Just get us *out* of here."

"What's the fastest route to your apartment?" Dad asks Gus, then leads the way, checking out what's ahead before coming back and leading us onward.

Gus limps, leaning on Nate and flinching with every step. He was shot in the right calf and can barely use the leg due to the excruciating pain. Morning has broken by the time we reach the outdoors. Smoke hangs heavy in the air. Shouts and shots are heard in the distance, explosions even further off.

Gus's face crumbles as he takes in the destruction surrounding us. "This isn't what I wanted. This isn't what I fought for. I sure didn't want the current Panopticus rule to continue, but I wanted a *peaceful* revolution led by *good* people. Not this pointless, misguided tragedy where everyone just fights over scraps."

I take his hand, still cool but now sweaty from exertion, and squeeze it.

Gus coughs. "Not far now. Just one more block. Right near the library."

We make it to his apartment. The door is unlocked and slightly ajar, but the inside looks much the same as the last time I visited. All his crowded bookshelves, all his pictures hanging on the walls, and a blue blanket folded neatly on his brown, well-worn comfy chair.

"Let's get you seated." I grab the blanket, Nate sits him down gently, and I tuck him in.

Gus glances out the window as people rush by. "Ah, a room with a view."

"Let me clean your wound."

"You should find your mother."

Ignoring his protests, I search for supplies. There's a pitcher of water in the fridge which no longer has power, so it's warm but still clean. I find a few unused rags in a cupboard. I kneel before him, move the blanket to the side, and get to work.

"Ouch. Oh, you are a stubborn child." Gus groans as I clean him up the best I can.

"Silvia, do you mind if Daniel and I go looking for my sister Edwina while you stay here with Gus?" Nate asks, anxious to get searching.

"That's fine with—" I start.

"I'm not leaving her," interrupts my dad.

"I don't blame you." Gus squirms in his seat. "You're her father. You *should* protect her. Now, Silvia, you've done enough. Get out of here and go find your mother."

"I'm coming back for you." I set the rags and water to the side and stand.

"Then you're a fool, and I saved you for no good reason." Gus shakes his finger at me.

Nate comes to my side. "Okay, before we go, let's review how to use your gun, just in case, okay?"

Gus raises his eyebrows. "Silvia has a gun now?"

"I need it for protection." I run through everything again with Nate, then tuck my gun away.

"I'm worried for you," Gus frets. "You two, do everything you can to keep her safe."

"You got it," Nate answers as Dad nods silently.

"And you, come here," Gus urges, grabbing my hands once I get close enough to reach. "If you must choose between me and yourself, then you choose yourself. If you must choose between me and your mother, then you choose her over me as well. Do you understand? I'm ready to be done with this life, but I'm not ready for *you* to be done with your life. Do you hear me?"

"Yes, but—"

"Now get *out* of here." Gus tries to say more but starts wheezing. It takes him a while to catch his breath and continue. "You've done enough. I'm comfortable sitting in this chair, and I'll just watch out the window as the city I once loved destroys itself."

I shudder and start crying. I can't help myself. "But I *love* you, and I don't want to live without you. I want you to come with me and build a life outside these walls. I *need* you."

He clenches my hands with surprising force. "And I need you to *live.* You hear me? I love you, too. You're like a daughter to me. I'm so happy I had you in my life, but I need you to let me go now. It's time to say good-bye. I won't make it. I'd die trying with this bum leg of mine, and I refuse to drag you down with me. You need to go. Now." He drops my hands and turns away, coughing as he stares resolutely out the window.

"Silvia, listen to him," Dad pleads. "He's right. We should go."

Tears running down my face, I glare at my father. "He doesn't know what he's saying."

"Oh, I know exactly what I'm saying." Gus refuses to look my way. "You two, take her away. And don't you *dare* let her come back here again."

44

PHOTOGRAPH

"Silvia, respect the man's wishes and do what he says." Dad escorts me to the door, then passes me off to Nate. "Take her outside."

"Get your hands off me!" I protest as Nate guides me out of the apartment. "I'm coming back for you, Gus!"

As soon as we step outside, I push Nate away. "What's Dad still doing in there? What's he telling Gus? I don't need either of you making my decisions for me."

"Listen." Nate holds up his hands in self-defense. "I'm very sorry about this, but Gus is in a lot of pain. He wants to protect you, and that's part of it, but maybe he just can't withstand the torture it would be for him to travel anywhere. Clearly, he's given up, and I don't get the impression that he's the kind of man to give up easily, so he must have good reason to do so."

"What are you saying?" I don't want to hear this.

"I think he's asking you to let him go partly for your sake and partly for his." Nate shrugs. "He can't take much more. You do recognize that he's very weak and close to death?"

"Don't *say* that!" I snarl.

"Silvia, you don't strike me as the kind of person to deny the truth, but I'm sure we all have our blind spots."

"I don't want him to die alone," I whimper.

Nate shrugs. "Maybe that's what Gus wants."

This renders me silent until Dad joins us. "What were you doing in there for so long?"

Dad strides away from Gus's apartment. "I just wanted to thank him."

"For telling me not to come back?" I struggle to both glare at him and keep up with his fast pace at the same time.

"No, Silvia." Dad peers around the corner before entering the next littered street. "I wanted to thank him for everything he's done for you. I wasn't sure I'd get another chance to tell him how grateful I am to him for stepping into my place in my absence."

"Oh." That's not what I expected him to say. If I was in my dad's position, I might be jealous of Gus. Instead, he humbled himself in gratitude.

Dad directs us down an alleyway. "Our best chance to find Edwina is to search the same five schools we went to find Matthew."

Nate nods. "Sounds like a good place to start, anyway. Silvia, are you okay with this plan? Or do you want to find your mom first?"

That's a hard question to answer, but I need to be fair. "Edwina's young. I'm sure she's scared. Let's try to find her first. If we reach too many dead ends, then we'll switch to finding Mom."

"Agreed." Nate nods.

We carefully make our way down a few more streets, passing all sorts of people along the way. Some sleep alongside the road, leaning against buildings. Others run past us yelling and brandishing wooden or metal sticks. Occasionally a band of military uniformed police march by in a hurry. For the most part, everyone ignores us, which suits me just fine.

"Here's the closest one, but I don't know what happened." Dad clangs open a metal gate revealing an empty courtyard. "No one's here now."

Nate peers in every window and pushes open every unlocked door, finding nothing.

I shiver. This space feels so wrong to me. "It's okay, Nate, we've got four more schools to check."

"Okay, let's go." Nate hurries past us. "Where to next, Daniel?"

The second school is also empty. The third school contains only boys, although Dad swears there were girls there just a few days ago. The fourth school now only holds preschool aged children.

Dad becomes flustered. "This doesn't make sense. Why are things so different now than they were just a couple days ago?"

The fifth and final school on Dad's mental list is crammed full of kids, Suits, and teachers. When Nate tries to ask a young teacher about his sister, the Suits force us out the door but otherwise leave us alone without harassment.

"I gotta get back in there." Nate paces the road outside the school. "What if she's in there?"

As he heads back to the door, the same young teacher sneaks outside to talk to him.

"Don't go back in there," she warns softly. "But if you have a picture of her, I might be able to help."

"Yes. I've got one." Nate shrugs off his backpack to dig out a well-worn, small school photo of a cute little girl, her dark eyes squinting as she grinned for the camera.

The teacher examines the picture for a long moment, then shakes her head. "I don't have any students named Edwina, and this picture doesn't look familiar to me at all. I'm sorry."

Nate reluctantly takes back the photo. "Thanks anyway."

"Good luck to you." She sneaks back inside.

Nate sighs. "Now what? Gus is in no shape to help, and I don't know my way around here anymore. She could be anywhere. I knew I waited too long to come back. What if I *never* find her?"

I grab his shoulder. "Don't panic. We'll think of something. Is there anyone you knew from before you left that you could go ask? They might have heard what happened to her."

"I can't think of anyone." Nate shakes his head. "I'm just going to keep walking. Maybe I'll do as Alice said and yell out her name in the street."

"Alice was joking," I remind him. "Can I see the picture?"

He hands it to me. "Gus sent this along when he helped me escape. It's an old picture, of course, but maybe she still looks like that."

I take the picture, trying to imagine her now—taller, maybe longer or shorter hair, maybe glasses.

Nate grabs the photo back. "You're wrong about Alice. She would've done anything to find Matthew. I'll do whatever it takes to find Edwina, even if it does mean calling out her name in the streets." Nate runs ahead of us, stopping every person he sees, flashing the picture in their faces and asking: "Have you seen this girl?"

"He's going to get himself hurt." Dad hurries after him with me at his heels.

Nate's everywhere at once, begging complete strangers for help. Some brush him off, refusing to even look at his picture. Some show him a picture of their own, asking the same kinds of questions. On and on Nate searches for Edwina, dashing around like he's the fastest runner in a race. But the answer is always the same. Everyone shakes their head. Nobody's seen her.

Afternoon turns to early evening, and the sun's heat begins to fade. Streets start to blur together. Nate disappears, working through the crowd ahead of us. We trail behind, my father frowning. I wish I could read his mind. Is he upset he's still inside the city with me instead of heading home with Alice to protect his other kids from Eddy? Or does he wish we'd have found my mother first?

"What's wrong, Dad?" I ask. "Do you want to go look for Mom? We've spent all day on this, and we're no closer than when we started."

Dad nods. "Let's talk to Nate and see if we should split up."

"Yeah, let's. I don't want to wait any longer. I'm worried about Mom."

Dad pauses, cocking his head to one side, listening. "Uh-oh."

"What is it?" I ask as he sprints ahead. "Where are you going? What did you hear?"

Struggling to follow his path, I weave through oceans of strangers. What's going on? Where did they go?

"Get *off* of him!" Dad commands, shoving back a tall wild-eyed man.

Nate lies sprawled on the ground.

"What happened?" I bend down, putting a hand on his shoulder.

"It's my fault." Nate eases into a sitting position, dazed, putting a hand to his head. "That guy's just nuts. I never should've approached him. I wasn't thinking straight."

After Dad chases off Nate's attacker, he returns. "Are you okay? Looks like you're going to get a nice shiner."

"Yeah, and I've got a bump on my head, but I'll be fine." Nate sighs. "But this isn't working. No one knows where she is, and some folks have gone crazy with fear, lashing out at anyone who gets in their way. This place is a tinder box, getting ready to explode."

"What do you want to do now?" I ask. "Are you giving up?"

"I can't." Nate shakes his head. "I've come this far. I've got to keep going."

Dad frowns. "You need ice for your face."

"I just need my sister."

We help him up and wander aimlessly, Nate slowly putting one foot in front of the other.

"I'll be okay," he assures us. "I just need a little time to recover."

Dad nods. "Pull yourself together now. You're a tough guy. You'll be fine."

Another hour passes, and with every minute I grow more restless.

A woman approaches Nate. "I can't believe I found you again! I felt bad I couldn't help you before, so I've been asking around, and I think maybe I can help you find your sister."

"Are you serious?" Nate blinks dully, as if it takes him a moment to focus.

She hands him a slip of paper. "My neighbor's a teacher. She said they're keeping a bunch of kids at this park. It's worth a shot, right?"

"Oh my gosh! Thank you!" Nate hugs the women, who blushes. "You don't know what this means to me!"

He turns to us, fresh bruises forming on his rugged face. "Come on, guys! Let's go!"

Nate takes off again in a hurry, with Dad and I hovering on either side. Sometimes he stumbles just for a second before catching himself, and I wonder if he might have suffered a mild concussion. While I'm worried about Nate, disturbing images float through my head of my mother sitting alone on the hard floor in half comatose misery, not eating and non-functional while we are out here not doing anything to help her.

Nate consults the paper gripped in his hand. "Looks like the park's just around the corner from here. We're almost there."

Glancing up at the street signs, I see we have entered the Southeast sector. We approach a park surrounded by a tall fence. Half the park is pavement, the other half grass with very few trees.

"Wait a minute. I know this place." Last time I came here, I was searching for the family of the pregnant girl. There's the bench the old lady sat on with the red balloon tied to her wrist. There's the sandbox her grandchild dug in. But instead of the children running around playing with jump ropes and balls, they just mill about with worried faces and muted voices.

And then I see them. More Suits. My heart sinks.

I grab Nate's arm and point. He pauses, both the map and his sister's picture clutched in his hands. While we stop and stare, a little girl trips over an untied shoelace. One of the Suits helps her up and then bends down to tie her shoe. My mind flashes back to the Handler who made me ride in the front seat with him while the fireworks exploded over the Incinerator, and how Franco and I ran into him later in the park. He was just a protective father who wanted his little girl as far away from Franco as possible, because he thought he was dangerous. Maybe this Suit likes kids too. Making a split-second decision I hope I don't regret, I snatch Edwina's picture out of Nate's unsuspecting hand and stroll straight over to the Suit.

"Do you know this girl?" I ask. "She'd look a few years older than this picture." No need to give him any more information than that.

He examines the picture. "She might be here. There's a lot of kids here. What's her name?"

"Eddie!" Nate starts screaming, advancing through the crowd as the kids move out of his way. "Eddie! It's me, Nate!"

The Suit and I watch Nate search, the tone of his voice growing desperate.

"I'm glad you came." The Suit takes off his sunglasses, revealing soft brown eyes. "I don't know how to get all these kids back to their homes. I don't know what to do if nobody shows up for them, but their school got bombed, and I didn't know where else to take them. I just had to get the kids somewhere safe."

"Are you a teacher?" I ask, confused.

"No." He shakes his head. "Just a bodyguard. It's the only job I qualified for, and it's just because I'm a big guy."

I never thought about that before. That Suits are Suits because they took the same tests I did but qualified to be a Suit. Maybe he longed to be something else too.

"I hope he finds her," continues the talkative Suit. "I didn't sign up for this. This isn't right."

"Nate?" A girl who looks to be an older version of the picture still held in my hand bursts through the crowd right in front of me.

"Is this you?" I show her the picture. "Are you Edwina? Or Eddie?"

She grabs the picture. "Only my brother, Nate, ever called me Eddie. I thought I heard his voice, but that's impossible. He's been gone for so long."

"Actually, he is here. In fact, he's close by." I turn to where I last saw him enter the crowd. "Nate! Get over here!"

Nate pushes through a throng of kids and halts in front of his sister. They gape at each other.

"Where have you been?" She lunges at him, hitting him with her fists before collapsing into his arms. "I waited and waited and you *never* came!"

"I'm here now." Nate holds her in a tight embrace.

Edwina doesn't allow herself to cry for long before she stands up straight again. "Get me out of here, right now!"

"Can do." Nate nods, putting an arm around her to lead her out of the park.

I turn back to the Suit one more time before leaving. "Thank you."

"No problem. Stay safe now." He turns to watch over the remaining kids.

We walk back to where my father waits near the exit gate.

"Your crazy plan worked." Dad pats Nate on the shoulder. "You found her."

"Yes." Nate glances down at his sister. "Now I'm never letting her go."

The ground tremors beneath our feet as a huge explosion shakes my eardrums.

"What's going on?" I stumble but catch myself.

Over the sound of screaming kids, Dad yells at Nate and Eddie. "Go on! Get out of here while you still can!"

"Are you sure?" Nate yells back. "I want to help you find Yoshe."

Dad shakes his head. "Just get her out of here. Silvia and I can handle the rest."

I'm not sure I agree with this plan until I notice Edwina's face. This is what she needs right now. To be with her brother and to get far away from here. I nod. "Stay safe out there."

"Stay safe," Nate repeats. "We'll see you on the outside."

We travel together for several streets until Nate breaks off to continue straight while we veer into the Northwest sector, heading toward my old apartment. We wave goodbye, and then it's just Dad and me. As the skies darken I take the lead, since Dad doesn't have a clue where we lived after he departed. After skirting carefully past several angry mobs, the crowds begin to thin, the number of people growing sparser.

"We're getting closer," I tell him after several streets of silence. "Not far now."

He nods, searching our surroundings for any signs of trouble.

One last turn, and I point. "There it is."

Dad stares in confusion. "I never thought about where they would move you. I always just imagined you still in our old place."

"Not a chance. Those were the rules. The less people in a family, the less square footage allowed."

We reach the building and head up the whitewashed cement stairs. The power is still on here, so the lights remain blindingly bright overhead.

"Six flights up," I warn him.

"Must have been fun on grocery day." Dad pants, doing his best to keep up.

Many steps later, we are home at last. Or what used to be home. The hallway is too quiet. Where have all the families gone? I reach the front door, realizing I don't have the key. But it doesn't matter, because it isn't locked.

"That's odd." I start to push the door open, but Dad stops me.

"Let me go first." He steps ahead of me, gun at the ready.

We enter into chaos. Dishes from the kitchen smashed across the floor of the front hallway. Clothing ripped to shreds and discarded against the wall. Pictures smashed, hanging askew on the walls.

"What happened here?" Dad asks, looking around.

My heart races, and my hands shake. "Obviously the Suits were here, trashing the place and looking for clues, just like they did when you died. They went through all our stuff, trying to figure out what happened to you. They asked tons of questions. They found the red dress, and that's when Mom—"

I race into my room, and there it is. The dress. Intact. Perfect. Lying on my clean bed, the one spot of calm in the whole apartment.

"You still have that?" Dad whispers at my side.

"Yeah, and I'm taking it with me." I stuff it in my backpack before rushing to my mother's room. It's a complete mess, and Mom is such a neat freak. "The Suits were *definitely* in here. They messed with all her stuff. Look how much they broke! This is awful! I hope they didn't touch her violin. Where is her violin? That's strange. It's not in here. Let's check the rest of the apartment."

We dash through each room. No sign of my mother or where she went. No violin either.

I know the Suits were here. I just don't know what they've done with my mother. Or what we're going to have to do to get her back.

45

PRECIOUS THINGS

Searching through the rubble left behind, I discover precious pieces of my life before. Mom's shiny black flats strewn across the hallway, which once upon a time hinted at the promise of chocolate for dessert. Halfway into the kitchen rests Dad's old, worn, brown shoe which so many years ago used to mean spaghetti for supper. Picking it up, I realize Mom hung onto this shoe for eight years to somehow feel closer to Dad. Teacups smashed atop the kitchen counter, plates destroyed into bits on the floor. So many memories of sitting here with Mom trying so hard to pry info from me about my day at work, encouraging me to apply for a different job, wishing for me to somehow "stand out" and "get ahead" in Panopticus. How proud she was when I entered that stupid race. How happy she was to resume playing violin in the orchestra and get promoted so quickly. Only the smaller framed pictures remain intact, clustered together on an end table in the small living room, a small safe-haven from the ruckus and destruction through the rest of the house.

I show them to Dad. "Remember this?"

"Of course I do." Dad smiles. "Look how *little* you were, Silvia. Remember how much you hated that clown?"

"That's because clowns are creepy. I still don't like them."

Dad laughs. "You kicked that clown in the shins, and we were asked to leave the event."

"No way!" Now I'm embarrassed. What a brat I must have been. "Please tell me you just made that up."

He holds up his hands. "Sorry, it's true. After that, Yoshe called you SBM for a while."

"SBM?"

"Small But Mighty." He smiles, lost in the memory. "Or sometimes Silvia Be Mighty."

"How come I don't remember that?"

"You could have twenty people all at the same place at the same time, and every one of them will remember things differently afterwards." Dad picks up another picture. "That's just human nature."

"I'm taking these with me." I pack the pictures in my bag. "I won't let the Suits have them. They're mine."

"Good idea." Dad hands me the last picture. "It's dark out. What should we do now?"

I glance out the window. "Do you think we could just stay here for the night? We could lock the door and everything. It's gotta be at least a little safer here than out in the streets. I'll take my bed, and I'm sure you could use Mom's bed."

Dad shakes his head. "I'll sleep in your room on the floor. I'm not comfortable leaving your side. But I agree we should get some sleep before heading out to search for Yoshe in the morning."

Dad returns to the front door to fiddle with the locks. I follow him, shaking my head at the upheaval in the apartment. Mom would be so mad about this.

"What do you think happened to Mom?" I ask. "Do you think the Suits took her? Or do you think Franco came around in time to protect her?"

His shoulders slump. "I don't know. And I have no idea where to begin to search for her."

"We could ask some neighbors, although they might be surprised to see me."

Dad nods. "Let's get some rest and make plans in the morning when we can think straight again."

Once the front door is locked, we head back to my room. Dad gawks at the photo of him on the wall across from my bed, surprisingly left unbroken.

"Yeah. Your face was the first thing I saw when I woke up every morning. Pathetic, right? Well, since I've got the real thing now, I don't need to take that picture with me, do I? Plus it's too dang big for my bag."

Dad sighs. "I'm so sorry about how everything turned out."

"It's okay, Dad. You're here now."

"And I'm not leaving. We'll find your mom tomorrow. I'm sure of it."

"I'm not, but it won't stop me from trying." I settle down in my bed, which feels ridiculously comfortable, then toss a couple pillows and blankets to Dad on the floor.

"Good night, Silvia."

"Good night, Dad." It doesn't take long to drift away.

THE APARTMENT DOOR *swings open before I even turn the key.*

"Oh, honey!" Mom hugs me tight, her innocent face filled with light. "Isn't it wonderful? You've been Chosen!"

She leads me into the kitchen crowded with Suits, all waiting for my arrival.

I back away, hands outstretched. "No! I'm not going with you!"

"Silvia, what are you doing?" Mom gapes. "Isn't this what you wanted?"

"It's not what you think it is, Mom." My voice shakes. "I work in the Mortuary. I know what happens to those who get Chosen."

Mom collapses against the nearest wall.

"Let's not upset your mother," the suits caution. "You know how fragile she is."

I reach back for my mom, still leaning against the wall. The light in her eyes fades. She'll die, too, if I don't do something.

I grab a teacup and smash it upside down on the counter.

Mom's eyes flash and catch mine.

Save yourself, is my unspoken message.

She nods, then opens her mouth to speak. "Wake up, Silvia. Someone's at the door."

🏃

"Wake up, Silvia." Dad hisses in my ear, shaking me awake. "Someone's at the front door."

The front hallway light switches on, pooling light across my open bedroom doorway, then is quickly shut off again, leaving us in the dark.

"We have to run for it," Dad murmurs.

Following my father, I slip on my backpack and tiptoe into the kitchen. If we can make it to the front door via the kitchen, maybe we can sneak away from the intruders.

But the plan doesn't work. At least two people loom in the shadows, one silhouette filling each opening into the kitchen. They stalk toward us on either side of the counter.

There's no escape. We are cornered.

"First chance you get, run away as fast as you can," Dad instructs in a low voice before surging to my right. "Don't wait for me."

A dark clothed intruder rushes him, kicking and hitting and throwing anything left on the counter at him.

Dad yelps in pain.

Trembling, I point my gun at the shadowy stranger in front of me. "Don't come any closer or I'll shoot."

The person freezes. I'm not sure which is shaking more, my voice or my hand, so there's no way they can be afraid of me.

Shrill female screaming fills the air as my father's attacker grabs a frying pan and swings.

I turn away from my target, recognizing that scream. "Mom? What the *hell* are you doing to Dad?"

The frying pan bangs to the floor.

Lights blaze overhead, temporarily blinding me. I blink to focus, then stare in shock at my mother, her hand still hovering over the switch on the far wall.

No more sleek, shiny bobbed haircut with every hair in place. No more tidy, conservative clothes. My mother has transformed into some new creature completely—her hair chopped short on the sides with just enough left up top to be rumpled and out of control, fierce black eyeliner accentuating her wide, unblinking eyes. And she's wearing my black pajama tank top and my favorite dark jeans.

"Mom? You just beat the crap out of Dad!" I rush to stand over him. "Dad, are you okay?"

He lies moaning on the floor, facedown. "Give me a moment."

Mom races to my side to peer down at her wreckage. "Daniel? Is it *really* you?"

"Yeah, what's left of me anyway," he croaks.

"Oh, no! What have I done?" Mom reaches across the counter. "Franco, come help me!"

"Franco?" I turn to face him, and it all rushes back at once. Every argument. Every leading or misleading turn of phrase. Every smile. Every frown. When he was impressed with me, and when he was disappointed. When he was teasing Liam, and when he was mourning him. When he threw me out of his apartment, and when he drew my picture. When he gave me his jean jacket with the message: *I need to know you made it out alive.*

Franco mouths my name. "Silvia." His eyes are pinned to me.

"What's wrong with you?" asks my mom, always demanding. "Get over here and help me!"

Franco approaches, his gaze on me unbroken until he leans down to help my dad to his feet.

"How badly did I hurt you?" Mom frets.

"What happened to your hair?" I ask.

"I cut it myself. Doesn't matter," Mom answers brusquely, reaching a hand to Dad's already bruised cheek. "How do you feel?"

"Not my finest hour," he answers, rubbing his head.

"I'm so sorry, Daniel." Mom grimaces. "I wasn't expecting you. I wasn't expecting either of you. I mean, Franco told me what happened eight years ago, but I never thought you'd return *now*, after all this time. And, Silvia, we thought, we thought—"

"I know what you thought," I interrupt her, because it's clear the words are getting hard for her to say. "I met Linda on the road outside, and she told me the Suits showed you pictures of me dead on a stretcher."

Franco pales. He still hasn't said a word.

"Franco, Linda said you wouldn't leave with her because you thought I was dead," I continue. "You should've gotten out of here. You should've taken my mom with you. What were you waiting for?"

Mom puts a hand to his arm, as if to console him. "We had things to do, Silvia. Don't yell at him. We *chose* to stay and help."

"Like what *kinds* of things?" I demand.

They look at each other, and I'm on the outside. They're a team now. How did that happen?

"Tell her." Franco nudges my mom. "She's the reason you did it, so tell her."

"What is it?" I lean in.

Mom rushes her words. "I re-kidnapped the baby Representative Waters-Royce stole and gave her back to her real family."

My mouth falls open. "How on earth did you manage that?"

She shrugs. "Gus helped me locate the family, so I dressed up like a nanny, used a fake pass card to enter the home when I knew bombs would be going off outside so there'd be a distraction, fled with her in my arms, took her back to her real family, and then we arranged for their escape."

"You say that like it was no big deal." I can't believe this. "And how did you know about the bombs?"

Once again, the two of them look at each other, and I am excluded from their silent conversation.

Franco clears his throat. "I might have had something to do with that."

"You *bomb* people now?" I ask, aghast.

He points at me. "You have a *gun* now?"

"Okay, fine." I shrug. "I get your point."

"And we don't bomb *people,* we bomb empty buildings of importance."

"And you're part of this?" I ask Mom, noticing her outfit again. "And why are you wearing my clothes?"

She sighs in exasperation. "What's the problem? I didn't feel like doing laundry, and you never said I couldn't borrow your clothes. And what would you have had me do? I thought you were *dead.* I thought they *killed* you, and I wanted them to pay. And maybe I didn't care if they died." She takes a deep, shaky breath. "And maybe I didn't care if I died, either."

"Oh, Mom." I move forward to give her a hug. She hesitates a moment before relaxing into the embrace. Typically, we are not big huggers, but this one is necessary.

"I'm sorry about breaking all our stuff," she mumbles into my hair.

I stiffen. "What are you talking about?"

"I might have... *redecorated* after the Suits took you away." Mom clears her throat.

"What?" I glance around. "I just assumed the Suits searched through all our stuff again and made this huge mess."

"No, but it kept them away." Mom steps back, squaring her shoulders. "They showed up a day or two after you were gone. When they saw my mess, they thought our apartment had already been searched, so they moved on to bother Gus instead."

"Gus?" My voice comes out all pitchy. "Is that who shot him?"

"No, as soon as they left our place I took off. You may think I never listened to all your boring exercise talk, but I remembered which way to your work was the fastest, and I got there before they did to warn him. You're not the only runner in the family, I guess."

"But the cameras. They would've seen you there."

Mom nods. "Gus walked me through faking happiness about your promotion for the cameras, and that we were planning a celebration meal together. And when the Suits did show up, Gus knew how to manipulate them. I guess he's been through this kind of thing before."

"I'm just glad you're okay." I pause. "I worried that you would be..."

Mom nods in understanding. "Like I was when Dad died... or left us?"

"That's not quite what happened," Dad interjects. "Gus helped me escape."

Mom levels her gaze at him. "And you never came back for us or tried to contact us to let us know. You should've had someone tell us. Linda knew, so she could stay strong. I didn't know, and your ten-year-old daughter was left to fend for herself while I fell apart."

Mom and Dad stare at each other, standing right next to each other but still a world apart. The tense silence ends with a *boom* that shakes the apartment.

Franco checks his watch. "Right on time. Yoshe didn't want to see the library fall because she knew how much you once loved it, so we didn't stay to watch."

"Wait. They're bombing the library right now?" My heart races. "But Gus lives near the library!"

"Don't worry about that." Franco shakes his head. "He's in hiding now."

"No, he's not!" I grab Franco's shirt. "I moved him out of that hell hole! I brought him back home. He was happy to be home!"

Franco's face pales. "Silvia..."

Everyone stares at me.

My breath catches painfully in my throat, and I whisper, "I just killed him, didn't I?"

4 6

I GO TO PIECES

I lurch to the living room window, gripping the frame for support as I peer outside, but it's facing the wrong direction. I can't see what's going on, except for long, curled ribbons of black smoke stretching overhead into the distance.

"Let's go!" I tear through the kitchen to reach the front door. "We've got to get Gus out of there!"

Franco follows me into the front hallway.

"What's taking them so long?" I fret, anxious to get going, but reluctant to leave Mom behind.

Franco glances back into the kitchen, then stares intensely at me.

"Whatever it is you have to say, just *say* it," I beg him. This silence is killing me.

He clears his throat then mumbles three words. "I missed you."

Tears fill my eyes. I missed him, too, so very much. But I don't have time for this right now. I only have time to worry about Gus and about Franco's answer to my next question. "Did you have anything to do with bombing the library today?"

Franco pales. "I might have."

I shudder. "You know I won't be able to forgive you if—"

"I know," he cuts me off, wincing and turning away.

Mom and Dad enter the front hallway, slinging bulging backpacks over their shoulders.

"Don't worry," Mom assures me. "I packed in a hurry. I took all the food I had left, plus a few things I just couldn't leave behind. We're not coming back this time."

I nod. "Okay. Let's go."

Down the six flights we race as one, rush into the morning air, smoky from the destruction ahead. I burst into a run without looking back, knowing the others will follow me northward under the darkening skies and through the frantic crowds. Everyone else heads in the opposite direction with terrified, tear-streaked faces. Normally, I might care, but right now I just don't have any more in me left to give.

Gus can't be dead.

The crowds halt right in front of me. Bouncing on my feet, I try to see what the holdup is.

Dad catches up to me. "Silvia, we can't get through here. I asked around, and everything's fenced off. They're only letting people *out* of here, not in."

"Okay, where do we go instead?" I ask, looking from one of them to the other.

Franco has the decency to look both horrified and guilty.

I grab his arm. "If you know what's going on with the bombing, you've got to tell me so I can get Gus out of there!"

"Follow me." Franco takes a deep breath, scanning our surroundings before veering west away from the throngs of citizens. Choking on the smoke, we dodge stragglers and their belongings discarded in the street. But everywhere we go, we are stopped by Suits, military, or police. Nobody's getting through. Everyone's escaping in the other direction as fast as they can, taking just what they can carry on their persons.

The third time we're stopped, I finally get to talk to someone.

"Please, sir," I beg the Suit. "My friend is stuck in there and needs my help."

"I'm sorry, miss." He shakes his head, eyes hidden behind sunglasses. "Can't let you in here. Too dangerous. Your friend will just have to get out on their own."

"But he's *really* old," adds my mom, and for once I don't contradict her.

We both direct our best begging faces to the Suit.

"I'm sorry." He turns to the next person in line.

"What are we going to do?" I ask, just as the loudest bomb yet quakes the ground beneath our feet, followed by people screaming, children crying, sirens wailing, and vehicles honking. I don't know where to go, who to ask, or what to do anymore. I'm out of ideas and too tired and hungry to think my way out of this mess.

"Silvia, we can't get in anywhere." Dad yanks me to safety as a motorized vehicle pushes through the crowd.

I fight his grip, crying again but hating every tear. "I can't just *leave* him here!"

Mom caresses my wet cheek with her hand. "I know how much you love him."

I nod, trying to catch my breath.

"And Gus loved you more than I ever realized or expected." She wipes away my tears. "You knew him better than the rest of us. What would he tell you to do now?"

My voice catches on a sob. "You're just saying this because you know he would tell me to save myself and forget about him. That he would tell me to go."

She nods. "That's right. He would tell you he was too injured to make the trip anyway, that even if you found him alive in there, he was already close to death before the bombing ever started."

Mom gestures to Franco to dig in her backpack for something. "It's in the side pocket."

Franco finds what he's looking for and hands me a letter.

"What's this?" I reach for the paper, my hand trembling harder when I recognize Gus's handwriting.

Mom brushes a few loose hairs behind my ear. "Gus wrote this after he got injured. He knew he would die here. He thought he'd never see you again, so he begged me to find you and give you this. He just wanted a chance to say goodbye.

Mom and Franco share a loaded look. Mom takes a shaky breath. "Franco and I were all set to go with his family when the Suits told Franco you were dead. That's why I never went back to see Gus. I couldn't tell him, not after everything he went through to save you. I wanted him to die in peace."

I shudder, so angry at everyone and everything. "Why does everyone keep talking about death as if it were *peaceful*?"

Another bomb shakes our world. Pain shoots through my heart like it's ripping apart.

"Well, *this* is called living." Mom points to the darkening sky. "So it's possible death might be more peaceful."

47

SOMETHING I CAN NEVER HAVE

Silvia,

By the time you read this, I will be gone.

Despite my years in theater, I'm not trying to be melodramatic. I just need you to know I went and got myself shot and plan to die soon, so I don't want you come back and do something stupid like try to find and save me.

Since I won't be seeing you again, I've asked your mother to bring you this letter. Looks like she needed to get out of here anyway. Things are really going to hell, and she should be with you and her husband, not running around here with that lunatic (Franco) you're so crazy about. I tried to warn you away from him, but that didn't work (because you're so stubborn and infatuated with him).

Anyway, I'm not writing to criticize your love life. That's none of my business. I just wanted you to know how grateful I am to have met you.

You changed everything.

Until I met you, I was so sure of myself, so sure my acts were honorable, that I always did the right thing. Then you burst into my life, so angry and demanding. You're a stubborn force of nature that even mighty Panopticus could not crush into submission. You're a brilliant bird who needed to fly far away from here and stretch her glorious wings to see how high she could soar.

I once told you that I didn't want you to work for me, but I was so very wrong. You were exactly who I needed to show me how much damage I had caused. I wasn't fixing anything. I should've taken on the system, not waited my whole life for Panopticus to evolve and heal itself. And if taking on the system led nowhere, then I should've left and taken you with me. I should've taken both you and your mother to your father years ago. Right after the explosion. Right after I snuck Jack and your father out of here and left you alone with the terrors that followed.

My inaction caused you so much pain.

I beg your forgiveness but will never forgive myself.

Thank goodness I found you in time and got you out of here. As I sit here slowly dying, I am comforted knowing you are finally free.

I wish I had more time with you, but more time is something I no longer have.

- Gus

I flip the letter over, searching for a second page, but the back side remains blank. My eyes return once again to the first line.

By the time you read this, I will be gone.

Mom puts a comforting hand on my shoulder. "It's a lovely letter."

"Wait. You read it?" I can't believe this.

"Well, you were dead." Mom shrugs, not even bothering to look guilty. "And it seemed so important to him, I thought somebody should read what Gus wrote."

Franco avoids my gaze. No doubt he read it, too, or had it read to him by my nosy mother. But I don't even care that I should feel embarrassed. All I can think about is that I am the one responsible for putting Gus in the line of fire when I thought I was making things better for him.

I was so sure of myself, so sure my acts were honorable, that I always did the right thing.

I understand now what Gus meant.

Terrified screams and wailing alarms and exploding bombs surround us, but everything sounds muffled, like I'm wearing silencing ear plugs as the world falls into chaos around me.

"Silvia, we have to get out of here." Mom tugs on my arm. "I'm sorry, but it's getting way too dangerous to stay any longer."

I stare at the letter, Gus's words swimming before my eyes.

As I sit here slowly dying, I am comforted knowing you are finally free.

"Do you think Gus is already dead?" The questions burst out of me. "Do you think he died from his injury or because of a bomb? Is he in pain, or is it all over now? Is he still in there, all alone and hurting, and we're out here unable to get to him?"

This time Dad is the one to comfort me. He takes me in his arms, a place that even after all these years and all my anger seems so familiar and so right somehow.

"What do you think, Dad?" I mumble into his shirt.

Dad speaks softly. "I think he was so weak after we moved him that he passed away before the bombing even started, but don't feel guilty about taking him home where he was more comfortable on his last day. You did the right thing."

Dad does not let me go until I stop crying and step back on my own. "Okay." I wipe my eyes. "Let's get out of here."

Franco and Mom surge ahead. Dad remains by my side to guide me as we rush from the city. Everything's a dull blur. I can barely hear what any of them say. My mind dwells in the past, and the present fades away.

Gus took me under his wing when I had no one else. He was a substitute father when I so desperately needed one. Gus encouraged me, taught me, and believed in me. He was my best friend and could always make me smile. He was the smartest person I will ever know. I do not know how to live without him. I don't know how I survived before he came into my life.

Time and distance pass by without my counting or acknowledgement. We stop to eat and drink, but I can hardly swallow a thing. By the time we reach the broken fences of Panopticus, night is falling, but any colors of the sunset are muddled by smoke.

I no longer feel fear or heat or hunger. Every sensation fades away.

I wish I had more time with you, but more time is something I no longer have.

All I have left now of Gus are the memories.

Together we sneak past the city fence line, then cross the open field between the Incinerator and the trees. Not watching where I step, I stumble, and again, Dad catches me.

"Dad, what if he's not dead and he needs me?" I whisper.

"Don't torture yourself, Silvia." Dad sighs. "You know Gus wouldn't want that."

"But we don't *know*... we haven't seen... he could still be alive and waiting for me to come back."

"Gus isn't waiting for you. He told you to go."

"Yeah, but..." I shake my head. "He knows me well enough to know I don't always listen to instructions."

"Listen, Silvia." Dad runs his hands through his red hair, clearly struggling to make a big decision. "This is probably a horrible idea, and everything could go terribly wrong. In fact, I'm sure we shouldn't do this, but I'll go back inside with you tomorrow and check on him. Then you'll know for sure."

Stunned, I throw my arms around him. "Thank you, Daddy!"

He hugs me back. "I just hope I don't live to regret it."

"Regret what?" asks my mom, approaching from behind. "Hey, Silvia, this guy, Nate, says he's been waiting for you."

"What? Really?" I whirl around in surprise as Franco watches closely.

Nate smiles, his sister close by his side. "Don't worry. I wasn't wasting any time. We've been busy fishing so we have enough food to eat on the way home. I gotta say, it's a big relief to meet your mom and to know you made it out okay."

"Gus is still inside." I watch for Nate's reaction.

He nods solemnly. "I was afraid that was how things would turn out. I'm very sorry. Clark told me how much he meant to you."

"Don't be sorry." I brace myself for my mother's reaction. "Because I'm going back in."

"What are you talking about?" Mom exclaims. "No way, young lady. Daniel, you're her father. Tell her this is crazy talk."

I raise my chin. "Actually, Dad's going with me."

Mom huffs, tears springing to her eyes. "There's no way I'm letting either of you out of my sight now that I've finally gotten my family back. I won't let either of you leave me ever again."

Nate clears his throat. "Not to throw a wrench in your plans, Daniel, but with Eddy still on the loose, don't you think you should get back to Alice?"

"Wait a minute." Mom catches my startled look and immediately narrows her eyes. "Daniel, who is Alice?"

4 8

I DON'T WANT TO BE ALONE

"Silvia, I am so sorry." Nate apologizes again for the tenth time. "I wasn't thinking. It was stupid of me to talk about Alice in front of your mother without checking first."

"Yeah, your timing was less than ideal." One glance in my parents' direction makes it clear that my mom isn't done yelling at my dad, who just stands there taking it, hanging his head. "But who you really need to apologize to is my dad, not me."

Nate winces. "I'm sure you're right, but I'm not going over there any time soon."

"I don't blame you." I dig in Mom's backpack, sorting through her food supplies. "You said you had some fish, right? What goes with fish? I wouldn't know."

"Let me see." Nate moves in closer with Franco watching his every move. "At any rate, I promise fish is better than those gelatinous protein cubes you're used to."

To avoid Franco's intense stare, I hand Nate the backpack. "Just take what you want. You'll know better than me. Anybody want to go berry picking before supper? Let's just focus on making supper and forcing my mom to eat it. She can't yell with food in her mouth. Plus, I'm sure she's hungry, which makes everything worse."

Franco starts to stand, but Edwina jumps up first. "I'll go. I don't want to listen to your mom yell at your dad anymore either."

"Yeah. I know." Even though I treated Dad about the same when I first learned about Alice, this time around I'm feeling bad for him. Hypocritical, I know. "Let's get out of here. Franco, you can come with us."

He nods and follows close behind.

"I know where all the good picking is, so follow me!" Edwina scampers ahead, each of us holding a small collapsible container from Mom's sack.

When we pause to collect raspberries, Franco stands so close but doesn't say a word.

I guess it's up to me to break the ice. "I saw the greenhouses. How could you blow up your life's work? You used to be so passionate about everything growing there."

"I don't know what to say," Franco mumbles. "All my excuses will seem hollow to you in light of what happened to Gus."

The emotion in his eyes hits me full force, like I'm back in his apartment that last time before I escaped, when he had been drinking after seeing Liam's dead body. He was so angry and out of control, at first kissing me and then kicking me out of the apartment, yelling at me to get away from him. Did that moment change everything between us?

"Just *talk* to me," I beg. "I don't like this awkward silence. We used to have lots to talk about."

"Yeah, I know." Franco hesitates, weighing every word. "The reason I bombed the greenhouses is pretty basic. They destroyed Liam, then they told me they had destroyed you, and I didn't want to feed them anymore. So I blew it up. I knew where to put the bombs to cause the most destruction. It was easy. I wanted to cause them pain, when really all I did was hurt myself and those who worked with me." He stops to take a deep breath.

"I didn't know what to do with myself after I thought I'd lost you."

"Why did you believe them when they didn't have the jean jacket?" I ask. "You sent that with me so you'd know for sure. I still have it, you know."

He shakes his head. "The pictures looked so real and so much like Liam did. It was a nightmare. You know, your mom is the one who saved me. It started out with me taking care of her, but very soon things were the other way around."

"Mom has changed so much she barely even seems like the same person. My whole childhood would've been a lot different if she had been this strong back then."

Franco cringes. "I thought she was going to kill your dad when she learned about Alice."

"Yeah, I should've warned her."

Franco shrugs. "You didn't have time, and you were upset about leaving Gus behind. It's just a bad situation."

"Yeah. Mom waited eight years for Dad, and he moved on."

"What do you think of Alice?"

"Actually, I like her, although I didn't want to at first."

"You planning on telling your mom this?" he teases with that sudden smile of his.

I smile back. "Not any time soon."

Edwina crashes through the bushes in front of us. "You've hardly picked any berries! What have you been doing?"

Franco uses his charm on Nate's little sister. "All right. Your wish is my command. Just point me in the right direction."

Edwina leads him to one cluster of berry bushes and me to another completely separate area before returning to chatter at Franco until she decides we are done picking for the night.

"Let's leave some for tomorrow." Edwina sounds very wise and bossy for someone who has only been out of the city for a day. "Just pick what we can eat right now."

We head back to the smell of fish cooking over a fire.

Nate sits in the middle, preparing supper, with Mom and Dad perched uncomfortably on either side. Nate raises his eyes to me without a word. Edwina drags Franco away to help her hand out cups and plates.

"Okay." I watch my parents trying very hard to act normal. "Let's just eat and sleep, because that's what everyone needs right now. Tomorrow we will come up with the next plan. One thing at a time."

Mom levels her gaze at me. "What I need to know, Silvia, is if you are going to live with me, or him and this Alice? Because I know you always preferred your father, and I've just heard that you get along so well with this Alice that you took a road trip back here with her to find her son. Now I've been alone for eight years, so you'd think I'd be used to it, but I don't want to be alone anymore. I want you to live with me, but I want it to be what you want too. So who do *you* want, Silvia? Me or your father? Who's it going to be?"

Rendered speechless, I glance between the tired faces of my parents. Still not sure what to say, I instinctively turn back toward the city and the person I left behind.

Gus. That is who I want.

Mom catches on immediately. "You're not still thinking about going back in there, are you? I gave you Gus's letter. He knew he'd never make it out of the city alive, and he wanted you to be free."

"But—" I begin.

"There's no buts about this, Silvia. Now just forget about it. Tell her, Daniel..." Mom's voice wavers upon the realization that she and my father are not on the same team anymore.

Dad shrugs, glancing between us.

"Don't do this!" Mom falls to her knees before me, clutching my hands. "I'm used to living without your father, but I'll never get used to living without you. Please don't do this to me!"

I try to remain calm. "And I'll never forgive myself if I don't at least try to help Gus."

She drops my hands, defeated. "And you'll never forgive me if I try to stop you. But I only just got you back, and I hoped we were safe now."

The meal proceeds in relative silence. No one knows what to say, although spunky Edwina tries very hard to engage both her brother and Franco in conversation. I admire her effort but do nothing to help. After supper ends, I sleep fitfully, the night-owl calls mixing with the distant sounds of war and I wake almost as tired as when I went to bed.

Nate takes charge. "It's such a good fishing spot, I hate to leave it. If the rest of you don't mind fish again for breakfast, I think I'll go one more time so we can travel with full bellies."

"You forget we are not all leaving together," Mom reminds him frostily.

"Well, a warm meal will be good for everyone." Nate avoids getting pulled into our argument.

Franco stands, brushing off his clothes. "Maybe I'll come with you so I can learn how to fish."

"Daniel, why don't you go too?" Mom commands, rather than asks. "Because I can't even look at you right now."

"That leaves the three of us," notices Edwina, very chipper for the early morning. "I'll pick some more berries. Anyone want to come with?"

"Yeah, I'm coming." I don't need to be asked twice. Anything to avoid talking to my mom about my plans to see Gus.

"That's fine." Mom nods, already tidying up the campsite. "I'll get everything sorted out here and repack the bags."

Without Franco to distract me this time, I focus on berry picking. Charmingly bossy, Edwina directs me the whole time, but I don't mind. Living with my mother, I am used to being told what to do. We fill our containers so full it becomes difficult to carry them without spilling any fruit as we make our way back to the campsite, our fingers stained like dark red jewels.

"I hear voices," observes Edwina. "The guys must be done fishing already."

"Good. We can eat quick and all be on our way." I know I've put my mother through a lot, but I refuse to leave Gus behind without knowing for sure he is gone.

"You must be hungry. Let me just check on the berries, and I'll be right back." Mom's voice grows louder as she approaches us in the shrubbery.

One look at her face tells me something is wrong.

"What is it?" I ask.

Mom reaches for Edwina's berries, keeping her voice low. "Do you know how to find Nate's fishing spot?"

Edwina nods nervously.

Mom squeezes Edwina's shoulder. "Good, now run there as fast as you can and bring them all back right away."

Edwina takes off, wise enough not to question why.

"What's going on?" I whisper after Edwina disappears between the trees.

Mom pauses to check behind her before answering. "Eddy is here."

49

I WOULD DIE 4 U

"Do you have a weapon on you?" Mom mutters. "Somehow I misplaced mine."

"Oh, you didn't misplace it, darling." Eddy approaches with a gun in one hand and Mom's knife in the other. "I took it when you didn't seem, let's say, *compassionate* enough about my search for my long-lost wife, Alice."

Mom tenses.

"Silvia, how wonderful to see you again," Eddy sneers. "Thanks for being such a loudmouth about your plans that I knew exactly where you and Alice were heading. Too bad she isn't with you, but I'll take what I can get.

I reach for the gun Clark gave me, but Eddy is too fast.

"Silvia, watch your hands now. Don't want anyone to get hurt." He confiscates my gun before I can stop him.

Mom and I share a worried glance.

"Now, move it!" He marches us back to the clearing, swiping our berries to stuff his face. "Now hurry up and cook me a nice hot meal while I decide what to do with the two of you."

"Why don't you just leave Alice alone?" I badger him.

Mom throws me a warning look while she heats some beans from a can.

"You think you know everything, don't you?" He twirls the knife in his hand. "It's your dad who stole her in the first place. He's the criminal, not me."

"He traded for her," I snap back, knowing my plan to keep him talking could backfire if I make him too angry. "He traded a bunch of booze for her because all your Grouping cared about was getting drunk."

"Is that what he told you?" Eddy chuckles. "How ironic, when your father was the biggest drunk there ever was. A total mess. Could barely talk at meetings. It was pathetic. We only traded with him because we thought he'd forget the whole thing when he woke up the next morning, hungover as usual. Then we'd have all the booze *and* my wife."

"She's not your wife!"

"What? Are you volunteering for the job?" His malevolent laugh makes me shiver.

"Here you go." Mom hands Eddy a travel plate with warmed beans and some dried fish before tucking a shaking hand behind her back.

"Now, here's a good woman." Eddy nods at her. "Cooking me a nice hot meal. Being real polite and respectful. Try to be more like your pretty mother, Silvia."

Mom smiles a tiny, unreadable smile.

"Now, why don't the two of you explain to me why you're out here on your own with all these extra backpacks lying around? Did you steal them or something?"

Dang, he noticed. I scramble to dream up a story.

Mom beats me to it, smooth as can be. "We needed food and supplies. We took everything we could get our hands on. It's like a war zone in there. You wouldn't believe the bombing. People running through the streets, trashing everything. It's horrible. I'm so glad we got out of there alive. I *never* want to go back."

Eddy narrows his eyes. "So, what are your plans now, might I ask?"

Mom gestures to me. "Silvia says we have to join a Grouping out here to survive."

"Or you could start one of your own." Eddy pauses. "I like you, if you can keep your daughter in line. I'm a good provider. I'm strong and good at hunting and fishing. Your daughter here got me kicked out of my last grouping, so I'm on the lookout too."

"What about Alice?" Mom asks carefully. "Would you forget about her?"

Eddy raises his eyebrows. "Why don't you *make* me forget about her?"

Mom straightens her back, taking a step toward him.

"No, Mom, what are you doing?" I exclaim, misunderstanding her intentions.

In a blur, she swings the hot metal pan, striking Eddy soundly on his skull. He yelps, dropping his food, and reaches for his gun. "Damn you, woman!"

"Put down the gun!" Dad bursts into the clearing with one hand outstretched and the other holding his weapon.

Eddy spins toward him, firing twice. Dad gets off a single shot before collapsing to the ground, blood spurting from his chest. Eddy gets hit in the right shoulder, flinging him backwards.

Mother grabs his dropped gun and points it at his head, snarling. "Get on the ground! All your limbs spread!"

"You've got him?" I ask.

"Yes! Go check on Daniel!" she orders, not taking her eyes off Eddy.

I scramble to his side. Dad gasps for breath, blood gushing from his mouth. He's losing so much blood. Bright red blood everywhere.

"Take it..." He catches my eyes, his hand flutters in the direction of his fallen gun, his words coming in gasps. "And *end* this..."

I wheel around with gun in hand to find Eddy up and swinging a knife at my mother with his uninjured arm.

"Mom? What are you waiting for?"

"Let me handle this!" she argues, but still doesn't shoot.

"You're going to pay for this, you lying bitches!" He swings again, missing her by mere inches as she jumps back.

"I don't like to kill people." Mom's voice cracks. "But you deserve it."

He's so close now I can smell him.

"Enough!" I brace myself. "Together. Aim for his chest."

And we fire.

Mom cries out as Eddy drops, keeping her gun aimed at his fallen form while he shakes and sputters.

"Can I go back to Dad?" I beg.

She nods, glancing back at my father before focusing again on Eddy.

Dad's shallow breaths sound like liquid rather than air. I know what this means. He raises his blue eyes to my brown ones. "My brave girl." With a trembling hand, he reaches to smooth my hair. "I'm so proud of you, my Silvia Be Mighty."

"Dad? You can't go. Alice needs you. Your kids need you. Please stay with us."

"You can't... always get... what you want." Dad smiles the tiniest of smiles.

I glance back at my mom. "Everything okay over there?"

"Got it under control." Mom doesn't look at me, focused on her prey. "How's Daniel?"

"What should I tell her?" I whisper to Dad.

He coughs and spits up more blood. "Tell her... I'm sorry."

"I know you are, Dad." Tears fall as the others crash through the forest and into the clearing.

Nate pulls Edwina into a hug, turning her away from the scene.

"What happened?" Franco gasps. "What can I do to help?"

"Go help Mom," I beg, remaining focused on my dad.

Dad wheezes and chokes. "Stay... with me?"

"I'd do anything for you." I attempt to warm his cooling hands between mine.

Dad's chest heaves so violently I fear his ribs will break with each breath. I pray for his suffering to end, so he is no longer in agony. But as his gasps grow weaker and farther apart with each intake, I silently plead for him to keep trying, to get past this. I beg him to live.

But no matter what I want or wish, at long last his body shudders and goes still.

50

COME WHAT MAY

Back in the artificially chilled world of Mortuary & Autopsy Services, those in charge made sure Gus and I never worked on the bodies of people we knew. Until Liam, of course, but that was on purpose. That was to hurt me and, more importantly, to scare me into submission.

I should be used to dead bodies.

But I'm not familiar with the process of dying. Especially not with someone I love.

People talk, but I can't make out their words. Everyone runs around, yelling at each other. Their world has grown hazy to me, their voices altered and wavy as if underwater. I do not move, do not leave his side, until his last breath takes him away forever.

In my head, I tell Dad everything I didn't get the chance to say in real life.

Dad, I'm so sorry about everything.

I'm sorry I wasted so much time being angry when I found you with Alice and your kids. I wish that had gone differently. I like Alice, and I like your kids, and I understand now why you moved on. Eight years is a long time, and you never thought you'd see us again. You helped Alice, and she helped you.

I'm so sorry about running off with her without telling you. I should've taken the time to convince just you to come with me to get Mom and Gus and Matthew. Alice could've stayed home. The Grouping would've kept her safe. If only you and I had made the trip together. We would've gotten a chance to talk. I had so many things to tell you but never got the chance, because I was so selfish and stupid about everything.

It's my fault Eddy found us in the first place because I ran off with Alice, and then he overheard me talking about our plans and found us here. I wish I had shot him right away. Then you would be fine. Then you would be going home to Alice and your kids. Alice needs you. Mom and I are used to living on our own. We would've been fine. Mom would've been fine, she just needed more time. She only found out last night about Alice. Of course, she was upset. I don't blame her, but she didn't get the time she needed to see, to adjust, to understand.

How are you gone? I just got you back. If only I had done things differently. If only someone else had taken out Eddy long ago. If only you'd gotten more time to explain to Mom. But don't worry, I'll get her to understand. You'll see.

Except you won't. You're gone. I can't believe it. You were supposed to be a part of my life now. Maybe we wouldn't have lived together, but we could've been neighbors or something. Maybe I could help with your kids and Alice, like you promised to help me with Gus.

I can't lose both of you at once. You're both my dads. I love and need you both. If only we had gotten here earlier, before Gus got injured, then he would already be with us. But he's stuck inside, and I don't know if he's alive or dead.

I gotta go, Dad. I'm sorry, but I gotta find out for sure. I can't stay here any longer. I can't see you like this.

I'm sorry I can't bury you. I can't do it. I'm sorry.

I gotta go.

I stand, legs shaky from sitting so long, and start to walk away.

"Just where do you think you're going?" Mom hurries over to me.

One glance at Eddy's body tells me he has been dead for some time. How long did I remain at Dad's side?

"You know where." I turn back, headed straight for Panopticus, one last time.

"Don't you dare," Mom growls, her eyes dangerous and dark. "I won't let you."

"You can't stop me."

Mom glances at the gun, still in her shaking head, and her shoulders droop. "What if you die in there? What do I do then? I'll have no one. Your father's gone. Please don't leave me alone."

"I'm sorry, Mom." I touch her arm. "I have to. I can't live with myself if I don't at least try to save Gus. You know me."

She sighs. "Yes, I do. I've never been able to talk you into or out of anything. You've always had your own mind. Just be careful and promise me you're coming back to me alive. I'd wait forever for you."

I nod, knowing there are some promises a person just can't make, and turn to leave.

"Hold up." Nate throws together some things before approaching me. "At least take some food with you. You need to eat. And you need to clear your head. It's dangerous enough in there without you going in all upset and distracted by your emotions. You're a smart girl, don't do that. Promise me you'll be careful."

I nod, accepting the food. "Thanks, Nate. If you didn't have Edwina to take care of, I would beg you to come with me, but I can manage alone."

"You don't need him." Franco steps forward. "You've got me."

"You'll go back in?"

Franco grabs my hand. "I'm with you, come what may."

51

I KNEW YOU WERE WAITING
(FOR ME)

We eat along the way, picking our steps carefully through the rubble. Franco gazes at the greenhouses, their once arched glass ceilings caved in, the plants inside fallen over and damaged.

"Ben would be so disappointed in me," Franco says softly.

Franco worked in Botanical Sciences before his mentor and idol, Ben, developed pancreatic cancer, sending Gus into the Underground Market for pain meds once the New Order claimed his husband had already received his allotted Lifetime Medical Allowance. Ben's suffering turned Gus against the Government, starting all of this in motion.

Hours pass with both of us absorbed in our own thoughts until we reach the city in chaos noise of continual gunshots and small explosions. Smoke clogs the sky and our lungs. We avoid confrontation, keeping our heads down and eyes averted, sneaking between buildings. Daylight is not our friend.

We have not talked much, but there are things that need to be said.

"Thank you for coming with me." I glance at Franco.

"Couldn't let Nate jump in and save you, although he looked pretty keen to do so."

I roll my eyes. "You're impossible."

"That makes two of us." He stares at me. "You seem so different somehow, but still the same. What happened to you out there?"

"A lot of stuff happened. I don't know where to start."

He shrugs. "Maybe start with the last time I saw you."

"You mean when you threw me out of your apartment?"

"Uh. About that." He grimaces. "I'm sorry about that. I swear I don't usually drink that much. Ever."

"Well, Gus woke me up in the hospital, helped me escape through the Incinerator, and I hiked on alone until I found a dog for company."

"What? A dog?"

"Yeah. I named him Albert, because once Gus had a dog named Albert. And Albert introduced me to Clark after he fell in love with his dog Rachel."

"Who's Clark?" Franco asks pointedly.

"Well, he *is* pretty handsome... for an old man." I tease. "Don't worry. He's a great guy. You'll like him. He kind of reminds me of Gus in a weird way. He took care of me, feeding me and giving me supplies when I was running out of food."

"Your mom's right. You do have a habit of befriending old men."

"Clark helped me get to Minnesota, and that's where I found your uncle and my dad." I pause. "And I wasted a lot of time being pissed at my dad for marrying Alice and having more kids, but now I'm over it, which is ironic, because it's too late for me to do much about it now that he's gone."

"Well, Alice and the kids are still around." Franco squeezes my hand. "You can still be a part of that."

"I know." I blink back tears. "And I will. We just need to find Gus first."

Franco nods. "We'll be there soon."

"I went running off to Panopticus with Alice to find her older son and my mom without telling my dad, and that awful Eddy found us and dragged us to his Grouping, and that's where I met Nate. He's head of that Grouping, and he kicked Eddy out once I told him what was going on. Then he joined us to find his sister Edwina. Then we moved Gus right where the bombing was scheduled, and we ran into you right after that."

"So there's nothing between you and Nate, right?" Franco asks. "I just need to know."

"Nothing you need to worry about," I assure him.

"Okay, then." He pulls me around the corner of a building where we are somewhat hidden from the street and raises a hand to my cheek. "Just in case we don't make it out of here alive, I wanted to kiss you at least one more time."

I raise my eyebrows. "Sure you don't have to get drunk first, or anything?"

"Not this time." He smiles, and despite the world falling apart around us, I still melt.

Staring into my eyes, he moves closer. Then his lips are on mine, and even though my mind keeps swirling, I can't stop kissing him back. He's my safe haven in the middle of this storm, my home when I no longer have one, the missing part of me. We press together so closely, it's like we were never apart. Every breath he takes is mine. Everything goes fuzzy. I just want to be with him like this forever.

"What's that noise?" He breaks off the kiss, eyes widened in alarm.

A distant whine echoes nearby, followed by an enormous explosion that shakes the ground beneath our feet. Debris floats down through the smoky air.

"Let's get out of here!" Franco yanks on my arm, and we start to run.

We push our way through panicked crowds of people fleeing the bombing. I hang on to Franco, trying not to get separated.

"Get out of the way!" yells a terrified civilian, flinging his arms and grazing my cheek with his fist.

I falter, and lose sight of Franco, getting shoved here and there by the mindless mob. I can't see him anywhere. Smoke chokes me. I keep getting slammed against walls. I fight to remain upright, because if I fall, I am done for. Gasping for breath, I cling to the side of a building, dragging myself in what I hope is the direction of the library, but I've lost all sense of orientation. I keep going, hoping Franco will meet me there, hoping I'm heading the right way, hoping he's okay. The crowd flows past me like a mighty river, and I'm fighting my way upstream.

I think I'm getting closer. Oh, where is Franco? Did I bring him back to Panopticus just to get him hurt or killed? Is Gus still alive? Did we come back too late?

The crowd thins. A few more streets, and I spot the tall broken library in the distance. I panic, swinging around, searching for Franco. But he's nowhere to be found. I'm almost to Gus's apartment. One way or another, I've got to know.

I hurry to Gus's door and knock. No answer.

I glance around and keep knocking. Still no answer and still no Franco.

I give up on knocking, jostle the locked doorknob, then lean into it, ramming my already beaten and bruised body against the stubborn door. Once it gives, I'm sent flying into the room and land sprawled on the floor.

I jump to my feet. "Gus! Are you here?"

He's not in the kitchen. I hurry into the living room and gasp. The large window is missing, with sharp, blackened shards of glass poking out from every angle and scattered across the room.

Gus's comfy chair sits right next to the window, facing away from me.

I race to it, step siding the glass on the floor, and spin it around, bracing myself for the worst. "Gus?"

Gus slumps in the chair, his head angled to the side.

"Gus?" I shake him, then put a hand in front of his mouth and feel his warm breath. "Come on, Gus! Answer me!"

He blinks slowly.

"Gus! You're alive!" I hug him, this time letting the tears fall as they may. "Oh, Gus! I've found you, but I lost Franco in the crowd, and Eddy killed my dad, and now I don't know what to do anymore."

"Oh, Silvia." Gus shakes his head. "I wanted something better for you than all this."

I swallow and blink back my tears. "Then come with me and find Franco, so we can build a life outside so much better than this one."

Gus coughs. "Although I'd love to, I don't think I'm in the best shape to be your hero right now. You'll need someone else for that."

Franco bursts into the apartment, panting. "You made it! I couldn't find you, then I figured this would be the best place to wait for you. I knew you'd come for him."

Gus waves Franco over. "Good to see you, son."

"I wouldn't let her come back here without me." Franco puts a hand on my shoulder. "Glad to see you're okay, Gus. Your window doesn't look so good."

He nods. "Yeah, it broke when I was in the back bedroom, so I got lucky."

Tears come again to my eyes. "Gus, I'm *so* sorry I moved you here right before the library was bombed. You could've gotten killed."

Gus shakes his head. "You know I'm probably dying, anyway."

"Stop saying that!" I argue.

"And I told you not to come back here, you know." Gus pats my head in a loving manner, like he's sad I came, but still happy to see me.

I heave a sigh. "You knew I wouldn't listen."

"Yeah, I know." He gestures across the room. "That's why I packed a bag."

"What?" Sure enough, there's his bag, ready to go. "So I don't have to fight you on this?"

"Do I get a choice?" He shrugs. "But I worry you'll regret it. I'll be a hindrance to you every step of the way."

"That's a risk I'm willing to take," I assure him. "Let's go."

It's a struggle to get him out into the street. He can't walk unsupported, so Franco and I hold him up on either side, Gus's bag slung over Franco's shoulder.

"Are you two still sure about this?" Gus wheezes after the first couple blocks.

"You know Silvia." Franco smirks. "There's no stopping her once she's set her mind to something."

Gus sighs. "This is going to take forever. I shouldn't let you."

"Stop your arguing." I adjust my hold, hoping it will help. "Save your breath for getting out of here. I'm not leaving you behind, so just focus on one step at a time."

"You have no idea how guilty I feel letting you do this." Gus coughs again. "This isn't right."

"We will manage." I glance at the waning sun. Will night be easier than day? And how will we handle the woods? I don't have answers to my questions. All I know is that Gus is alive, Franco found me, and I'm going to get both of them out of here, one way or another.

Streets pass slowly. Time passes quickly. Soon the sun sets, and we still have so far to go.

"I need to rest a minute," Gus gasps. "I'm sorry."

"No apologies necessary." Franco offers Gus some water.

Gus gulps it down. "Promise me one thing at least. If I don't make it, meaning, if trying to get out of this godforsaken city kills me, which it very well might, you will *not* waste time burying me or hauling my body out of here, all right? If I'm dead, then I'm gone, and my body doesn't matter. Agreed?"

I wince. "Please stop talking about dying, Gus. It's getting on my nerves."

Gus persists. "You can't weasel your way out of this. I need an answer, and it better be yes, or I'm not taking another step."

"Fine. Just *don't* die." I repack and adjust the bags. "We'd better keep going, if you're able."

"Just barely." Gus winces as we put our arms around him.

Creeping along, we move forward inch by inch.

A vehicle appears in the distance.

"Hide back here." Franco moves behind a low building.

Gus grunts as he crouches. Peering around the corner, we watch the vehicle head back toward the center of the city, people crushed together in the middle, with gunmen positioned at all four corners. No one says a word until the engine noise fades away.

"Are they dragging people back into Panopticus now?" I ask, knowing neither of them know any more than I do.

"We better be even more careful." Franco helps Gus stand.

Gus frets, "If I get you two caught, I will never forgive myself."

"We won't let that happen." Franco puts his arm around Gus. "Silvia, could you take all the bags, and I'll just help him walk? That might work better."

I repack in a hurry, condensing everything to make it easier to carry. "Let's go."

Night falls, as does the temperature. Gus shivers non-stop, even after I gently put Franco's jean jacket on him. Our progress slows to a crawl. Gus grows weaker by the hour. Food and water and short breaks no longer help.

"I gotta be honest with you." Gus breathes hard even at rest. "I'm not sure how much more I can take of this, and we haven't even reached the greenhouses yet."

"What should we do?" I ask Franco. "Do we find some building to rest in for a while, or what?"

Franco looks down at Gus. "I'm sorry, but I don't think I can carry you."

Gus laughs weakly, the effort producing a coughing fit. "I wouldn't think so. I'm a grown man."

The coughing continues and deepens. Gus hacks until his body shakes. What have I done to him? How are we going to get him out of here? Finally, his breathing calms down, and everything is quiet again. But now that the coughing is done, I hear something else which might be even worse.

"Franco, can you hear that?" I ask. "Is that an engine?"

"Yeah, and it's getting closer. We gotta find cover, fast." He pulls Gus back to standing. "I'm sorry, Gus."

"Don't worry about me." Gus groans as we hurry behind a wall, sliding down for cover. Vehicle lights bounce in the distance, growing bigger with each second.

Closer and closer they come.

We flatten ourselves, trying to become one with the ground.

They are almost here. *Please drive past us.* They slow just on the other side of the wall. *Please, please, keep driving on by.* But as I hold my breath, the engine slows to a stop.

This cannot be happening. I refuse to let Gus get taken away from me now.

I refuse to be held captive. I will die first.

My heart pounds in my chest. No one says a word. No one makes a noise.

Until the barking starts.

5 2

RESCUE ME

"Since when do the Suits use dogs?" grunts Gus, out of breath.

Frantic barking continues, growing louder each second.

"They're getting closer," Franco whispers. "We're going to have to run for it. Gus, just hang on to me and do the best you can."

I tense, my fight or flight systems fully engaged. But then I hesitate, because I recognize that bark. "That's not the Suits." I struggle to stand with Franco holding me back. "That's *my* dog!"

A brown flurry of fur launches itself over the short wall, landing on my chest and knocking me backwards to lick wildly at my face.

"Albert! Enough already!" I sputter. "What are you doing here? Are you lost or something?"

A grumbling voice grows near. "Idiot dog! Where'd you go now? Said you had to potty, and that's fine, but this is ridiculous. We gotta get back to Rachel!"

"Clark!" I jump up with effort, Albert dancing around my heels, barking again. "I can't believe you're here! You swore you'd never enter the city limits."

"Silvia!" Clark raises his hands in celebration. "Thank goodness I found you!"

"You came for us?" I ask in shock. "You're an angel!"

"I've been called far worse."

"I can't believe you came for us." I rush to hug him. "Clark, you're so much braver than you think."

"Ha! That's where you're wrong." He hugs me back, a big smile on his face. "This isn't bravery. This is fear. Your mother scared me into it."

"My mother?"

"Yeah. Met her on the road with Nate. She seemed pretty upset."

I flinch. "Did she tell you Eddy killed my dad?"

"Yes, I heard about that." Clark puts a gentle hand on my shoulder. "I'm sorry, kid. You did what you had to do."

"I know." I shrug.

"That wasn't easy. It'll change you."

I take a breath. "I haven't had time to process it yet. We went right back in to get Gus."

"Yes, I heard about that too." Clark glances past me to watch Franco struggling to get Gus into a standing position. "And it looks like you found him."

My voice drops to a whisper. "He's so weak, and we've pushed him so hard. I don't know how much further he could walk on his own. Thank goodness you're here now."

Clark rushes over to lend a hand. "You're Gus Andrews? Can't believe I'm meeting you in person. You're a *legend* out there."

"You sound disappointed, but you're not exactly meeting me at my finest hour." Gus's voice is winded, his crazy Einstein hair even wilder than usual. "I'm sure you think I'm selfish, risking these young people's lives to haul out one miserable old man."

"Stop it, Gus." I hover nearby in case Gus should fall as both Franco and Clark assist him. "You're only sixty. That's not that old."

"Nothing wrong with being sixty." Clark calls out to Rachel, standing atop the vehicle, her tail wagging in welcome. "Look, my girl, we got company!"

"Okay now, Gus," Franco encourages him. "Here we are. It's a big step up. Do you think you can do it if we've got your back?"

Gus takes a big breath. "I'm ready."

Between the two of them, they ease him gently into the front seat.

"Much obliged," wheezes Gus.

Clark hurries to the driver's side. "Okay, folks, hop aboard and let's get the heck out of here." He revs the engine, and off we go.

Miles fly past with Albert perched in my lap, sniffing the breeze. We pass one damaged greenhouse after the other, Franco staring at them like a lost, lonely child. In no time, the Incinerator looms ahead, and the long rows of greenhouses come to an end.

"Hold on!" Franco taps Clark's shoulder. "I've got an idea. Can I just have five minutes alone inside?"

Clark scans the surroundings. "Okay, but hurry. This place gives me the creeps."

Franco jumps down, rushing into the last greenhouse and disappearing from view.

"Got any idea what he's up to?" Clark asks me.

"No, I don't." I watch the opening for his return.

"I might." Gus glances from the mangled greenhouse back to me. "Let's see how smart this boyfriend of yours really is, Silvia."

Minutes pass, Clark growing more antsy with every second.

Finally, Franco emerges clutching several bulging bags. "I grabbed as many seeds as I could. We'll need them to grow food out there."

Gus nods. "Wise plan. Ben would approve."

Franco turns to me, a single sunflower rising out of the terracotta pot in his hand. "This one survived, and I know how much you like plants."

I take the pot from Franco, my cheeks warming as I stroke the beautiful yellow petals.

"That's very touching." Gus nods toward the back seat. "Now, sit down, Franco. We need to get going."

Clark pauses. "You could give them a moment, you know."

"For what?" asks Gus.

Clark shrugs. "I don't know, maybe he wanted to kiss her or something."

"Oh, please." Gus snorts. "We don't have time for this. Let's go. Remember, you were the one so anxious to get going two minutes ago."

Clark starts the engine. "You just ruined what could've been a very romantic moment for the two of them. Franco, you can stuff those bags in the storage locker in the back."

Franco tucks everything away to keep it safe and jumps back on the backseat. A few minutes later we pass through a wide opening in the fence line and come out on the other side. All the hardships and hunger and fear fade into the background with Franco here at my side and Gus just in front of me. We are free of the city for good.

We drive past the area where we last camped. I turn back to stare at it, wondering what they did with Dad's body. Did they bury him? I hate to think of his body rotting away.

Gus watches my expression. "Is this where you lost your dad?"

I nod, blinking back tears.

"We've got you, Silvia." Gus squeezes my hand. "Daniel got you this far, and we'll take it from here."

"That's right," Clark chimes in. "We're here for you. Anything you need."

The vehicle bounces over a large rock in the path, jostling us, and making the dogs scramble for their seats.

Franco tightens his arm around me and steadies the sunflower with his other hand.

Gus braces himself, his eyes growing wide. "Yeah, we've got you, unless your buddy Clark here kills us with his crazy driving."

Clark smirks at Gus right before hitting the gas.

53

IT'S THE END OF THE WORLD AS WE KNOW IT

As morning dawns, we travel further into the woods along a rough dirt track, Franco gaping at the endless green beauty surrounding us. I sink back into the seat, relieved to escape all the fighting, bombs, and screaming—unless you count Clark peppering Gus with questions, yelling to be heard over the rumbling engine.

"How are you feeling? You'll let me know if you need anything, right? Did you know that Silvia isn't the first person you've saved that I've met? Heck, no. Not by a long shot. Do you remember this person and that person and, oh my gosh, I gotta tell you how much I admire you. I really do. I'm serious. What you did for all those people is just astounding. But how did you manage to evade detection for so long? You must be a genius. Silvia says you're a genius, anyway. How did you get them all out? Did you always use the Incinerator? Did anyone else ever come back before Silvia? Am I talking too much? Do you want me to stop?"

Franco murmurs into my ear. "Does he always act like this?"

"Clark's star struck," I whisper back. "Gus is his hero."

A bit rattled, Gus glances back to catch my eye. I smile, relieved to have him near. He shrugs and turns back to answer yet another of Clark's endless questions.

The late summer sun warms my head and shoulders as we ride on. Once we reach the highway, we pass subdued strangers resembling zombies who do not seem to care what happens to them anymore. I scan each unfamiliar face, searching for my mother, while Franco hunts for his family, neither of us finding anyone we recognize. And there are some faces neither of us will ever see again. We did not get Liam out in time, so he is lost to us forever. Despite all his grand plans, he never did get to leave Panopticus. Once again, Dad is gone from my life, but this time around I will not keep hoping for him to return someday. I spent the last eight years mourning and missing him. Now it will start all over again. How will I find the words to tell Alice and the children that Dad isn't coming home again? How will Mom recover from so much shock and change and loss?

At least Panopticus is finally behind us, and we never have to go back there again. Perhaps someday in the far distant future I will miss some detail or convenience of the city, but right now I am so happy to be rid of it. Absentmindedly, I pet Albert's furry head, still searching the road for my mother. She must be out here somewhere. What feels like only a short time later, Clark halts the vehicle.

"What's going on?" I mumble, confused and disoriented.

"Wake up, sleepy head." Franco nudges me. "We found Yoshe."

I struggle to sit up straight as Mom launches herself onto the vehicle and throws her arms around me. "Oh, honey, I thought I'd never see you again. I thought I would lose both of you on the same day. Promise me you'll never do anything risky ever again. Promise me *right now*."

I rub my tired eyes. "Come on, Mom. I'm fine, really. And look, we got Gus out okay, and Clark showed up just in time, so everything was fine. You don't need to worry so much."

"Hello, Gus." She places a gentle hand on his shoulder, causing him to wince. "Oh, dear. You're really hurt. Come on, Clark, let's get him out of here."

"Your wish is my command." Clark drives on as Mom squeezes in between me and Franco on the back seat.

"Where are Nate and Edwina?" I ask, finding neither of them in the crowd.

"I told them to go on ahead." Mom waves away my surprise. "I refused to take another step until I found you again."

"After what happened with Eddy, I would think you'd want Nate around for protection."

Mom flinches, pain flickering across her features as she digs in a pocket, pulls out Dad's leather bracelets, and gently presses them into my hands. "These are for you. He'd want you to have them. And don't worry about me. I can take care of myself. Nate had things to attend to, and I needed to know you were safe. I thought about coming with Clark, but before Nate and Edwina went on ahead there wasn't enough room for all four of us plus you three, and these dogs. It's pretty crowded in here."

I turn the bracelets over, remembering how I didn't like seeing them at first because they were a symbol of how different my father had become from the memory I had so cherished as a child.

"Here, I'll tie them on for you," Mom offers, blinking back tears.

"Thanks." I hold out my scarred wrists, knowing my dad loved me the best way he could, and silently promise to always wear this symbol of his life—the life he gave up so willingly for both me and my mom.

We settle back in the seats, Albert snuggling in further, and my heart warms. I'm more than a little flattered he remembered me enough to sniff me out in Panopticus, and I'm pretty sure he also recognizes that Mom and I need extra affection right now. Clark speeds toward Madison as Gus shudders and grows quiet. All this travel is too much for him. Instead of enjoying the scenery, I monitor his breathing.

"Almost there." Clark frowns, no longer asking Gus questions. "Not long now."

5 4

ONE WEEK LATER

"At least he's eating now." Clark leans on the fence as I harvest his garden while the dogs run rampant around the yard.

"But he's still so weak." I examine the tomato I just plucked off the vine. "I thought we were going to lose him. What if I made him worse by dragging him all the way over here?"

Clark shakes his head. "Don't say that. You did the right thing bringing him here. We'll get him all better. You'll see."

"I hope so." I notice the keys in his hand. "Where are you going?"

"Yoshe has informed me it's time for more driving lessons."

"She does enjoy bossing you around."

"Don't I know it." He turns back to the garage. "Your boyfriend's coming too, so wish me luck."

"He's that bad of a driver?"

"Let's put it this way," Clark pauses, "your mother takes to driving like a kitten to milk."

"And Franco?" I ask.

He groans. "He should stick to riding a bike. I hear he's good at that."

After collecting a few more tomatoes I call the dogs, and together we head back upstairs.

Both dogs jump on Gus's bed and nestle in.

"Someone's found a new favorite." I smirk, pretending to be jealous.

"Mr. Albert." Gus ruffles the little dog's fur. "Good name for a good dog."

"How are you feeling?" I ask, slicing tomatoes and tearing lettuce at the kitchen counter.

He eyes my handiwork from across the room. "More health food, I see. Trying your best to heal me with roughage while I languish uselessly on Clark's bed, hogging the only good sleeping spot in the place."

"Don't worry about that. I can sleep wherever."

"Not sure your mother feels the same way." Gus rearranges the bedding. "Maybe that's why she's leaving."

I shake my head. "No, that's not it. Franco needs to see his family, and Mom's going to visit Alice. She's learning to drive so they can get to Minnesota on their own while Clark and I stay here with you."

"Are you sure you want her to be the one to tell Alice about Daniel?" Gus asks. "Don't you think you should do it?"

I stop preparing veggies to throw him a glare. "I'm *not* leaving you."

"Yes, you've made that very clear. Although any time you and Clark want to stop treating me like a tiny child it will be much appreciated."

"No comment, and no promises." I turn back to my salads. "But about Alice, Mom said she's the best one to understand how Alice will feel about losing Dad, and I kind of agree with her. Plus, Mom doesn't want what happened to me when we thought Dad died to happen to Alice and her kids. So she's the one going for now. To make sure Alice can handle things."

Gus shrugs. "Fair enough."

"I'm sending the red dress Dad made me along with her to give to Serena. I hope that helps at least a little."

Gus raises his bushy eyebrows. "Are you sure about that? Isn't that dress precious to you?"

I nod. "Yes, but it's time to pass it on. I wish I had something for Thomas as well, but there wasn't much time to grab stuff while we were there, and what room we had in our packs we filled with food."

"It's good of you to give it to your sister."

"Feels like the right thing to do." I shrug, finished with food prep. "Time to eat." I bring over two heaping bowls, then watch Gus eat.

"Between you and Clark, I feel like I'm back in Panopticus with somebody monitoring every move I make and every bite I take."

"Once you build up enough strength, you can do whatever you want." I level my gaze at him. "Until then, you'll do what we say and eat what we say."

"I can't wait." Gus slaps the bedding at his side. "I hate all this lazing about. Soon as I'm able, I'll make you and Clark a feast like you've never seen."

"You sure I won't be cramping your style? This sounds like a date. I'd just be in the way. I can go walk the dogs or something while you two eat."

"Don't you start with me. I'm far too old for all that nonsense. What about you and Franco? Are you upset he's leaving without you?"

"Don't try to change the subject. No, I'm not mad at Franco for wanting to see his family. And I've had more than enough of hearing about your age, so stop complaining about something that doesn't even matter."

"Big words from someone under twenty." Gus frowns before taking another bite. "I'm so tired of eating salads. Can't we just play cribbage?"

ONE MONTH LATER

"I hope this is the last of it." Mom wipes the sweat from her brow. "Not much more is going to fit in that Jeep. Good thing I already brought the chickens over last trip."

"Yeah, I think that's it." I glance around at everything Clark will leave behind. "He said all he wanted to take to Minnesota were his books, pictures, shoes, clothes, and his favorite frying pan. He's leaving everything else for the new family. Oh, except for some seeds for the food gardens he's starting with Franco."

Mom nods. "I only hope he doesn't regret it. This will be a big change for him."

"I hear you two gossiping about me." Clark stomps upstairs with his heavy tread, followed by the pitter patter of dog feet. "Don't you worry about me. Gus needs to be with Silvia, and Silvia needs to be with you, especially if you're moving in with Alice and the kids—which seems a bit extreme to me, but if it works for you, who am I to judge?"

Mom shrugs. "We shared a husband, we might as well share the kids. I can be the Bonus Mom and Silvia the Big Sister."

I smile at this new version of my mom. No longer the uptight violinist or the fierce vigilante, she has once again evolved into someone new. For the first time I can remember, she looks relaxed and happy. Her hair has grown out a little, and she's wearing some random clothes Alice must have found for her. She smiles a lot more often and a lot more naturally. So far, I think this novel arrangement suits her. She always wanted more kids, and now she got them, by making the very best of a complicated situation.

Her eyes light up. "I haven't even told you the best part. Someone discovered an abandoned music store, so I've got a bunch of instruments to clean up and find homes for. I'm going to open a little music school. We'll have our own orchestra. You'll see."

"That sounds perfect for you." Clark ties some rope to secure a box. "Let me know if I can be of any help. I know I'm just tagging along here, but I'll find some way to make myself useful."

"I still feel like it's my fault you're leaving your comfy home behind—"

"Silvia, now don't you start. It makes sense for you to go, and now that I've got so many new neighbors here, it's not the same anyway. Especially after what happened."

I glance at the still healing wound on Clark's forehead from when a stranger attacked him in his own garden, stealing his food and knocking him unconscious. He was out there for at least an hour before Gus found him lying on the ground, but he's better now.

Mom frowns. "I expect there will be more of that to come. People are desperate for food and supplies."

Clark nods. "I'm keeping Rachel by my side from now on, that's for sure. And I think it will be safer to live further away from here and further away from Panopticus. We'll still see Nate sometimes, I think. I'm looking forward to working with that boyfriend of yours on the new gardens next spring. You haven't seen him for a while now, have you? I heard he's kept busy experimenting with alternative fuel sources. He may not have a clue how to drive, but he's quite clever in other respects, I guess."

"Actually, he's brilliant." Mom shocks me with her generous praise. "And he's made big plans for a night out for you once you arrive. Madeline's in charge of the meal, and she said her new roommates can bus the table."

"It's very nice of her to take us in like this." Clark picks up the last box. "I've heard she's a fabulous cook. Can't wait to try her squash soup."

Gus comes up the stairs. "That's about it, isn't it? Have we got everything?"

"We've got all we need, Governor." Clark salutes him.

"I never said I was actually taking the job," Gus grumbles.

I sling a couple more bags over my shoulders. "But you'd be so good at it."

"What do I know about politics? And you know how much I hate government stuff."

"Then make a *new* type of government," I suggest. "A type that's fair."

"A type that stays out of your business, doesn't tell you what to eat or where to work or where to live," Mom adds.

"I'm not sure I'm up for this." Gus shakes his head. "It's all Nate's fault for suggesting it in the first place, just because people know my name, but this shouldn't be a popularity contest. I worked in Mortuary Sciences for years, for Pete's sake. I don't know anything else."

"Don't you worry," Clark says. "You'll be great."

"I don't know about that, but I do know we better get on the road if we want to get there before dark."

We venture down the stairs for the last time. Clark hands off the house keys to the new owners, and we all head to the vehicle. Mom hops in the driver's seat. I am in "shotgun" (a new term for me) holding my precious sunflower. The two dogs settle in with the men in the back seat between all the boxes tied securely for travel.

"You boys ready?" Mom glances back before starting the engine, backing up smoothly, and easing onto the road. She was meant to be in charge.

"Yeah, Bonus Dads, you ready to go home?" I turn to them, excited for the future and—let's be honest here—for my first ever date with Franco.

Gus smiles. "Yes, Bonus Daughter, let's go home."

PLAYLIST

Inspired by Gus's love of music, each chapter title comes from a song:

1. HAPPY BIRTHDAY
2. RUNAWAY - Bon Jovi
3. ALONE - Heart
4. WALKING ON SUNSHINE - Katrina and the Waves
5. LIFE IS A HIGHWAY - Rascal Flatts
6. HUNGRY EYES - Eric Carmen
7. THE TRICK IS TO KEEP BREATHING - Garbage
8. SOMEBODY'S WATCHING ME - Rockwell
9. THE BIRDS AND THE BEES - Dean Martin
10. ZOMBIE - The Cranberries
11. HIT THE ROAD, JACK - Ray Charles
12. SOLITARY MAN - Neil Diamond
13. TAKE ME TO THE RIVER - Talking Heads
14. BREAD AND BUTTER - The Newbeats
15. ANIMAL - Def Leppard
16. GOODBYE TO YOU - Michelle Branch
17. THE LADY IN RED - Chris de Burgh

18. THE WAY YOU LOOK TONIGHT - Tony Bennett
19. ALWAYS SOMETHING THERE TO REMIND ME - Naked Eyes
20. WINTER - Tori Amos
21. HURT - Trent Reznor first, Johnny Cash second
22. OH FATHER - Madonna
23. THIS KISS - Faith Hill
24. I HATE MYSELF FOR LOVING YOU - Joan Jett and the Blackhearts
25. THE WINNER TAKES IT ALL - ABBA
26. FEAR - Sarah McLachlan
27. WE ARE FAMILY - Sister Sledge
28. PICTURES OF YOU - The Cure
29. FATHER FIGURE - George Michael
30. YOU CAN'T ALWAYS GET WHAT YOU WANT - Rolling Stones
31. MILLION REASONS - Lady Gaga
32. STILL THE NIGHT - Bo Deans
33. CREEP - Radiohead
34. NEVER GONNA LET YOU GO - Sergio Mendes
35. EVERYBODY HURTS - R.E.M.
36. TAKE ME WITH U - Prince
37. HOLD ON, I'M COMING - Sam and Dave
38. BURNING DOWN THE HOUSE - Talking Heads
39. IT ONLY HURTS WHEN I'M BREATHING - Shania Twain
40. HERO - Enrique Iglesias
41. I WILL REMEMBER YOU - Sarah McLachlan
42. IF I CLOSE MY EYES FOREVER - Ozzy Osbourne & Lita Ford
43. STAYIN' ALIVE - Bee Gees
44. PHOTOGRAPH - Def Leppard
45. PRECIOUS THINGS - Tori Amos
46. I GO TO PIECES - Peter & Gordon

47. SOMETHING I CAN NEVER HAVE - Nine Inch Nails
48. I DON'T WANT TO BE ALONE - Billy Joel
49. I WOULD DIE 4 U - Prince
50. COME WHAT MAY- from Moulin Rouge, sung by Nicole Kidman & Ewan McGregor
51. I KNEW YOU WERE WAITING (FOR ME) - Aretha Franklin & George Michael
52. RESCUE ME - Fontella Bass
53. IT'S THE END OF THE WORLD AS WE KNOW IT - R.E.M.

RESOURCES

1. "Beryl Novak has lived alone in his one-room deer shack for 44 years. That's the way he likes it" -Article by John Myers for the Park Rapids Enterprise, published November 05, 2021 - https://www.parkrapidsenterprise.com/sports/northland-outdoors/beryl-novak-has-lived-a lone-in-his-one-room-deer-shack-for-44-years-thats-the-way-he-likes-it

2. Rand McNally Maps of Minnesota and Wisconsin

3. "Minnesota, Wisconsin and Michigan Wild Berries & Fruits Field Guide" by Teresa Marrone for Adventure Publications, Inc., copyright 2009

4. How to Stay Alive in the Woods" by Bradford Angier, A Fireside Book Published by Simon & Schuster, published 1956 and renewed in 1984

5. How to use a compass YouTube videos, the best one was "How I Use a Map & Compass to Navigate Off Trail - The Basics" by Christina Cozzens

ACKNOWLEDGMENTS

Always a voracious reader, I owe a huge debt of gratitude to all the authors whose amazing minds allowed me to expand my own. *Dead Girl Running* is a cross between *The Giver*, *The Handmaiden's Tale*, Agenda 21, and everything I have learned from running both down the road and along the trails.

Holli Anderson from Immortal Works Press, thank you for encouraging me to finish this series after taking a long break from writing. Time marches on, but heartfelt gratitude remains towards those who helped guide my books: Tori Merkiel, Colleen Chmelik, Christa Worrell, Kristin D. Van Risseghem, Danielle Allen, Michael Kalmbach, Rachel Erickson, Matthew S. Cox, Emma Adams, Samantha Bryant, Yolanda Renee, Katie Hamstead, C.M. Spivey, and Josh Noser.

Silvia's dependence on running reminds me of my first coach, Mary Allen, who introduced me to the sport. Even though I called Cross Country "hell in a bucket" at the time, thank you for planting the seed that grew into such a lifelong love. My caring college Cross Country coach, Jen Arneson, always put her athletes first. Thank you for showing me life can lead you down any road you have the courage to follow. Eternal gratitude to all my "running peeps" from high school, college, and today. Extra kisses to my current canine running buddy, Stella, who is always so eager to join in our adventures.

ABOUT THE AUTHOR

Growing up an only child, I learned to entertain myself. During summer vacations, my greatest form of exercise consisted of turning the pages of a book. Now I'm all grown up, and full of stories half-written in my head. I write them down to find out what happens next.

This has been an
Immortal Production

www.ingramcontent.com/pod-product-compliance
Lightning Source LLC
Chambersburg PA
CBHW050752190726
48285CB00005B/1627